AGE OF MONDAYS

PRAISE FOR *AGE OF MONDAYS*

'[Lopa Ghosh's *Age of Mondays* is] a consummate, confident and original portrayal of familial tensions seen through the prism of a child's mind. The slant-eyed perception of motherhood is skilfully wrought through a unique blend of real life and fantasy. Again and again, it shows how the darkest of moments in life can offer brightness to those who look for it. It leaves the reader with a feeling of positivity and hope regarding complex family ties. The writer's ability to weave the story through the mirage of a dream world, while not letting go of the here and now, makes it a remarkable work.'

—Kavery Nambisan

'Lopa Ghosh's novel, *Age of Mondays*—written with empathy ... an anticipation of death looming over it, and spoken in the voice of a child—is a heartbreaking read.'

—Hansda Sowvendra Shekhar

'Ghosh's Narois is that rare child who holds a universe within her that people many times her age and experience cannot touch. Her wisdom is both ancient and childlike, ethereal and heavy, rich with the joys of childhood and blue with an unimaginable tragedy. The reader couldn't have asked for a more magical guide to this narrative universe of shocking beauty.'

—Saikat Majumdar

PRAISE FOR *REVOLT OF THE FISH EATERS*

'Edgy, brilliant ... shot through with subversion ... every story in this volume comes with a gift ... where the moments of wonderment are never in short supply.'

—**Rajat Chaudhuri**, CNN-IBN

'Ghosh successfully imprints her protagonists with a human ache.'

—**Annie Zaidi**, *Tehelka*

Also by Lopa Ghosh

Revolt of the Fish Eaters (2012)

AGE OF MONDAYS

A NOVEL

LOPA GHOSH

HarperCollins *Publishers* India

First published in India by HarperCollins *Publishers* 2025
HarperCollins *Publishers* India, Cyber City, Building 10-A, Gurugram,
Haryana – 122002, India
www.harpercollins.co.in

2 4 6 8 10 9 7 5 3 1

P-ISBN: 978-93-6989-743-8
E-ISBN: 978-93-6989-141-2

Typeset in 11.5/15 Sabon LT Std at
HarperCollins *Publishers* India

Printed and bound at
Thomson Press (India) Ltd

FSC www.fsc.org
MIX
Paper | Supporting responsible forestry
FSC® C010615

This book is produced from independently certified FSC® paper
to ensure responsible forest management.

*

HarperCollins *Publishers*, Macken House, 39/40 Mayor Street Upper,
Dublin 1, D01 C9W8, Ireland

To Ira, Averi and all the children of this imperilled world

Contents

1. Relativity

The first time she went away was on a Monday morning in July. I woke up to the sound of a gathering storm. It was 6 a.m. Gorilla had fallen off the bed as usual. I yanked him back under the covers.

Mama-mon was in front of the mirror, applying lipstick. Green-room lights around the mirror blazed like six suns. My eyes hurt. I wanted to snuggle back into my dream where I was with DinDin. We were in her old house, just the two of us, sorting old crumbling photos from her wedding album. I sucked on a piece of lime pickle with salt crusted over it. Big drops of rain plopped through the leaky roof, soaking our shoulders. I was wet, but I was warm. DinDin's white-pink skin, old smell and soft wrinkles wrapped me—a glowing blanket.

Flashes of lightning and terrifying claps of thunder fell. I sat up, clutching Gorilla. Out in the forest, tall trees tossed and headbutted. The eucalyptus swayed fiercely. Red and yellow flowers from the gulmohar and amaltas parachuted helter-skelter. It wasn't going to be an ordinary morning. Gorilla looked unimpressed. He was used to stormier stuff.

My pillow ruffles and murmurs startled Mama-mon. She looked at me and sailed over, cuddling me up in a warm hug.

I wanted to tell her about my dream. But it didn't seem like the right thing to do. We were, after all, forgetting about that old house and more importantly, forgetting about old DinDin.

She gazed at the storm and sighed. 'The problem with our universe, Earth at any rate, is that nothing ever goes away forever. It just cannot because matter is indestructible, as we know. And the jury is out over whether time will end. So, even if a star becomes a supernova and dies, we won't really know that it has died. We will see the star shining up there and believe in its twinkle.'

She wrapped her arms around me and gave me our special squeeze-hug.

'I am a boa constrictor from the Amazon. My love is deadly,' she hissed.

I freed myself and gulped some air. 'But black holes are a reality, Mon.'

'Oh, of course they are, and thank god for black holes. It would have been such a bother otherwise, to go on and on. So, in a black hole, time stops, or rather time—past, present, future—sit to tea together. Hence, even if something is dead, it is alive. By that logic then, speaking in Lojban, there is no real goodbye.'

'Are you going away somewhere?'

When Mama-mon goes away, although she hasn't exactly ever been away, I don't do so well.

I didn't want to rub salt on her wounds by asking if she was going away when she never actually does.

Mama-mon is always on-the-verge of going away. On-the-verge of living in New York, on-the-verge of reporting on the South Sudan crisis. On-the-verge, but always here.

Stuck, according to her. And it was because of being stuck that she spent nights glued to the flight radar on her phone, watching planes zipping around the world, flying away from cities to far-off places.

'See these orbits—thousands of them zigzagging. Highways and roads in the sky.'

She let me play when I had fever and couldn't sleep at night. We picked a tiny plane that was heading to Longyearbyen in Svalbard. Propellers rotated like a bee-buzz. We wondered about the people and whether they were seeing the aurora borealis.

Sometimes she stayed with a plane throughout its journey—watched it taxi, rev up, gain altitude, fly over oceans and continents.

'Look, this LearJet flew out of St Croix in the Caribbeans and will land in Fort Lauderdale. I bet this one is flying a billionaire drug lord.'

Frozen Siberia was her favourite haunt. She looked for planes that flew deep inside the Artic Circle.

Daddy said it was spooky and a gigantic waste of time for someone like her.

'What if by chance the plane you are spotting happens to be hijacked and the government comes after you?'

Challenging her was a mistake because then she called him Oblonsky and reminded him of the time he lied about catching a plane from Curaçao. I searched 'Curaçao' on Daddy's phone. Then I googled Oblonsky and was told that Oblonsky was a name, not an adjective. Oblonsky was Anna Karenina's brother.

I wondered that Monday if Mama-mon was catching a flight that I could spot on the flight radar.

'No, no, I am only saying—be more focused on your work at school today, okay, my pickle? It is not how long but how well that counts. What about playing a game with me? A long game stretching over days and months! Every now and then I will disappear, and you will do something really clever while I am away.'

'Will you pretend-disappear?'

Like when she does in the afternoons that are orange. She could be in her study, keeping herself warm in a pretend-tent with whisky-coffee, while I would be outside, in a deep forest, following the clues that Maachli the Tiger left, clues that were left unsolved long after Maachli was dead. My feet would be cold and I'd feel something inside me—probably my small intestine tying itself up in Houdini knots.

'Something like that. Except I may not be in the study. I may be a bit further away.'

'How far far? Café Qutb?'

'A bit further than that, please.'

'Calcutta? To meet DinDin?'

Perhaps the dream was a signal.

'Oh, no, not quite as far.'

This is just the start, she said. An experiment. She would be gone just that day and night.

I don't know why I shivered. Although I nodded and said what she wanted to hear—Gotcha, Mom.

Mothers left all the time. Pandas, cuckoos, black bears, rabbits—worst mothers in the animal kingdom.

'I am a lioness. I don't leave. I stay and I fight,' Mama-mon has declared from time to time. But when she hurls a glass of vodka packed with ice at Daddy, she says, 'I will leave and never come back.'

I wondered, as we walked to the front door where an overnighter stood packed and ready, if this was the 'never-leaving' lioness or the 'glass-hurler'.

At the door, Daddy and Mama-mon wrestled with the duffle bag. Rain fell lightly. A carton of milk and that Monday's newspaper lay uncollected outside.

'Let go, Danish. Let go!' She pulled with all her might and yanked the bag. She walked away, her heels clattering on the wet driveway. A white rickety taxi was at the gate. We watched as she got in and drove off. Her perfume stayed a long time, mixing with the rain and the clouds. Home-leaving, school-going butterflies fluttered in my tummy.

'What was she whispering to you? Something about Achilles?' I asked Daddy.

'Ah, that,' he said. And then said no more.

'I know Achilles rather well. It must be a clue.'

'Detectiving around, are you?' he said, his heart not in the joke.

It was 7 a.m. Daddy packed my lunch box. He slapped big wads of melty butter on the soft milk bread and put in extra cheese and cucumber slices. Tears slid down his long Dorabjee nose and hung by the tip for a dizzying moment before plopping onto the bread. And he thought I wasn't noticing—that tears were soggying up my sandwich and my own mother, the one who didn't have anywhere to go, had left after lecturing me on universal time.

2. Double Lives

How about starting from the end? What if, in life, we could be taught to run a sprint, check out the ending, run back and be wise? Would it make life one dreary dull time? No surprises, no scary moments. What if your parents are sitting on a sofa under which a timebomb ticks? In that case, would it be such a bad idea to know? To know how it is all going to end?

Here's a fact: we don't choose our parents. We don't choose what becomes of them either.

Sometimes I wonder: could I, Vera Narois, ten-year-old pianist with a friend problem, only child of Imon and Danish—two pixelated, hazy shadows who belong nowhere, not even to themselves—possibly have known the true meaning of sadness?

First, I ask, do we *really* know what we know? Second, is meaning essential to know what we do know?

Sadness is not a bicycle that you learn to ride, and once you have learnt it, you cross over to the other side and become a sadcyclist.

Sadness is a smell, a colour, a person. It is singular, plural, common and proper. Onion rings in your gravy may make you sad one day and then not. So too: a pigeon at the window, peppermint fumes, the sad tale of what happens to hair, the prime minister whose face you cannot bear to look at. Friends may make you sad, friends who betray. You may in turn betray your friends and that can make you sadder. It is possible to be sad no matter whose team you are on. Sadness is what makes you wonder what comes at the end and what comes after.

It made Mama-mon sad that Daddy was living two lives. When she said it, accusing him of it, with her slim finger pointing and prodding his chest, whisky fumes lacing her rising voice, Daddy seemed sadder. He hung his head or looked far away, the irises of his eyes glowing like coals. Yes, I do know how coal burns. While Daddy lived his other life, Mama-mon taught me and Kiran about the world.

Kiran—my first best friend, my parabatai, the one I was bound to love and protect, the one for whom I could have laid down my life, lived next door. In the house with a pine tree and chandeliers. If you ever decided to make a Kiran doll, plastic googly eyes from the craft shop or shiny black buttons wouldn't do the trick. You would need black onyx from ancient Egypt.

For her hair—the thick braid that snaked down her thin back—what could recreate that kind of hair, I am yet to discover. For her snowy white teeth, I have decided marble from the Leaning Tower of Pisa might work. Kiran was skinny and her bones, well, they could break in a breeze. But not her eyes that shone like a tiger's. You could grow afraid of the deep end of her eyes.

For Mama-mon, she was the 'other daughter'. Perhaps the truer daughter, because Kiran always had the best stories to tell her—about the autowallah with a beard coiled like springs, or the green-eyed policeman at Kabutar Chowk, or a cloud shaped like a unicorn appearing every day at noon, or a geography teacher who kept an empty Coke bottle inside her bag into which she shed tears. How she laughed and cried over Kiran's stories. All I ever saw was traffic, grey cars, people rushing to work, flame of the forest flowers falling all the way down with a whisper. I did, however, see what Kiran or Mama-mon couldn't—but that didn't count. I saw the sound of it all, rising like a flock of multicoloured birds, a rainbow of traffic sounds, Principal Ma'am's brown voice, Arijit Singh's teal voice, Daddy's golden voice, Kiran's voice a colour from space, a colour I no longer remember.

I can't pinpoint exactly how and when Mama-mon's going away on Mondays began to affect me. I got headaches and my feet were always cold, even if I wore two socks. One thing I do know definitely—it was around this time that I stopped eating apples and went off Harry Potter. I was done with all the wizarding and 'I am the Chosen One' fawning and swooning. I needed new things in life to replace old things that weren't working for me anymore.

To cope with Mondays, Mama-mon taught me how geological time worked. She told me of drifting continents, the Devonian period, the eternality of everything. We no longer spoke of time in days and weeks. We became creatures of mega-annums and giga-annums and of the year when the world was full of fish. Of everything else that came before and will come after.

'So you see, Narois, it's all relative. And we are nothing. We are here … but not here really.'

In the orange light of afternoon, before the Age of Mondays dawned on us, Mama-mon would pour herself whisky-in-a-cup.

'Just a splash in my coffee. Not a peg. No need to judge,' she would say to Daddy if he was around. To me she would just nod and wink.

Daddy didn't look like someone who had another life. He was solid—always present, loyally stuck to:

- His side of the bed
- His scratchy old turntable
- His alcove of homeless and abandoned gods
- His olive-oil-garlic-lemon marinade for beef
- His weekly trips to the market where he could tell riverfish from pondfish

Daddy paying the school fees.

Daddy arguing with Granny Dorabjee about who is a non-Parsi, and why such definitions should be banned, even if such arguments meant never visiting the Dorabjee house in Colaba.

Daddy's heavy shoes thudding at the doorway when he left for the harbours and islands on which there were lighthouses ...

Daddy's boring life, comforting and warm like a hug.

Which became, in Mama-mon's eyes, Daddy's double life.

She said it so often that we began to believe it existed even if we couldn't see it. Those words hovered around us like a mist in which Daddy began to turn hazy. He would be at the dining table, happily tearing into lamb chops, when just like that, for no reason at all, she would say it. His eyes would quiver like a going-out candle flame, and he would begin to turn translucent around the edges.

When I pointed it out to him, Daddy said, 'Oh, that's a trick. I am learning to be an illusionist. Imagine, Narois—the Colosseum at sunset, thousands of screaming fans. And I disappear. Now you see me, now you don't.'

After years of fighting with Daddy over things like a Tokyo afternoon, the misty city of Durban, a busker at Port Haifa, after calling him a leaver and an Oblonsky, after sleuthing on him and giving everything he did a double meaning, it was Mama-mon who began leading a double life.

Dr Ambrita said I shouldn't blame myself. That I am a child stuck in an uncommon situation. That I should talk to Kiran. Unburden. (Confess? Repent?)

When I reminded her that I didn't have superpowers, she said, a letter would do.

'A letter that goes nowhere?'

'Well. How about journalling every night?'

The thing about writing in a diary is that any kid with any self-respect will leave that be and tell their teachers and shrinks not to harangue them about journalling. If confidence and better self-esteem are what the adults want us to grow, grow like the potato and radish that everyone is growing on their balconies and terraces and backyards these days, writing in a diary is a BAD IDEA. It's an exercise in humiliation—since no diary ever written by a child could ever match up to Anne Frank's.

So, no, thank you, Dr A, I am not falling for that cliché.

But yes, sometimes I could write to Kiran. Ask her how she is.

'How are you today and how will you be for years to come? Your new house is not next to the mad emperor's fort—that I know. Is it next to the river? Is it true what they say—that the water is poisonous and if you touch the white woolly foam that floats on it, your fingers will fall off? Then how do you, my Kiran-Bee, go swimming in it? Maybe you don't. Maybe living by the river is overrated and it doesn't mean that you go for a swim and catch fish whenever you like. From living next to a forest, you went to living next to the river. Fancy that. Does the river enter your house? The way the forest did—yours and mine. Sometimes I wonder if forests always have demons or are the demons in our head and we enter the forest with demony heads and put the blame on the forest.'

I would also tell her about Dr A—'She came after you, you see! She is my shrink! Oh yes, I see a shrink these days, to deal with the unusual circumstances that have disrupted my normal childhood.'

That's how Dr A describes my condition in the case summary that I have read, although I am not allowed to. According to Dr A, I have abandonment issues. I tried telling her that I am the abandoner as well as the abandonee. But she doesn't agree with that, and although she doesn't say it out loud, I know from the notes that I snuck a look at that she rates the unusual circumstances of my life pretty high up on various scales she uses to measure the despair of folks—I score an 8 out of 12 in something and a 10 out of 10 in another!

It was with Kiran, Mama-mon's other daughter and my best friend, that I entered the forest for the first time and became part of an adventure that was possible only because we had begun living in the Age of Mondays.

3. Gravity

The first motherless Monday, in school, I murdered five ladybugs, flattened their crunchy red elytra under my shoes. Twinkling-quick, harp-sharp—à la: guillotine.

In maths class, I got a fever. Fractions seesawed—numerator became denominator and vice versa—up and down, up and down. Chairs and tables and my friends floated.

Armish came over and said that my eyes looked like they had left their posts and gone for a stroll far back into my skull.

'As if you don't want to see anymore.'

She said she could feel my fever from the other end of the classroom. That's Armish for you—the friend who could remember your favourite colour, the poem you recited in grade one, your yearning for metallic colour pens, the one who could weave the best loom bands. Armish with her tastiest tiffin; Armish, the glitteriest of us all. Everyone loved Armish and wanted to be her friend. I did too. Everyone, except Rishit, who lost no chance to bully her.

One day in English class, he called her a Paki and a mullah. Meera and I complained to Nita Ma'am. She turned purple around her nose and gasped for breath. We thought she was having a heart attack, the way she clutched her chest and said, 'Oh!'

She called Rishit aside. 'I don't want such poisonous words in my classroom. Tell me, why did you call her names? Do you repent?'

Nita Ma'am took him to the principal's office. His parents were called and warned that if it happened again, he would be expelled. But it happened again, kept happening. Rishit couldn't stop himself from calling Armish those names. Mama-mon said it was a disease that had infected everyone after the year 2014. That the world had entered a giga-annum in which an extinction event was going to take place.

Armish told Meera that I had fever. Meera, my friend since nursery, came over. In her usual no-fuss way, she felt my forehead and said, 'You are a bit warm. We should tell Ma'am.'

Our class teacher, Jyoti Ma'am, felt my forehead and tsked-tsked her annoyance.

'Go. Health centre. Now.'

Meera said she would walk with me, but Jyoti Ma'am sent her scurrying on some errand with the class register. Meera's mother, Aunty Rebecca, is a top police officer. Because of her, we considered ourselves experts on how criminals thought and planned their crimes.

Meera managed to whisper before hurrying out that Jyoti Ma'am's behaviour could earn her several penal code violations.

'I'll ask Constable Chacha and also make him tell me how long her prison sentence should be.'

Constable Chacha, one of Aunty Rebecca's aides, was on 24x7 duty to protect Meera from kidnappers.

Zorawar laughed at me and called me weak and silly. 'Just like a girl.' So I pinched his soft round cheeks on the way out. They turned bright red, and he yelped.

The health centre was at a far end of our primary section, next to a shady grove of neem trees. I walked along the wet path, bypassing earthworms and ladybugs who might want revenge if they knew who I was—murderer of their people. Rise of the Insecta!

At the health centre, they stuck a fat thermometer into my mouth. It smelled of Dettol and other people's fever.

Daddy came to collect me. He carried me over his shoulder to the car and I let him.

'Do you want chicken wings from KFC?'

Such a cliché, Daddy. But why not! So, I nodded eagerly; my mouth watered thinking of the flaky, salty crust. Which Mama-mon said was probably made with plastic scrap. That the chicken was no chicken. It was Frankenstein Chicken.

'You are made to believe it's chicken, but it's not. It's brainwash.'

Daddy's choice of KFC made it clear that this was indeed a motherless day. Mama-mon was nowhere near us. Aka: it was possible to gorge on these treats. Make hay while the sun shines. Seize the day!

I oozed idioms. They came out of me in jerks, and if I held my tongue to keep them in, they would slip out with a sneeze. Mama-mon said I was born idiomatic.

My idioms gave Jyoti Ma'am a tsking fit. One day a fight broke out over a dead plant on the windowsill of our classroom—a plant we were supposed to look after. Reba called me rude, so I said to her: 'Look who is calling the kettle black.'

Reba went up to Jyoti Ma'am and complained. With a stony face, Jyoti Ma'am called me to her desk and said I shouldn't insult anyone for their appearance.

'But Miss, what I meant was—people who live in glass houses shouldn't throw stones at other people's houses.'

'Tsk tsk tsk. Speak easy. Do you think you are better than the rest of us? All this fancy talk!'

She made me write that down in the school diary—Speak in language simple. Be humble.

At the restaurant, after a large bucket of KFC wings, we glugged down two bottles of pistachio milk from Keventers. Then we floated around Connaught Place aimlessly. The world seemed muffled, a city stuck inside a woolly blanket. Daddy and I spoke very little. We didn't have to.

We stared up at the massive flag of India fluttering listlessly (looking at it, Mama-mon would have said, 'Even the flag is tired and wants to stop being a circus'); at the smelly entrance of Palika Bazar (looking at it, Mama-mon would have said, 'Counterfeits and smugglers, yes, but better than ghastly pish-posh malls'); at old office buildings (looking at them, Mama-mon would have said, 'Jobs, salaries, life, choices—stuff I don't have access to. Door closed. Chapter over!').

The next evening, looking very cheerful, Mama-mon returned. She was once again the Mama-mon she used to be before her spooky flight-radar journeys, before whisky-in-a-cup! Always ready for a hug, twinkling eyes, the best playmate on earth. She cuddled me and spoke to Daddy nicely. But before it all, she soaked her clothes in a bucket full of Dettol and glared at them as if she wanted to burn the whole lot. Then she took a bath so long that it emptied the city's reservoirs.

Mama-mon ate dinner in silence, chewing slowly. She asked Nago Didi to make me a bowl of starchy rice with potatoes and a hard-boiled egg—the one bowl that could soothe me, no matter what. When you are feeling like I was feeling that day, it is possible to find in the yellowish-blue broth of the starchy rice a dozen seahorses fighting with each other. Startling as they may be to look at, seahorses and appetite don't go well together.

I spent the rest of the week forgetting all about that Monday. What if it happened again? What if it was a dream? The following Sunday it became clear that Mama-mon would disappear mysteriously *every* Monday. And wherever she went on Monday was a cold, cruel place. A place from where her coming back wasn't so certain. The worst part was that she continued to say like a circus clown, 'Back in a blink! Before you say snap! Top secret!'

On the second Monday, I lay in bed and watched her get ready in front of the mirror. She smeared a white ointment on her chest, right below the collarbone. Then deftly, on top of it, she landed a transparent tape, sealing in the cream.

She caught me looking, winked and sat next to me for a chat. Exactly like the week before. Only this time, it was not about black holes and relativity. It was about secret devices planted under the skin. 'You know, don't you? Gravity is what they are after. Therefore, all of this—tap-tap!' She pointed at the mystery tape. None of it made sense. But I nodded. It was code to say—I am telling you stories that mean nothing to protect you from true meaning.

Mama-mon was lying, in the usual adult-slippery way.

I am lying because it's important. I am lying because it's good for you.

That Monday, Daddy couldn't get away from work. He managed to collect me from school, and we had a hurried slurpy noodle lunch at a Chinese joint close to his office.

'I have a very important visitor today. Hang around here, darling, while I quickly finish my work.' We got off the car. Daddy looked nervous. His cheeks carried green shadows. A cloud of perfume hovered around him.

Daddy's office greeted me like a cool oasis. Giant ferns rustled in the AC breeze. My face swam on glass panes. The floor was the colour of sand. Of this place, which Mama-mon said was built to resemble a mirage, Daddy was the boss and owner. I usually made myself at home in the conference room where I could write on frosted walls, listen to music and have Oreo shake ordered in from my favourite cake shop. But that Monday was weird. The conference room was full of strangers—new, smart, very foreign. They buzzed around in black suits and looked serious. No one paid attention to me. I set up my little workshop in Daddy's room.

After a while, a lady walked in with Daddy. She wore a Prussian blue skirt and black high heels. Her hair fell like a curtain of silk.

'Meet Shani. She is a very important guest. Shani and her team are visiting our office this week. Shani—Narois; Narois—Shani.'

Naroishani!

To impress this important visitor, I said, 'My mother once wrote a poem about someone called Shani.'

Shani said Uh-uh and that she was curious.

I asked if she would like me to recite the poem. Shani with curtain-hair nodded and said, Why-not.

Daddy said, 'Why? Not, not, not now.'

But I was ready with my lines.

Shani listened, her brows shooting up as she did.

She turned to Daddy and asked, 'Is that allowed? So adult. So dark.'

And I wanted to tell her, 'It's okay, Miss. We are cool. Don't worry. My mother lets me read and memorize her poems because she has no audience. I am her one and only.'

The first thing I noticed was your neck;
I could wring it, but I felt no hate.
I was in the plane you shot down,
I was in the tower that fell,
I am in the houses that you telephone before you bomb;
On top of a dresser in one such house,
I have a photo of your lover and me.

Just like that, the Age of Mondays had rolled in, and those Mondays became routine. I learnt to accept the slight breathlessness I felt when Mama-mon was gone, to kickbox the dread out of my life, to tell myself that no matter what, my mother was going to come back. Yes, there would be the next Monday, and then another, but this infinity of Mondays also meant that she was not vanishing; she had to be there with me to go away in the first place.

On Sunday evenings, I was allowed extra-long hugs and cuddles. We sat on a messy pile of legs, arms, laps and shoulders on the sofa, the three of us becoming heavier and warmer until it seemed like we had become the Taj Mahal.

Then one of us, usually Daddy, came unglued and said, 'Who wants dinner?'

Sometimes, at night, Mama-mon and Daddy fought. At first there was just the low hum of a helicopter in the room. Then the sound would grow, become a mini-earthquake. I recorded all of this through the pillows under which I buried myself.

4. The Ghost of Uncle Perez

Do you know how many parks there are in the city of Delhi?

Well, I am sure you don't. What would you do with that information?

Unless you need parks to burn the dead.

Well, we did eventually. When that happened, I found specks of ash in my banana shake. Mama-mon didn't believe me until she went out on the terrace and found flecks of it on her tongue.

Before that, no one had reason to count the number of city parks, right?

I googled to find out. According to the website Delhi Parks and Gardens Society, there are as many as 18,000! Imagine now, of all those thousands of parks, Kiran's Papa chose to bring Kiran and Suraj to the one park where Mama-mon had taken me one winter afternoon.

Way before that, the first domino in the swirl of dominoes that we toppled, was the day when Mama-mon and Daddy went house-hunting. After a long weary day, during which they visited more than a dozen homes, the broker brought them to a house made of limestone. It glowed and it spoke—*come live here*. What clinched the deal, according to Daddy, was the call of jackals and dusk gathering in the forest on the other side of the wall.

We moved in six years ago with our bags, books, piano and Mama-mon's mountain of keepsakes—little clothes from when I was an infant, red colour-pencils with which DinDin's mother marked class twelve math copies, her grandfather's microscope and a box of slides that had all kinds of illnesses smeared on them. Our bookshelves had room for crumbling books, which were DinDin's, and her notes in scarlet and black. Granny Dorabjee's recipe book and an old copper map of the world were all we had from Daddy's family. How I wished, instead of filling up our rooms with things that belonged to people, we could have had those people visit us regularly. Like DinDin, who raised me until I was five and then went away and never came back. I never really got to know Granny Dorabjee. Daddy gets me to speak with her on the phone twice a year—once on my birthday and then on the day of Navroz. I greet her as Granny Dorabjee, and she tells me, 'Call me Gran, my Narois.'

But Mama-mon says Granny Dorabjee is a better name. A truer one.

It was Granny Dorabjee's cousin, Uncle Perez, who gifted us the hundred-year-old piano. Uncle Perez was ancient and lived all by himself in a dark house on top of a narrow staircase. One day, his stomach and its various pipes stopped working, and old Uncle Perez decided it was useless to try and eat any longer. Daddy's family from Colaba, Atlanta and Singapore flew in with their broths and mashes. Uncle Perez shooed away the entire bunch and locked himself in. Daddy and I were the only ones allowed because we went without any intention of making him eat. When Uncle Perez began resembling a skeleton, long before he made it to the ground underneath, Daddy put his foot down and said he would have to be force-fed.

Uncle Perez gave in and agreed to a few spoons of soup every now and then.

He sat tottering on the piano stool and played all day, all night.

Daddy arranged mattresses and cots all around the piano. When Uncle Perez's spine could no longer hold him up, he lolled over to his left or right for a rest.

Sometimes I sat next to him, his skeleton giving me friendly jabs. He would give me a ride on the flying carpet, zipping across pieces of Beethoven and Mozart and Handel—my fingers resting over his long and bony ones. One evening, he took me flying over a piece by Nikolai Rimsky-Korsakov. What a giddy ride that was, but at the end of the piece Uncle Perez said he had had enough. I helped him bring down the lid, on top of which he planted a kiss. Then he got off the piano stool and lay down on the mattress to his left.

He died a few days later, the soup not being food enough to keep a body running. After his funeral, we found out that Uncle Perez had left the piano for me with a little note that said: I will always be with you. Let the lessons continue.

I took that message literally. Sitting at the piano, going over the keys, which I found I could do with ease, I thought I heard Uncle Perez sigh. When I misplayed a note, I felt boney jabs.

DinDin said she was broken. Something about Uncle Perez's death reminded her of everyone else she had lost.

'But you barely knew him, DinDin. You met him twice and spoke exactly six sentences.'

Those six sentences DinDin knew by heart.

- How was your dinner with Satyajit Ray?
- He was rather grumpy, but the chops were good.
- My sister used to go to Eniss and they gave the best hair bouffant in town.
- Oh yes, my lady friend preferred Ennis in those days; she moved to June Tomkyns later.
- I wish Mrs Dorabjee would become our friend.
- Oh, don't bother, sister. Families are like that.

DinDin said she was aghast at the way old things were made homeless or replaced. She was tired of it.

'Do you dislike me because I am the piano's new owner, DinDin?'

'No, no, Kankabati, I dislike nothing. I just like things that are no longer around us.'

Mama-mon said that such things were to be found only in DinDin's old haunts, that she was hell-bent on looking back.

'It is an infection I want to keep you away from.'

'A delicious infection but!' DinDin whispered to me in secret before she caught the evening train and never came back.

'I am done with Delhi. I am done with new things.'

That year in autumn, we visited DinDin in Calcutta. It was the last time I saw her, but I didn't know it then. There were festoons and lights. I couldn't take my eyes off Ma Durga's super kind eyes and the glittering sarees of her daughters. Dhaak beats thundered on loudspeakers, priests chanted, people sang—there was music everywhere. When the festivities ended, DinDin sent us on a trip to a village called Sherpur where her cousin-in-law lived.

'Chin is dying. Please visit her, for your father's sake.'

We had a gala time driving down. On the highway, I rolled down the window and stuck my feet out, getting tickled by the slightly nippy and salty breeze. Daddy drove like a car racer. We skidded on a muddy stretch, and he said, 'Oh, it's nothing!' Mama-mon giggled. My heart beat wildly, and I thought that was the end. We crossed rivers and temples and paddy fields.

Daddy stopped the car after Burdwan. We had lunch at a roadside eatery.

The serving boy, who skated about between orders at tables and in cars, plonked a hill of puffed-up crispy luchi on our table. He chuckled at how much we were going to eat. My fingers turned yellow from the daal and glistened with oil from the luchi.

Mama-mon was happy. She took photos and claimed control of the car music, something she always complained about otherwise. Often on the road, she slipped her hand under Daddy's on the gear. That day, she found nothing to scold us about.

The village was pretty with huts (like in drawings), thatched roofs and coconut trees bending over ponds. Little magnets danced down my spine. I had a strong urge to play, make little mud pellets, sort the hay, cook on woodfire.

Chin Dida's house was a large red building. There was a handpump in the courtyard. We sat on a divan in the covered balcony with bright green grates at the window. It was so cool and musty. Mama-mon's relatives gave us a plate full of yellow and pink sweets.

Ritu Mashi, Mama-mon's cousin, hugged her and cried.

'We grew up together. Imon, I have missed you so much, re. But how you never came back, broke my heart so. Now I am an old woman with a married son, and you are so young.'

Plans were made to visit the nearby temple, which the family owned, and to walk along the paddy fields.

Kids of my age came over. They were in frocks with shimmering nets and satin roses. I longed for that sparkle. One girl called Disha was wearing bright pink lipstick—'In your honour,' Ritu Mashi said. I thought Disha would be embarrassed, but she wasn't and came over and asked me, 'Which class are you in?'

First we had to visit the dying. Chin Dida was in a special hut at the far end of the courtyard. It was a proper mud house with a hay roof. We entered barefoot. The autumn sun filtered in and made little patterns on the mud floor. A sweet-disgusting smell attacked my nose, and I had to stop breathing. Mama-mon went up to Chin Dida and laid a hand on her head.

'Pishi, I am here. Ma sent me and asked me to give you this.'

She took out an old saree from her bag. It was a tattered silk with a musty smell like all of my DinDin's sarees; I wondered what on earth was Mama-mon doing, handing over old stuff to this dying lady.

'Bharati asked me to tell you that she remembers the day you wore it. You looked mayabi. Your dusk-rose Banarasi, Pishi. No one will take it away from you anymore. Won't you see it once?'

Although her breath rattled and she moaned constantly, Chin Dida opened her eyes till they were slits and her toothless jaw wobbled. Then the strangest thing happened; her moans stopped. She seemed to fall asleep. Daddy, although he had never seen this lady before, sat by Mama-mon, closed his eyes and said a prayer.

'What did you pray, Daddy?'

'Oh, you know, I make it all up.'

They were making things up all the time—Mama-mon her poems, Daddy his prayers.

I learnt that afternoon that rice grew well in flooded fields and were babied inside crunchy husks.

Autumn rice is called aus chaal and winter rice is called aman chaal.

Disha reminded me of Kiran. 'Show me her photo,' she demanded.

I opened photos of our Goa trip on Daddy's phone.

'Mmeh, she is so skinny and dark,' Disha said. 'Not like me at all. See how white I am.' She placed her hand next to mine.

After that I didn't want to play with Disha anymore. I no longer envied her haystacks or the endless supply of mud she could play with.

Things came apart at dinner, which we ate in another outhouse made of mud. The electricity went off. Kerosene lamps were lit. Although I liked the smell of kerosene burning and sniffed the air around the sooty glass chimneys, I disliked the tight darkness all around us.

Mama-mon stared at Daddy. She had eyes for nothing else. Just fixing her stare on him like that meant something had happened. Something was changing. And I wasn't wrong in assuming that.

Dinner was delicious, but a fishbone stuck in my throat and I couldn't swallow anything. My mouth filled with spit, which I couldn't gulp down. Ritu Mashi made me swallow a ball of hot rice. Magically the bone was gone, and I was fine again.

Even as I settled down, Mama-mon said DinDin had called. There was an emergency, and we had to head back home straight away.

Whenever she lied, she mumbled and made it very clear to everyone that she was lying.

'Why should I bother hiding anything? Something must have happened to make me lie, so in a way my lying is on *others* and that should make *them* uncomfortable.'

Always that—I and Them.

Mama-mon and Daddy continued saying nothing. Ritu Mashi reminded her about the fishing expedition.

'I had it arranged for tomorrow morning, even though Choto Kaka says we will end up with barely grown chara ponas. But I did it for you. Fifteen jeles are coming on special request with their nets. They are already in Arambagh, and I have prepared meals for them. Can't you stay until the maachh dhora tomorrow? Let the fish be caught and then you can leave.'

We got into the car. I said a cold goodbye to Disha. Ritu Mashi hugged Mama-mon and couldn't stop weeping.

Daddy started the car, and we sat in silence until the village road had fallen far back. A few relatives followed us on their bicycles. When we climbed onto the highway, they waved and went back into the darkness. We sat in silence, whizzing past brick towers that were rice mills and a river growling. Finally, when Daddy turned onto the eight-lane road and picked up speed, we played music and chatted about getting a dog.

Our house with limestone walls can be spotted from an aeroplane if you have the eyes for it. Look to your right when the plane is beginning to land in Delhi. As soon as the forest looms under you, keep an eye out for the row of houses on its northern border. Sure enough, you will spot our house, glowing a yellowish-white at noon or a sunny marmalade at sundown.

'We live next to the rich, but we are not them, no-no, don't get us wrong, we are anything but rich. We are here for the forest, you see,' Mama-mon would explain, her hands flying, eyes blazing, to anyone who happened to sigh over the bigness of our apartment or over the backyard always flowering with yellow oleanders and sweet-smelling, worm-drawing raat ki raani.

You could love something and be ashamed of it at the same time.

The forest didn't really care why we were there, its wall rubbing against other posh houses; the Jahanpanah Forest that has existed for centuries, rustling, shedding, lurking.

Kiran lived in the Sharan House next door where chandeliers blazed day and night in every room. In the main mansion, where I have never been, there were carpets and furniture that could, according to Mama-mon, 'feed a nation'. The Sharans owned cinema halls across the country and were almost as rich as our other neighbours, the Coal People, who flew in singers from Bombay for their parties.

Standing like a beanstalk in the Sharan House's backyard was a narrow tower. A winding staircase led to a cozy little room in which Kiran lived with Papa, Suraj, Choti Ma and the baby. From atop that tower, Kiran let down her long black hair to dry in the sun. The yard garden was a riot of colours and smells. Kiran's Papa grew a little patch of herbs—parsley, sage, rosemary and thyme—like the song—with a chorus of mint, coriander, lemongrass and turmeric. There was an arch of bougainvilleas, a grass giraffe, guava trees full of fruit, jacaranda and amaltas, and an old bottlebrush wearing red earrings. When the Sharans went away on vacation, we secretly made it our den.

'Selfish giants and beyond reform.'

Mama-mon wanted to write a letter and aeroplane it across the wall, but Daddy stopped her.

'Kiran's Papa will lose his job. What good will that do?' he said.

At least once a week, I ate dinner with Kiran and Suraj in their tower room. Choti Ma made rotis on a round black hotplate. The room smelt of burnt flour.

'They don't trust us with a real fire. So, they gave us an old hotplate.'

Kiran could cook. She said she wasn't taking a chance. 'Not after what happened when Amma died. If ever left to myself, I should be able to cook and eat.'

Before the baby was born and their little room started smelling of diapers and stale milk, I would sit with Kiran and Suraj on the top landing of the staircase, overlooking the dark forest. We dangled our legs through the railing, not making a sound. We kept a potted aloe vera plant by a corner and draped handmade Tibetan prayer flags along the banister. Papa and Choti Ma locked the room from inside and made a baby. It was the best time of the day, even in bone-chilling winter when we had to sit huddled and our feet turned blue and our nose watered. The forest glinted and winked at us with mysterious lights and packs of jackal assembled below for a chat. When I couldn't join Kiran, the noisy yowling of jackals became our secret code. It was a signal that Kiran was out there.

Good night, Kiran!

Good night, Narois!

Kiran was not born in the chandelier house with a chir pine tree in its front garden. She was born in Tughlakabad, in a house that shared a wall with the emperor's fort, at one end of a befuddling maze of lanes snaking up from a road so noisy that the people who crossed that road every day slowly went deaf. Her old house was in a cul-de-sac and much quieter than the rest of the neighbourhood. We have visited a few times. Usually with Nago Didi, who complained non-stop about the dirty lanes and the rudeness of people who she thought were staring at her for no good reason.

The family that rented the house after Kiran's Papa moved away were nice people and knew Kiran as a baby.

'Your mother made the best kebabs in the entire neighbourhood, and she was such an amazing seamstress,' the lady remembered when we visited.

Then she showed us an old kurta which Kiran's Amma had stitched and embroidered for her elder daughter.

Houses shared walls snugly. People sat outside all the time, eating, sewing, chatting, watching comedy shows on their phones, recorded fake laughter adding to their own real laughter.

Here you couldn't possibly feel lonely, and if you wanted to hide you easily could. You would never be found.

'Papa says our house was damp and cold, but I don't remember it that way at all. Amma would finish up her chores and take me for an afternoon walk to the highest parapets of the fort. We would stay there until the sun set over the forest. I in her arms, Suraj playing nearby. It was perfect.'

I never got to know how Kiran's Amma died. The exact details.

'Amma was sick, and she died. It doesn't matter why, does it? Death is all the same. One minute your mother is warm, the next minute she is ... COLD, and you don't feel like touching her. And before that there are days when you are waiting for it to happen.'

How cold is death? How long is the wait? How much does it hurt to die and to be left with your mother dead—all these questions came to me much later.

When Amma died, Kiran's Papa, who was a talented Chinese chef, sat in one corner of their room next to the fort wall and cried for days. Suraj ate biscuits when he was hungry. Kiran just bawled and bawled. Sometimes a kind neighbour came and fed her milk. Probably to stop that racket.

'The hunger of those days burnt a hole in my food pipe. That's why I'll always be skin and bones,' she had told me one day.

We were not yet friends when all this happened, so I never got to know her Amma. A few months later, one winter Wednesday, at a nearby park where Mama-mon and I often went when she was having an afternoon-fit, Kiran's Papa turned up with both his children. Only sleepy dogs and us in the steely silence of mid-afternoon. Mama-mon spotted Kiran's Papa sitting on a bench, crying. Suraj was on the seesaw, shooting up and down. Kiran was crawling around on the dusty dry ground. A stray dog sniffed her. Mama-mon swept her up in her arms and gave her the rest of the apple juice from my bottle.

But back to the story that I never tire of. How Kiran cried for Amma. How, as days went by and she didn't stop crying, the people of Tughlakabad started saying bad things about Papa. They said he was trying to kill himself and that he would starve his children to death.

One day, he shook himself up and took a bath and bought a few packets of chips and biscuits from Chacha's shop. Then he said to Suraj, 'I will get you hot food today evening.' And he went to work. That night, Papa came back with two packets of staff food from the Chinese restaurant where he was sous chef. He had lost his job. Ajinomoto and spring onion reminded him of Amma.

Since the day Kiran's Amma had died, no matter how much he tried, Papa could not cook Chinese food. What good is a Chinese chef who can't cook Chinese food? They let him go. But the owner was a kind man. He gave Papa some money, two staff meals and advice—'Why not learn some other cuisine?'

Kiran's Papa spent months watching Italian food recipe videos on YouTube. When the savings ran out, he worked as a part-time gardener and toilet cleaner. Papa hadn't actually cooked any Italian food. But when he was called for a trial stint at the chandelier house, he cooked spaghetti in alfredo sauce and lasagna perfectly. That was the afternoon we met at the park and Mama-mon said, 'Let the children be friends.' Ever since that day, Suraj and Kiran became part of my evenings, Mama-mon's afternoons, our Saturdays and special biriyani days.

Uncle cooked and cooked and finally became an expert at cooking European food and at forgetting Amma. He got better and grew stronger, and when he no longer wept over Chinese food, he married Choti Ma and made a baby.

All this, on account of parks in Delhi where every afternoon thousands of people who have nowhere to go turn up and have ice cream and meet someone they will love forever.

And if they don't, they are eaten by a dog.

5. Salon-Salon

We settled into a routine of sorts. A drowning-and-then-bobbing-up-for-air kind of routine. Daddy and Mama-mon fought every other night, and those fights became bigger and louder and always ended with Daddy begging Mama-mon to stop.

The problem with them fighting was that it left a guava taste in my mouth. The creamy smelly taste of it hijacked all other tastes, including the finger-licking taste of butter rice.

I was six years old. We were eating breakfast, Daddy and I biting and sucking guava sprinkled with black salt. Mama-mon fiddled with a burnt toast. Shattering the silence of our eating and chewing, she spoke up in the voice of a woolly mammoth waking up after a million-year-long sleep.

Mama-mon could speak like posters when she wanted—in captions and slogans. I remember how the poster-sentence went, the music of it, the gnashing beats, Daddy's sinking heart, the splash it made when it fell into the sea. How startling it all was!

'Last night I was on the verge of suicide. Wanted to stick my head in the gas oven and die like her.'

'Imon, watch what you are saying.' Daddy got up, swatting the air as if the words were mosquitoes.

'Narois, go inside. Oh, Imon, can we not have some sort of a code? Oh, my poor little child.'

He covered my ears and pulled me into his arms. But I had caught the word. It was delicious and terrifying. No harm in words, Mama-mon always said. They can come and go as they please.

'Die like who, Mama-mon? Where is Soo Ee Side? How do you go there?'

'Is she not my daughter, not even a little bit?'

'Yes, Danish, half yours, half mine. How you are dealing with your half is the question.'

'But I have no say, not even half a say in what she hears and learns at such a young age.'

I, half-Danish, half-Imon, already knew about Growing Up and theoneandonly Minister of Words — who censored or not as she chose, whose ruling and unruling steered my entry into life and sent me crashing into adult zones.

I knew by age six that Mama-mon was suicidal. That she held a blade over her wrist for an hour, hovering like a plane undecided about whether to release the bomb. That Sylvia Plath's husband was a two-faced demon who lived two lives. That Daddy was living two lives.

The other life was a possibility. A life that existed, even if it didn't, according to Mr Albert Einstein.

From such drowning we were saved by Rani who came on Saturdays, with her bag of wax jars, silk threads, needles, creams, face bleach and tiny vials of perfume, which she cooked herself. Part human, part painting. Rani was Mama-mon's tailor, hairdresser, beautician. She smelled of roses and wore lacy bras and clothes in soft shades of peach, mint or sky blue. Her lips shimmered like a river in the sun. 'Our special light,' Mama-mon called her. We were puppets, bobbing and spinning to the dance of her long fingers.

Saturday of the second Monday, Mama-mon said she wasn't feeling up to a massage. Her feet were blue.

Rani hatched a quick plan.

'Let's pack sandwiches—two types at least. Chicken-mayo and egg-potato. I have a bunch of people to visit, clothes to deliver and new orders to take. You come with me as my assistant."

Mama-mon clapped and cheered and said I couldn't have asked for a better Saturday. 'Go play salon-salon.'

Daddy wasn't so sure, and he said so.

'Why not stay back and practise some maths, finish homework, have a go at the piano?'

Mama-mon's face hardened. 'Why do you object, Danish? No, really, what's the real reason?'

Daddy turned purple.

I forced Kiran to come along. She was unwilling. 'Don't want to miss maths tuition.'

I guessed that the real reason was something else. Rani made Kiran uncomfortable. She felt excluded in her company. I pleaded with Kiran, and she finally agreed. It could be fun, and both of us felt in our bones that something exciting was around the corner—something off limits, something that we would keep a secret.

I was going to miss my music lesson. Mama-mon telephoned Ustadji to tell him that. It made him angry, and he said it was not right to miss lessons, that Raag Bhairav must be learnt in a flow. Mama-mon said structure was a beast and should be avoided at all costs.

Kiran's days were structured, and she was perfectly groomed—not a hair out of place. She combed her waves herself. It's what kept her safe from sadness, from the hollowness of not having her own mother.

We set out at noon. The streets were empty and rain puddles turned into streams. Manhattan Cove, where millionaires lived, was our first stop. Inside the marble-and-glass foyer, a waterfall gushed down and collected in a lily pond. The lilies looked real, but they were plastic. It was cool inside, and the sun felt like silk.

We rode a private elevator to the penthouse apartment. A baby squealed, and a nanny fussed over him and called him Baba. I wondered if he was Baby No. 6, with five dead sisters before him. Mama-mon taught me to count like that: 'Always count the invisible. Remember that people who live in houses with glass façades go on baby-killing holidays to Thailand.'

Rani deposited the onesies she had stitched for the Baba-baby. There were prayers and hymns embroidered on the tiny garments.

One to ward off the evil eye.

Another to make sure Baba-baby's poop was a perfect yellow.

Perhaps another to scare off the ghosts of his sisters.

The mother, whose hair shone like molten copper, looked delighted and treated us to eclairs from Paul's.

I thought she must be a fan of sugary baked goods because not only was her fridge stuffed with many more eclairs, but Rani also handed over two small bottles of white sugar to the lady.

The sugar was packed in tiny glass vials, same as the bottles in which Rani carried her attar. Of what use were such small quantities of sugar? They wouldn't even sweeten Baba-baby's cereal.

After another waxing and hair-crimping appointment, our work at Manhattan Cove was over, and we walked out into the hot afternoon. Roads battered by incessant rain looked like ruined cake. Giant potholes slowed down cars. A stray dog followed us, snarling.

We walked across to the W-block park. It was empty except for a few drivers who were off duty or waiting between car trips. They sat in a circle playing cards and gazed at Rani.

Kiran and I took turns with the outdoor gym equipment. The swing scalded our thighs, but we swung high and caught a glimpse of the market beyond the boundary wall.

Our next and final stop was at Naina Sehgal's house, whose living room had a deep green ceiling. Everything else was gold and white. Her kid played a drum-set in the basement. Our bones shook. An old man snoozed on the yellow sofa. Rani revealed a gown of mirrors, and Naina laughed. She spun it around. The gown was like a person.

As she tried on the gown in her bedroom, three chilled glasses of mango shake came for us. Long after our mango shakes became leftover sea froth on our lips and we had doodled our names on the frosty tall glasses, Naina came out, gown nowhere in sight.

'*Kaisa laga?*' Rani asked anxiously. 'How come you didn't show us what a beauty you looked in it?'

Rani could be a diplomat. If you happened to run a country, she could be your minister of foreign affairs.

Naina smiled and said she would transfer Rani's charges. Then she sat looking at the green ceiling and asked, 'Any other news?'

'Yes, but maybe it's nothing.'

'Oh, it never is nothing. Trust me, baby,' Naina Sehgal said.

'Can't talk in front of the bachhas. Call me later.'

We stewed in Naina Sehgal's house of daring greens for almost an hour. The kid kept beating the drums, and our eyeballs popped, and our saliva pooled under our tongues. Naina Sehgal's ocean of words lulled us. Her kid was the best at everything, she was as rich as a Kuber, but she was also a poor unfortunate. And things happened to her. Cruel terrible things, all owing to the fact that her husband had found another Mrs who was actually a Miss who would never legally be Mrs.

We stopped for coconut water near the market. From the mountain of green coconuts, Rani picked up a few and shook them, listening to the water inside and expertly choosing the three heaviest. We sipped on the delicious water and ate the white fleshy meat, which the coconut seller cut open for us with a sharp knife.

A light breeze picked up, blowing away the dull gloom. Dust stung our eyes, so we tried walking home with our eyes tightly shut.

6. Oculus Sinister

Mama-mon got a new haircut. She looked dashing and very pleased.

'Nasir has outdone himself this time.'

Bouncy curls frilled her neck and forehead, dancing to the tunes of Nasir Uncle's scissors. I twisted them around my fingers, those proud curls which smelt of evening and parties.

Rani sulked a little bit. She would, wouldn't she? After all, Mama-mon hadn't consulted her about the haircut—Rani the salonista who had a Pinterest board on what-hair-looks-good-on-whom.

What an evening, I thought, when Mama-mon bounced around in her haircut! Nothing ever goes wrong with such evenings.

But all the while, as we chatted about parties—which would all lead to my upcoming birthday party—a wicked rat scurried up and low in my belly saying, Hello! Something is about to happen!

Rat is never wrong. Kiran was at the door, furiously ringing the bell, *krring krring, krring*. She was panting, and her face was white.

'Suraj is in trouble. They caught him selling something dangerous during lunch break. And now he is suspended from school. Choti Ma taunted him about it, so he left home in a huff. I ran after him, but there was a bike waiting for him at the gate, and he sped off on it with a friend I have never seen.'

The world spun—a bike whizzing through traffic, car horns, police. I felt queasy and put an arm around Kiran. To comfort her and because I needed comfort too. Suraj—out in the darkness, gone to a mysterious place where we couldn't reach him.

Daddy called Kiran's Papa and spoke to him in a low voice. Looking grimmer and grimmer, he called Lawyer Shroff, who was a hotshot lawyer who solved everything for Daddy. Lawyer Shroff came on a conference call with Daddy and Kiran's Papa. The lawying went on for almost an hour. Daddy took the call from inside the bedroom. I could hear nothing. Mama-mon was with him, but she came out later, hugged Kiran and spoke in a shrill, unnatural voice.

Nago Didi made hot chocolate and fried a few fish fingers.

After Kiran went home that evening, Mama-mon pulled me close and said, 'Narois, Daddy and Uncle will meet the principal. Everything will be fine soon.'

Dinner was a hot bowl of egg curry and steaming rice. I broke the rice hill with my fingers and poured gravy over it. My nails turned red from the tomato and chilli. I squeezed a lemon, picked out three unbearable cardamoms and ashy peppercorns.

Mama-mon put up her feet and tilted her head back on the armchair, while Rani made little circles on her head.

'Have dinner. It's late.'

Rani refused and gave another one of her excuses, which never did sound very solid—she muttered them whenever we asked her to stay for dinner.

'Di, you know how much I love egg curry. But Chacha's eldest wife is on her way to Ajmer, and she said she wanted to spend a night with me. Just to catch up on family gossip.'

Then she lowered her voice, but I caught every word.

'Let nature take its course, let the water flow as it will. Suraj has found his level, Di, with those boys from Tughlakabad. He runs wild with them, doing whatnot when evening falls in the abandoned ramparts of the fort. Why, the other day, I was just passing by when ...'

Mama-mon silenced her with a hand and a stare. Enough! Then she closed her eyes and put an end to the chat.

After a few minutes, Mama-mon said, in a voice icy and low, that she was tired and Rani could leave. I felt horrible for Rani, who was hurriedly packing up her things. I pushed back my chair, getting up to see her out.

'Narois, please don't get up in the middle of a meal,' said Daddy, as if in perfect understanding with Mama-mon.

Never have I ever witnessed our Lady of Touch and Light being dismissed the way she was that evening. It dawned on me, something that Kiran seems to have always sensed, that Rani had other lives, other parts of her mind and dreamy self that were not entirely known to us.

Kiran got bullied in school. Her friends stopped talking to her and passed rude comments. During lunch break she sat all by herself in one corner of the school grounds and sobbed her heart out.

'Even Pari?'

'Even Pari. They think Suraj is a drug dealer. Because he is bad, I am bad too.'

'Oh, schools are overrated, aren't they? It's just cruel gossip.'

'Narois, they did find drugs in his bag. Like real bad stuff called Meow Meow. It can kill you, or worse still, melt your brain. Lawyer Shroff told Papa that the case is so bad that they can put him away in a special jail for children where doors don't open until the badness inside you has been completely cured.'

'But that doesn't make sense. Suraj is a kid, and he's got a really innocent face. Who would ask him to sell drugs? Drug mafia—they are really wicked-faced people.'

'You think looks matter? No, Narois, it's better if your face doesn't give you away. Pretty babyface looks are perfect for drug-selling. Don't you see why your favourite person is so successful at it? Everyone trusts her and thinks she is too pretty, and they don't mind buying that horrible stuff from her ... as if buying it from a beautiful person will make it harmless.'

Wait, what? What was Kiran going on about?

When I said I couldn't understand, Kiran called me naïve.

'You have no world view.'

'Okay, fine, I get what you are saying. But prove it to me.'

'I can't. But these are things that don't need proof. You can sense it. Choti Ma says Rani is a drug dealer. The whole salon-and-tailor thing is just a cover. She basically supplies very expensive drugs to her clients. What do you think is in those small glass bottles? Sugar?'

'Mama-mon is also her client. Are you saying she is a druggie?'

Kiran rolled her eyes and said I was being stupid and obstinate.

Do druggies have orange afternoons? Do druggies chase aeroplanes?

Kiran and I swore that we would do everything that needed to be done to keep Suraj safe. Even if it meant taking risks. We were ready for it. The solution was, in fact, staring us in the face, all thanks to gossip. If Rani was indeed a drug dealer, wouldn't she be our best bet to find a solution? Kiran agreed with me at once, and we promised never to tell a soul.

'Don't go off telling Rani that we are using her and that her cover is blown.'

'Obvio! Whatdya think of me, bro?'

It was hard to think ill of Rani, and to be honest, I wasn't exactly thinking ill of her. I was, if anything, awfully impressed.

Kiran and I decided to act immediately. Prep work before such a mission is what makes or breaks things. So, I sought out my oldest 'other' friend—Meera Rebecca—who is actually a wizard training to be a police officer. Naturally, if you have a sleuthing mission, your first port of call for top tips will be her. Meera listened with huge eyes and broomstick lashes, what she called 'the eye system trained in Morse code and all-types-of-seeing'.

'Using eyes for plain-see and plain-look is a waste. My Oculus Sinister sees what you can't see. Oculus Dexter, on the other hand, sees what lies in broad daylight but it's actually *not* what you see. First things first. Give your mission a name.'

'That's easy. We'll call it Mission Suraj.'

'Dead giveaway, that one. With names like this, you will never lead a mission to success and end up catching a bullet in no time. Suraj was accused of selling narcotics, was he not, officer?'

'What's narcotics?'

'Ah, finally a word that even Vera Narois doesn't know the meaning of. Well, drugs, obviously. According to Mummy, it is evil on earth. Now, since the drug in question is Meow Meow, let's call it Mission Cat-out-of-the-Bag.'

'How do you even eat drugs? I think they drink it.'

'Nah, you don't eat or drink. You DO drugs, gottit, Ms Idioms and Words? They have many options, so it's just *doing*—swallowing as pills with Coca-Cola, snorting them like powder, rubbing them on the gums, inhaling, injecting. It's really awful. Do you know some people are called drug mules? They carry tonnes of drugs inside their bodies.'

'Do you think Suraj is a drug mule? Because I have never seen him stashing away anything mysterious ever. Maybe it's all inside his body.'

'Oh, yeah, that's possible. Drugs are put inside capsules. Mules swallow like five hundred capsules. Then they take anti-vomiting meds so that they don't throw it all up. Narois, if the capsules burst inside Suraj's stomach, he will die. You got to act fast.'

It was difficult to eat lunch, even though Nago Didi had snuck chicken momos in my tiffin box.

We got on to the next phase of planning called tell-me-whys.

'Tell me why Rani is the right candidate? You love her and trust her—those can't count as reasons.'

'That she saved Mama-mon from suicide? And all of us too. Pulled us back from a cliff edge.'

'Too vague.'

'Ah, okay, then it must be the other reason that makes me so confident that only Rani can guide us.'

'What's that? C'mon, I must have it all on the table.'

'All right, it's a secret, a big one really. She shared it with me and Mama-mon on the condition that not another soul could know. Although how that can be good for business, I have no idea.'

'Go on.'

'Rani is a famous perfume mogul. She owns Company of Attars, bequeathed to her by Abbu, the man who took her in and raised her like a daughter. Abbu came from a family of old perfumers who had been perfuming for hundreds of years. They brewed perfumes for Shah Jahan, bottled up exotic scents for Queen Victoria, and once—which made them mad with guilt and was probably the reason why their empire started crumbling—created a special perfume for Mussolini. Their brightly lit shops in Daryaganj, Chitpur, Lucknow, Banaras, with all-glass doors, windows and ceilings made of prisms, shut down one after the other. Heartbroken, Abbu's grandfather collected the discarded attar bottles and lined his house with shelves. Over the years, Abbu's family home was sold because they were poor. So, the attars travelled with them wherever they moved. Now these ancient and well-respected attars live in Rani's one-room flat. She says it's gloomy and suffocating, and she desperately wants to move out.'

'So why doesn't she?' asked Meera. I could tell she was fascinated. It was all going very well.

'Oh, what to do! Rani says she is destined to rot in Sangam Vihar where throat-slitting murderers roam and the water tankers come at 3 a.m. These old but very uptight and proud attars of Abbu's library refuse to move. Whenever she broaches the topic of moving, they plead with her—*Oh Rani, don't displace us from our shelves. Don't mess with the essence of emperors and musicians.* But truth be told—Rani is a talented perfumer. People from all over the world curry favours, pull strings for a bottle of special attar from her. It takes her at least a month to make one bottle.'

'Business must be thriving, no? She must be a millionaire.'

'Oh, easily,' I said.

Lunch break was almost over. We walked back to our classroom in silence. I could hear my heart thudding against the ribs.

Meera was deep in thought. At PE class, she said, 'Someone who runs an undercover business and has conjuring skills is indeed the right choice as mission leader. Rani—Keeper of Secrets.'

And Narois, too—Keeper of Secrets. Brilliant at it. Cold-blooded even.

Rani the attar-maker was a secret I could bear to share. Rani the drug dealer—this was a secret I would guard with my life.

I decided to wait until Saturday to casually mention to Rani that she had to lead us on a sleuthing mission.

'I know you can do it. You are a natural,' I would say to her, and if she dilly-dallied and talked about my parents scolding her for putting their only child at risk, I would sneakily mention that Mama-mon called my random afternoon outings with Rani the School of Escape, a school where I learnt things which I never would at any schooling school.

Let me school with you, I would say to her.

During the week, it was impossible to get in touch with Rani, who galloped through different pockets of the city. On Mondays she was at Sadar Bazar picking up fabric and threads for her tailoring jobs. Tuesdays and Wednesdays she was at home with her copper pots and various oils, cooking up a new batch of Abbu's attar. Until Saturday, the week was bound to drag.

Peculiar things were happening at school, so I amused myself with that.

The third Monday was not as smooth as the ones before it. I thought I had become quite a pro at Mama-mon leaving and saying to me in all kinds of geological terms *I might not return*. That morning, she put on a loose shirt and seemed petrified by her own image in the mirror. *Petrificus Totalus*.

Her lipstick was smudged over her teeth. She pulled me to her and started talking about the Great Oxidation Event, which occurred about two billion years ago in the Siderian Period and filled the earth with oxygen.

'The earth's population at that time, all of those microscopic organisms, died on a mass scale. They just couldn't survive the flood of oxygen.'

Oxygen reminded me of a poem, which tried to make the cliched point that mothers ought to be around, like the very air we breathe. That threw me in a lurch, and I couldn't breathe, my going-away mother couldn't make me breathe. She thumped me on my back, blew into my mouth and sang to me in our secret language.

I don't remember much about that episode. Except that it left a hollow inside of me for the rest of the day and the day after. So, I turned my attention to the things happening at school. To Annabelle—the doll trapped inside a Horror Museum. To anything that would take me away from the free fall.

It was 9 a.m. and we were out in the backfield. An after-rain warm sun tickled us. Distant cars hooted and hooshed. Peacocks screamed. We had discontinued our games to stand in a huddle around Reba, who claimed that Annabelle the Evil Doll, unable to find a home anywhere, was on the lookout for a place to haunt.

'She can travel in spirit anywhere she likes, and I found out, with my tremendous magical powers, that Annabelle the Doll is hosting with a man who lives in *that* apartment.'

We glanced up at the old apartment building that she was pointing at. It was a beige-coloured ten-storey high-rise, overlooking our backfield. Paint peeled off its walls. Flats were stacked one on top of another. Everything looking crummy, except for the balconies that grinned at us, wanting to say hello, talking to us with their washing swinging day-long. Pretty kurtas, tattered sheets, infant onesies, old pajamas, bras of all sorts. Once in a while, peeking above such washing and through them, were people. They came to check if the washing was dry or to hang out more. Sometimes they stayed back and looked down at us. Maybe they sighed. Out of irritation, of course, that we were making a noise; or out of envy that they weren't us. They extra-watered the flowerpots, secretly puffed on cigarettes.

We named the host of Annabelle, who lived on the fifth floor, Headless Azad. Precisely at 9 o'clock, when the organ music composed by Mirra Alfassa boomed in the Hall of Grace, Headless Azad came out to hang his towel in the sun. We could see all of him except his head, which appeared cut off. Otherwise, he was just a regular man who went to work, his office blue shirt a dead giveaway. It was exactly the blue that Mama-mon hated. Daddy looked nice in office blues, checks, stripes, solids, freshly showered, cheeks green from the shave. But seeing him in a blue shirt made Mamamon unhappy. Unhappier.

I thought Daddy looked like Elvis. With his sideburns and high crop of hair.

On Thursday, two days after we started spying on him, Headless Azad was late for work. The organ music started and ended. But no Headless Azad appeared.

Maybe he and his wife (who we assumed existed because of the bras that were hung out to dry) were out on a vacation.

Zorawar said, 'Maybe his wife is going to have a baby and he had to rush to the hospital.'

Our EVS teacher took us on a 'looking around you' walk across the fields, lily ponds and neem groves and showed us every mulberry tree on campus. We plucked and ate delicious mulberries—they blackened our tongues.

'Eat mulberries whenever you like. It's safe. So, remember and recognize well. This, for you, is the only fruit, children.'

That week, Reba played fortune-teller for all of us.

'Anabelle whispers to me from the balcony of Headless Azad. If you be nice, and pay me back with your friendship, I can tell you your futures.'

Meera and I sniggered—obviously, bro, we know what you want! To be the most popular girl in our class and to snag our prefect badges.

We weren't going to let her, but we went along in any case for the fortune-telling.

I have to say, her predictions created a buzz.

Sanvi's little sister would die in a school fire. In that same fire, Kyra's hair, which was fluffy, would become a burning bush. Her eyebrows would burn too, and eventually she would die of bad dreams. What she said about Zorawar was so terrible that when Zorawar told his mother about it, she lost sleep. Aunty sent an email to the class teacher, asking to see her immediately. After school I saw her climbing up the stairs slowly, her round belly, inside which was a baby that Zorawar secretly hoped would die and never come out, wiggling as she climbed.

7. Ground Zero

'Explain.'

Kiran's braids were pointier these days. Like a scold.

'What's your point? What's there to explain?' I was losing patience.

'Why her?'

'Cos she knows.'

'Why does she know?'

'Because of that life of hers—being an abandoned child, empress of perfumes, neighbour of stabbers and thieves. You would know, too, if you had that life.'

'So she is—even you admit— some sort of criminal.'

'Ugh, would I ever judge? Don't be so basic, Kiran.'

I drew a battle plan on Post-its. Mission Recruit-Rani was to take place that Saturday. Daddy helped me arrange a small picnic in the garden. We laid out a plate of sandwiches—grilled egg, cold ham, masala cucumber.

Rani finished Mama-mon's massage and came out smelling divine. We sat in the sun, waiting for Kiran. Thunderbolts roared and cracked in my tummy.

Kiran arrived, after I'd given up hope that she would turn up, with pulpy eyes. She must have cried buckets.

'Suraj packed up his clothes and headphones and our photo with Amma. All in a bag. Then he left. He is not coming back. Papa says he'll be all right … but only if we prove that he has been framed. If not, he is lost forever.'

Mission Recruit-Rani was on a scooter, vrooming headlong. No need for Post-its now.

'Can't you help us, Rani? You have such superbly clever connections. Mama-mon and Daddy want to use boring law and won't break rules. Can't you think of something clever, pull some strings?'

'We should trust in law and the police, little girl. But … ummm … let me see. Perhaps a little consult with my attar-abba and attar-naani will give me ideas. But don't tell Mama-mon, okay, Narois? Not even Daddy. Promise? They have too much on their plate.'

I thought it odd that she should want to keep anything from Mama-mon or Daddy. But anyone could see that we were spinning out of control that week.

Mama-mon locked herself up in the study every day, for hours. She said it hurt her head to open her mouth and talk or to listen to anyone talk.

'I need this echo chamber for a few days. My door may be closed, but it's open in the true sense, always.'

I was okay with that. It wasn't new, after all, her need to soundproof herself.

Daddy took me for a swim one evening, and I wished he hadn't because he was sullen throughout. It had rained earlier. The water was cold. In the blue light of the pool, I saw him wipe his eyes furiously. On the ride back home, he let me blast my playlist at full volume.

At last, after a long and dreary wait, Rani told us that she had found the solution.

'I happen to know just the right sort of people who can help us,' she said and rubbed her hands in glee.

We were to meet a group of undercover problem-solvers who, according to Rani, were the best in the whole world. So special were their powers, they had to stay hidden.

What incredible luck then that these invisible sleuths had set up a temporary station in the forest next to us.

'You are neighbours!' Rani was super excited when she discovered their location. She said it was a sign.

Soon it was the launch day of our mission. Rani, Kiran and I set out at dusk. Daddy was poring over a bunch of papers and didn't even look up when I told him I was going out for a stroll. Mama-mon's door was locked.

After a short walk along the busy road, we arrived at the forest gate.

A green turnstile let us in. I had been to the forest a few times but never so late in the evening. It was almost dark and a wild chorus of birds greeted us. Kiran grasped my hand tightly. It was one thing to speak to the jackals from Kiran's perch atop the winding staircase and quite another thing to be amongst them. A thin blue fog came hissing and slithered around us. It was cold and clammy. You had to squint and blink to see ahead. At a bend, a dark shape came hurtling. We froze. But it was only an evening walker on his way out. Kiran said he was chanting the Hanuman Chalisa. The forest path was empty. After a while, we sat on a bench to catch our breath. Evening flights roared past overhead. Traffic sounds drifted in from all corners. Leaves rustled, crickets chirped, birds slept.

Silence fell around us, offering an iffy hug.

We were thirsty and hungry. There was only one bottle of water to share.

'Take tiny sips,' I warned Kiran.

We munched on half-melted crumbling Mars bars, which we found in the satchel. Their sticky sweetness pumped in a tiny bucket of courage.

'Who are these people we are going to meet, Rani? Your friends?'

I was bobbing—a speeding wave of goosebumps.

'Narois, you are not paying attention. I told you, didn't I, these are people who will help us find Suraj, that is, *if* they choose to meet us,' said Rani, getting all fidgety herself.

'Are they dangerous?' Kiran could be direct when she wanted to be.

'They are the best thing that could have ever happened to this city,' said Rani, scoffing and turning up her nose. 'You are about to meet the legendary Jugnus. Wherever they are, they take on the name of the place. Now they are the Jahanpanah Jugnus, healers par excellence. They are healing everyone, even if no one knows about it yet. Just the other month, they cured the chief minister of his mango addiction. Did you know about that, Narois?'

'Ummm, I think so,' I lied, although I could vaguely remember Mama-mon grinding her teeth and saying something about mangoes and ministers.

'The chief minister would have fifty mangoes a day, and even that wasn't enough. He would wake up at night in a sweat and creep up to the kitchen for more mangoes. He thought of nothing but mangoes all day. Wore mango-coloured shirts. Drank mango juice. Gave speeches using mango idioms—he would say things like: "The opposition party is an Alphonso scam." His party headquarters got a new coat of mango-coloured paint. Then one day he slept a long sleep—slept for a week straight. When he woke up, he was cured. Can you guess what happened? The Jugnus had come, unnoticed by one and all. Mashallah! They cured the poor mango-ed minister. How they did it, no one knows. No one saw them come, no one saw their bag of medicines. Only those of us who know they exist could recognize their handiwork. They are changing the world, Narois. The Jugnus of Jahanpanah. You are so lucky to meet them. But first, before they trust us and appear before us, I want you both to swear that you will keep the Jugnus a secret,' Rani whispered nervously. 'Jugnus are kind and friendly, but if you betray them, they will come with ice picks and tear out your heart.'

We swore in the name of six different gods and swallowed our secret with our spits. A light rain fell. To stay warm, we sheltered under the arch of an ancient gate. The familiar smell of bat poop in old historical buildings made me nauseous.

By then, I was ready to walk back home. Kiran was on the verge of tears and wouldn't let go of my hand even for a moment. We were exhausted.

Sensing our impatience, Rani said the wait was worth it.

'You must see Silver Samir in person. He used to be a highly paid fashion model. Had millions in the bank.'

'Why did he give it up?'

'Oh, they all gave up something treasured to become Jugnus.'

I frantically combed the brambles for a flash of silver.

While we waited, Rani told us everything she knew about them.

'To be a friend of the Jahanpanah Jugnus, you have to pass tests of trust. To be able to go on missions with them, you require skills of another level. If you are an excellent trapeze artist, dog trainer, chemist or a manager of storms, you can join their gang. Apart from curing people of sicknesses they didn't even know they had, they also control dust, filter the air and so on.'

Kiran's feet were cold. I was about to beg Rani to end this adventure when a shadow appeared. With its spectral fingers, it beckoned us to follow. Which we did, trembling head to toe. A few steps and we were out in a clearing. There was light, thankfully, warm yellow light from the string of bulbs that hung from trees that circled the open patch. The grass was mowed and a few chairs were laid out. It wasn't raining anymore. A man, whom we came to know later as Velu, watched over a kettle on a small stove. A few others, all of them shadowy, lurked around the edges of the circle.

A more handsome person than Silver Samir I have never seen. He did indeed look like a movie star in blue jeans ripped stylishly across his knees. He wore a black T-shirt under which his muscles rippled like a comic-book avenger. Silver and diamonds sparkled on his ears, neck, wrists. He spoke as if he owned the forest. Argue as I might in my head, at that moment, it seemed like he did.

'Welcome to Jahanpanah, girls! Congratulations! You are the first children to ever wade through the dark forest and get a glimpse of the Jugnus.'

Rani stood next to Silver Samir. She trembled like a plant caught in a breeze and would have tripped and fallen had he not held her by the elbow and pulled her so she could lean against his strong body. He lifted a finger and made tiny circles on her forehead, between her brows. She closed her eyes and said something we couldn't hear.

Lo and behold!

Kiran and I looked at each other—was that a Jugnu-healing happening right in front of our eyes?

Silver Samir offered us a slice of black-forest pastry. The kettle-minder Velu held it out to us on a paper plate.

It looked tempting. Our tummies growled. Kiran licked her lips. But I held firm. Enough rules had been broken that evening. I told the Jugnus that we were not allowed to take food from strangers.

Silver Samir smiled at me and said he understood. Then he slowly ate the cake. I watched the delicious sweetness disappearing into his mouth; his dazzling white teeth nibbled at it slowly. Then he held out some for Rani who licked the cake off his fingers, it was so scrumptious.

The black-forest pastry was a test that I had failed.

'I was hoping to make you a member of our secret society since you come with recommendations. But that must wait.'

I was hungry and cold, mosquitoes feasting on me, their stings leaving little bumps with red spots on my skin. There was not a soul in sight.

'It's okay,' I said. 'I don't think we should be part of your secret society anyway. We hardly have any time left after school, music lessons and badminton. Could you just help my friend Suraj who is wrongly accused of something he couldn't possibly have done? If you see him, you will know right away that a sweeter, more innocent person never existed. How can he be a criminal?'

'Only take and no give? Come now, you could be a valued member, little girl. We need bright young things like you. It's good for the weather.'

'For the environment, you mean?'

'Yes, but we call it weather, in the old-fashioned way.'

'Mr Samir, I mean Samir Uncle, we should be going home. It's late.'

Rani shifted on her feet. I watched her. She was looking at Silver Samir and he at her.

'Rani, I ought to go. Mama-mon will be worried.'

'Yes, of course, darling, let's go.'

We bid adieu to the Jugnus, who seemed sad to see us leave. They watched us as we hurried away in the darkness that was even thicker now.

On the main road, Rani shouted above the cars to tell us that getting an offer to join the Jugnus was as special, if not more, as getting a letter from Hogwarts. 'Would you ever consider turning such an offer down?'

It was late and I was scared. Silver Samir's job description didn't interest me anymore. It was past 9 o'clock when we reached home. Daddy was outside, pacing up and down the street and smoking his I-am-tense-hence cigarette. These days he was smoking several of these tense-hencies in a day.

When I approached him, he rushed and hugged me and kissed me with his ashy mouth.

'Where were you? I called you so many times, Rani.'

I crossed my fingers and toes, hoping and praying she would not tell him the real reason. Even if I didn't want to go back to the Jugnu Club, this was meant to be a cherished adventure, and I didn't want to burn bridges with such important people. I wanted the back door in to stay open.

Kiran and I said goodnight and parted ways at the gate.

Rani spoke to Daddy in low tones as I walked into the driveway. Evening jasmine bloomed in thick clusters of white. Their sweet smell brought tears to my eyes. Even though Mama-mon was at home, and it was a Saturday, there was still that Monday looming over me.

Suddenly a loud clap and boom came from Kiran's driveway. I jumped. Was it a gun? A horrible stench filled the driveway. I scoffed at my own jumpiness. It was nothing but the usual mosquito-repellant canon that the neighbours fired every evening to keep away dengue. I held my breath and ran inside.

8. Jugnus

Sunday mornings were warm. We made breakfast together, took turns to play music, washed and dried dishes, did chores around the house. Mama-mon let me water the garden and found no cause to call Daddy an Oblonsky.

At the breakfast table, Daddy said in a stern voice, 'Enough loitering around. I'll set out a routine, and you will stick to that.' Mama-mon agreed with Daddy.

But try as we might to live by a routine, our days were open-ended with last-minute twists. Daddy was always busy. Mama-mon's Monday expeditions were cutting the week short, so he had to work harder during the remaining days. Because they fought until late hours almost every night—the only constant in our daily routine—he usually woke up groggy and tired.

The following Saturday, we went back to meet the Jahanpanah Jugnus, setting out well before dusk.

Ground Zero had a copper glow, very much like Mama-mon's afternoon tents. Velu offered us tea in doll-sized clay cups, and it was delicious.

Silver Samir was away on a weather emergency, which was disappointing. Clearly, he was the CEO and the rest were a bit clueless without him.

'Does it mean we can't start solving Suraj's case while the weather emergency lasts?'

Velu didn't look like someone who could be in charge. But he was interim CEO, he said, and we had to address all our queries to him.

'Jugnus have strict rules. You can't just come and ask us to do tasks for you. You have to earn the right. You have to pass many tough tests. We will first test you before we help you.'

Jugnu tests were of many kinds and many grades. You had to pass one level to take the next level of tests. If you passed at least six levels, you were eligible for Jugnu healing. If you passed the entire dozen, which could take months, and if you had a skill that could turn minds and the weather, you would be appointed a Jugnu.

Velu explained the rules of the first test. When he spoke, his eyes darted about at the speed of light.

Disappointingly easy it was—no big trial involving magical beings or hackers. All we had to do was put together a first-aid box.

'Remember not to take help from anyone. Remember not to cheat because Jugnus have eyes everywhere,' Velu told us. He smiled and his broken teeth showed.

That week, I collected a shoebox, which I covered with white tape and painted a red cross on one side. I found Peppa Pig Band-Aids, a bottle of Betadine, a strip of paracetamol tablets, and a small pair of scissors whose edges were almost blunt and cut nothing except gauze.

The week after, we took our second test, which was a quiz conducted on Ground Zero once again by Velu. He held a rapid-fire round of 'how well you know your own family'. There were ten questions about stuff that I saw and did every day, my parents' names, where they worked, the make of the car we drove, our favourite colour and so on. For Kiran, the questions were a little different and seemed to be more about my family than hers. We both passed with flying colours.

The third test was trickier. I had to smuggle out four chicken drumsticks and recite from memory our car's licence plate.

After the fourth test, in which we had to walk backwards, blindfolded, Kiran and I became members of the Jahapannah Jugnus.

'Welcome to the tribe.' Silver Samir held out his hand to shake mine. On his wrist was the tattoo of a thunderbolt. I doubted him no more. Here he was, a true weather worker.

'Where is the clubhouse?' I asked. It would be nice to finally be welcomed into a warm, well-lit secret den where all the weather workers sheltered.

He looked flummoxed.

'What club? What house?'

'The weather workers' club! Like … if you are a society, won't you have a club, a hideout where you meet and brainstorm?'

'Ah, a club … you see, Narois Didi, we are followers of the forest djinn. The djinn won't help us if we move within four walls and have a roof over our head. We must stay in the open, remain nimble and invisible. A club is too dangerous for us.'

It was hard to say what the Jahapanah Jugnus were meant for. They drifted in and out, faces changing every time. Some were superb acrobats who hung from trees. One Jugnu could break glass with his singing voice. Another Jugnu taught us to cartwheel. They came and went, as I said, but there was always Silver Samir and there was always Velu. And they were always to be met at twilight when the shadows were the deepest or in the afternoon if an unknowable fear gripped you.

Rani said they were farishtas who required kindness from people to do their job and do it well.

'Carry a gift. Always carry a gift when you go to meet them.'

I carried a bit of Daddy's whisky in a water flask, a pear and a container full of chicken nuggets, popcorn and marshmallows. I asked Rani if she had bought any gifts for Silver Samir, to which she said, 'I am his gift.'

Bearing gifts, we went every Saturday, hopeful that the Jugnus would solve the mystery and Suraj would be proved innocent as soon as possible.

'He is missing a lot of school, and he is not that great a student. Can you please hurry with your sleuthing?' I petitioned.

Most evenings we sat below a giant jamun tree, watching birds land on their nests. When it rained, we huddled under the blue tarp that was Velu's home. Velu kept his kettle on and supplied cups of hot tea, besides samosas and other delicious snacks. The remaining Jugnus would huddle too and tell us stories.

Mian Pagla was a boatman who decided, one day, to go where the river took him. For years he rowed his boat, ferrying passengers, goats, furniture. When the tide was low or when the river dried up, he did odd jobs on shore.

'In Taki, I was a smuggler of medicines. In Calcutta, I consoled weeping lovers. On the Manikarnika Ghat, I was a helper of Doms. In Allahabad, I stole sand. At last I arrived in Delhi. My boat floated through milky foam, and I thought I had come to wonderland. I anchored my boat, took out my best shirt and went on a tour of the grand city. When I came back at night, my boat was gone. Someone had stolen it. I wanted to drown in this river of fire and had only just walked to the edge, which was frothing and bubbling like a monster with a thousand nostrils, when someone pulled me with so much force that I fell back. I hit my head on the hard bank and blacked out. When I opened my eyes, I saw a face, the face of Jibril, glowing at the edges, shining like the moon, stroking my forehead ever so kindly. For the first time since I had left home, following the river, someone had actually touched me with the kindness that only comes from the touch of your family and loved ones. I wept and wept and mourned the loss of my boat. The river journey had come to an end, and it seemed to me that this was my destination. Silver Samir took me to their secret nest, which at that time was in a different forest. I became a Jugnu and a forest dweller. Maybe one day when I have had enough of this weather-work, I will buy a boat and return the way I came.'

Mian Pagla took out a little packet from a pouch, which he wore around his neck. Inside it, carefully wrapped in layers of plastic, were photos of his wife and children and of a goat called Abhimani. He was keeping them safe from the river and the rain.

Rani was not with us that day. Kochi, who was the acrobat Jugnu, offered to walk us back to the edge of the forest. He had long legs that carried him at supersonic speed. Because we were with him, he walked as slowly as he could. That made him restless, so he sprinted up a tree branch, somersaulting thrice mid-air. Coiling himself up like a porcupine, he cartwheeled beside us.

'The sadder I am, the bendier I get. That's the story of my life. Back in my village they used to call me "the devil's doing" and "the snake's nephew". What's my fault, tell me, girls? I can't help the bendiness of my bones, can I? So, one day I decided I would show them how useful a bendy person can be. Our sarpanch had a cow who was going to have a baby. She moaned and whimpered, trying to give birth. The calf was stuck and just wouldn't come out. After three days of pain and wailing, she gave up and lay down, waiting for death. Late at midnight, when the entire village slept, I crept up to the barn where she was writhing in pain. Bending my long hands, I went as far as I could up the cow's womb and pulled out the calf. Oh, how the little calf wriggled, and how happy the mother was! Next morning, the sarpanch was jubilant. He declared a feast to celebrate the birth of his favourite cow's calf. Ma cow and baby cow were both alive and lively. I walked up to him and took credit for what I had done. Do you know what gift I got for my superpower? A hundred slaps, a broken tooth and a job at the travelling circus.'

A nilgai appeared and looked at us unblinkingly. We walked home as fast as we could.

Kiran's eyes glimmered with tears.

'I hope Mian Uncle finds a boat and returns soon. And I hope Kochi's bendiness comes to an end.' I hoped so too, but I had enough world knowledge to know that sometimes people were stuck in situations forever. Like my Mama-mon in her afternoons.

One day, we were in Velu's tent, eating ultra-delicious chicken rolls. A light rain fell constantly. Although our shoes were wet and muddy, we kept them on as there were too many earthworms wriggling around. Velu's stove warmed our feet.

Suddenly, someone pulled aside the tarp curtain and peeped in. We looked up and got the shock of our lives. There he was—the dearest one of all. His beautiful long curls flattened by the rain. A new ring on the top of his ear. An iPhone sticking out of his jeans pocket.

Suraj! Suraj!—we jumped up with joy and disbelief. We found you. Suraj was found. Oh, what a brilliant decision it was to seek out the Jugnus. I remember the glow of that moment, the satisfaction of solving a problem. Phase 1 of Mission-Cat-out-of-the-Bag was over. The Jugnus did indeed have all the answers. Our mission was a success, but oddly enough it didn't seem like one, not yet. There was something not quite right. Suraj didn't seem relieved to have been found.

Kiran gripped his hand tightly. I hovered around Suraj, creating a sort of goalkeeper's fence just in case he slipped away and disappeared again.

We thanked Velu and Rani and said we would walk back home. Take Suraj with us. Rani smiled at me and blew me a kiss.

'You go on then. I'll stay here for a bit and have another cup of tea.'

We stepped outside Velu's warm tent. It was drizzling. Kiran gave Suraj a good shake and, clutching him, asked him sternly, 'How did you know we were here, bhaiya? Do you know these people?'

Logical questions. How come I hadn't thought of that before? But I wished Kiran hadn't started the Q&A in the gathering darkness.

A lanky boy appeared and joined us uninvited. He had a sly grin and a golden mohawk. He put an arm around Suraj, and I saw on his wrist a tattoo of a fire-breathing dragon, the flames inked in with red. Suraj shook off Kiran's hand. He seemed embarrassed.

'Meet my friend Bittoo. He goes to college and has a black belt in tae kwon do.'

Bittoo held out his hand to greet us. We stood aloof.

Velu came out of the tent and thumped Bittoo on his back. It was clear as day that Bittoo was a regular here, and now perhaps Suraj was too. Velu knew them both.

'Are you a Jugnu?' I asked Suraj.

'Ah, not yet, Narois. But I will soon be.'

The warm glow got snuffed out. Our feet were cold in the rain.

'Bhaiya, let's go home.' Kiran grasped him by his hand and pulled him away from Bittoo.

'I can't. I won't. Don't act silly.'

Kiran started sobbing. I stepped forward, and although words were hard to pull out of my storm-tossed insides, I glared at Suraj.

'Take her home. I'll come and visit, I promise. It's not as if I am disappearing, is it?' Suraj told me.

'Where will you stay?' I asked.

'Bittoo is letting me camp with him. Don't worry, his mom is really nice. She makes amazing food. I'll visit every other week, I promise.'

There was nothing left to be done. Even if you solve a problem, the solution may not be the right one. Kiran and I started walking back. Velu ordered Bhaiya Jugnu to go with us. He was shy, so he walked fifty paces behind in complete silence. Night had fallen, and a three-quarter moon shone on the forest path.

9. Tehran

Because I couldn't get the forest out of my mind, I wrote a story about it in creative-writing class.

'The forest of Jahapanah murders little children. But it does so with kindness, very gently. Dying is like eating ice cream.'

My class teacher exploded. Watermelony bits of her blasted all over the classroom.

'Death, permadeath, slicing with a hacksaw, murder by zombies, eyeball explosions, nail-ripping—thirty-five types of death in a five-hundred-word essay. Over and over again! What are you consuming on the evil Internet? Ugh, you spoiled child!' Jyoti Sharma shrieked.

A gigantic wave of laughter swept through our classroom. Meera got hiccups from all the air she swallowed.

'What were you thinking when you wrote that? How can you explain this?'

'Oh, but the children were not dying painfully at all. I wrote in my essay that they think they are having their favourite flavoured candy when the dying begins. It's a wonderful moment actually. If you read on right up to the end, you will see that I have written that the children feel no pain.'

'It is so violent, so inappropriate.'

'I was only being creative, Miss.'

'Oh, don't call me Miss. All the kids call me Ma'am. You must too. You know this.'

'Okay, Madam.'

'Ma'am. Not Madam. That sounds ... anyway, I must report this to the headmistress. An email will go to your parents. They will be called in.'

She glared at me and moved her eyebrows in a way that meant: now back to your seat. Conversation over.

Meera came over to me during lunch break.

'Are you in trouble?'

'Yes, it seems so. My parents will be called. Maybe they will expel me. So much for freedom of speech.'

'Oh, what did you write that was so bad? Can I please read it? Are there any naked people in it?'

I said I could smuggle her the rough draft that I still had with me.

'What if I get caught, Narois? Better you read it to me.'

A secret place was hard to find in our school. Full of long corridors and square rooms, there were no corners. We hid under the gigantic slide in the front field where younger kids played. I read out what I had written.

> *The Forest of Jahanpanah murders little children. But it does so with kindness, very gently. With poison that tastes like a child's favourite candy. Children are dying in any case. We die in hundreds when there is a war. And the war is here. Although not everyone will agree since a war plane has not dropped bombs on our houses yet. One day, soon, it will. When the time comes and all the adults are dead, we, the children, will walk to the Forest of Jahanpanah. A weeklong carnival will take place. Giant wheels will spin. Roller coasters will zoom. Under the blue fog called 'phitkari' which envelops the Forest of J to keep it hidden from the world outside, war planes will miss us and drop their nasty bombs on what is left of the city. After we have had our fun, the forest will slowly begin to kill us. After all, there are no parents or kin to go back to. We won't cry or be afraid. We will pick our flavour from a candy stall. There will be a hundred flavours to choose from. The poison, tasting of Toblerone, caramel popcorn, marshmallow or strawberry sorbet, as you prefer, will give us a final dream. And then ...*

'For this you want me to take her to a doctor? Because some teacher who has probably never read any folk tale has chosen to be offended? And you will have me listen to some doctor jawing out one-size-fits-all judgements on my child's freedom of expression? You want her punished for her creativity?'

Headmistress Parashar sat with a grave face, nodding her head, dodging my mother's sermon missiles.

'You should give her a trophy for this spectacular metaphor. Maybe ask her to design a forest. Or consider submitting her essay to the next Climate COP.'

Headmistress Parashar said she understood and wouldn't argue. But it was a fact that the passage had made my class teacher uncomfortable.

'Well, then, that's settled. It is the class teacher who needs counselling. I know a top doctor, particularly skilled at curing narrowness of thought.'

We came out of that meeting feeling charged.

'Narois, you and I are ready for a revolution. We need bullets and black flags and slogans. Let's cure this city.'

I was ecstatic. My life was finally somewhat comparable to ten-year-old Marji's, who lived in Tehran forty years ago. Mama-mon said that Delhi could be Persepolis. That soon bombs would fall, and rulers would bring out tanks against people.

'Get ready, Narois—this is Persepolis right here.'

I dreamt of shadows, nights and candlelight protests. I imagined I knew people who disappeared and were tortured and never came back. I slept with Marjane Satrapi's book, her life was mine.

That evening we danced—Mama-mon and I. But her breath fell fast and shallow.

We talked about Israel and Iran and Islam. Daddy had many Israeli friends who didn't look a bit like killers of Palestinian children.

I told Mama-mon about Shani, the most important visitor from that Monday who was also from Israel.

When Daddy came home that night, Mama-mon read out another poem to him, this one titled 'Shani cntd'. This Shani that she was writing about had something to do with Israel and Iran.

On my body I wear the smell of your distance.
At night it glows and dims, glows and dims.
Never faster, never quicker,
The stately beacon of a lighthouse.

Soon after we moved into this house, Mama-mon put up a ladder against the wall that bordered the forest.

Spotting this new addition, Mr Kapoor, the house owner, called Daddy and said that the ladder was a security risk. None of the houses along the road had ladders. No one living in those houses was ever nagged by the need to have a bridge over to the other side.

Ladder trouble with the house owner went on for almost a month; while it did, the ladder lay along the wall, horizontal, and I practiced walking on its rungs, my hands aeroplaning.

Our neighbours from the first and second floors dropped in to say hello. Mr Freddie and Angelika Aunty came with their adorable toddler, Margot. Mr Freddie said that propping up a ladder that climbed to nothing and went nowhere was simply impractical. Jogging little Margot on her knee, Angelika Aunty said ladders brought good luck. To show her support to Mama-mon, Angelika Aunty baked us a bright yellow bread. Mr Bharot kept his opinion to himself. He practised Scientology, which was a very difficult thing to practise and requires you to stare at food, not eat it, to pine for your children from the Babylonian era and to believe that you have been exiled from another planet. He rang the bell and gifted us a succulent plant.

Eventually, Mama-mon won the battle with Mr Kapoor, and the ladder rested vertically against the wall. She hung wind chimes and talked of placing a bird feeder. The only condition Mr Kapoor laid down was that the ladder had to come down at night. It had to be put to bed. Daddy did that usually and sometimes let me shin up for a last peek into the dark forest. When we had parties, the ladder made their friends drunker than ever. Some tried to climb it and others found it to be the most wonderful metaphor. They took their wines and their whiskies and perched on its lower rungs.

When the Age of Mondays began, the ladder in our garden was often forgotten. It remained standing all night.

When *they* came, they came not using this ladder, as one might suspect. There were questions nonetheless as to why the ladder was there in the first place. Police hovered around it and the house owner said: 'I told you so.' Until top cop Aunty Rebecca solved the mystery and put an end to ladder-blaming. 'Nothing to do with the ladder. Their technique was a dare! Brilliant! Tells you how unafraid and therefore dangerous they are.'

Aunty Rebecca stood in our living room, drinking ginger tea, while the other policemen walked about the garden and gazed up at the concertina wires that had been cut through with plyers. Mama-mon's carefully grown orange trumpet creeper lay in ruins.

The wall or the ladder had nothing to do with it. By that logic, neither was the Age of Mother-Disappearing-Mondays to be blamed. We were, as the police said, living next to a forest. That decision was always going to be a calculated risk. And now the risk had caught up with us.

But I knew better.

I knew that certain gates could be opened ... that they could be opened in *other* ways. And I had opened the gate far and wide.

10. Truth or Dare

'Nerdy Narois! Needy Narois! Are you getting expelled? Serves you right. Planning murders in creative-writing class? Are you going to grow up to be a serial murderer?'

Rishit was on a roll. His army of cronies stood around, grinning their stupid grins.

I too had an army of new-found fans of my fiction. There was Meera as always and Zorawar, who thought all that kid-killing with candy was epic cool. And ta-da! Armish was a fan too. She said she was super impressed with my forest essay. I felt warm and special.

One day Reba came to school with a miniature crystal ball bubble-wrapped and hidden inside her bag.

'I'll gaze at your future for a BFF kiss or hug. If the gates to tomorrow seem cloaked in a fog, I'll tell you a secret from your present life today, no extra charge.' She spoke in a raspy voice, which was obviously put on and silly.

Meera and I took her aside and threatened her.

'Have you forgotten what a mess you created with your prophecies?'

When Zorawar's mother complained about the prophecy, Reba got a diary note and a scolding from the principal. Soon after, a chubby and annoying brother pushed his way out of the mother's belly, upsetting Zorawar's world. Reba's powers were limited, obviously.

'This is different. Don't be disbelievers or harm will come on you. Annabelle the Evil One may have exited the house of Headless Azad. But she is around, sending me demon tips about you all. So, try me—your own sorceress. Isn't that cool? Let me show you what my crystal ball can do!'

We decided to make the most of it while it lasted.

Reba said we had to ask her at least one question to open up the clouds in the crystal ball.

I was dying to ask if her crystal ball could tell me more about the Jugnus and how they might help solve Suraj's Meow Meow case. But that secret I had sworn to protect. Even to Meera I had said not a word.

I asked Reba if we could see anything about Mamamon leaving for a mysterious place on Mondays. As the words came out of my mouth, I knew I had made a mistake. Reba's eyes danced and after a very brief glance at the crystal ball, she said she had an answer.

'Lady vanishing on Monday, taking taxi to meet new boyfriend. Soon she is leaving her old husband

and silly daughter to be with a rich man who lives in Dubai. He is gifting her LV bags and Chanel lipsticks.'

Meera, who was right next to me, boxed Reba's ears and threatened to tell everyone about Reba's crush on Rishit if she repeated a word of what her fake crystal ball had apparently seen.

'It is what it is, and you both are really stupid if you don't know that when adults leave mysteriously, it is because they are having an affair and soon there will be DIVORCE.'

I felt stumped for a moment. One couldn't deny that Reba knew way more than we did about these sneaky bits of the adult world, particularly about divorce, which had already happened in her life. 'I am made of fractions—1/2 with mom, 3/8 with Daddy and only 1/8 with my grandmother whom I love the most in this world,' she had once told us.

'Now pay me,' she said. 'In cash or kind.'

We stuck our tongues out at the crystal ball and said the only payment she would get was us doing her a favour by not spilling the beans about Rishit.

'That is ONLY if you never spread your lies about her mum,' Meera said in her policewoman voice.

I practised Musette in D. The E key got stuck, so I imagined its sound in my head and played on. Daddy said it sounded off-tune to those listening to the music from the piano, but not to the music in my head.

That evening they were sitting next to each other. Mama-mon laid her head on Daddy's shoulder.

I went back to school the next day and told Reba that I was sorry her parents got a divorce, but mine surely were not about to walk that path.

'Ah, but you see, when they decide they are going to part ways, they stop fighting and the old love comes back a little to say goodbye. It is a sign; I am telling you.'

I fetched the Game of Life, lying unplayed on the top shelf in my room. We sat on the cool floor. Daddy arranged cushions for Mama-mon, just like he had once done for Uncle Perez's swaying skeleton. I amassed a fortune and beat everyone to the graveyard. Daddy kept paying bail for his uncle who went to jail, and Mama-mon retired penniless. After four rounds around Life, Daddy said he was tired of it.

'Let's play Truth or Dare!' he announced.

My heart beat like drums. What was he up to? Wanting to trap Mama-mon so she'd confess her affair? Should he do it in front of me? Or was he going to ask me where I disappeared with Rani every Saturday, sometimes returning way past my 7 o'clock curfew?

It was Daddy's turn first. Mama-mon said she would take a dare.

Daddy asked her to eat a kiwi.

Mama-mon said, no one eats fruit at night. Bogus dare!

Then it was her turn. I said I'll take a dare, but she insisted on truth.

'What food does Daddy give you on Mondays?'

I said, 'Not my usual,' and that made them laugh at my cleverness.

We went around in circles, and I could sense that they were trying to tell me something, making a sloppy mess of whatever it was. I wished they would just say it; I yawned and excused myself.

It was a Wednesday. At dinner time, Mama-mon stared at the soup, resting her hands on both sides of the table mat. On her bony wrists I noticed two white bands, wound so tight that they were digging little holes. Every now and then she adjusted the bands. Nago Didi brought her a few strands of raw ginger. Mama-mon put a few in her mouth and sucked on them. She looked strange and hollow. Although it was hot and muggy, she was wearing a pink cotton handkerchief on her head, tied at the nape.

Mama-mon wore costumes all the time—armbands, hammer-and-sickle shirts, black turtlenecks; once, Jesus's wounds painted on her palms and forehead. One awful week she spent wearing a mask of Masih Alinejad's face. I forgot what my mother looked like and started believing that Ms Masih, whom I admired greatly, was, in fact, my mother. Daddy packed his bags and went off to the harbour on an urgent trip after Mama-mon asked him if he indeed preferred Masih as his wife. That was better than the week she wore a T-shirt that stank of petrol in solidarity with Greenpeace protesters in Norway. The pink kerchief she was wearing now was probably something in support of Heidi.

'Ah, yes, you are wondering. Trying on a new look. Goes with short hair. Peasant-y.'

Later, when we sat down to play a game of UNO, she said she wasn't feeling up to it and went into the bedroom to lie down. I watched her walk in slow motion. Atlas would have sauntered like that if he had got a chance to, with the world on his shoulders. Pushing against gravity.

'Mama-mon wants to say something really important to you,' Daddy said.

'What is it? Can't you tell me?'

'No, darling, better she does. You know she is the teller of things in our family. She will tell it so much better, even if it's difficult to tell. And from what I hear it's thrilling, it's sci-fi. Very adult too. So, cheer up and give me a song.'

Always that with my parents—a song now, a song then. A song for everything. But that evening, unlike other times when they asked me to sing, that evening, I felt a song bobbing inside me, as if it was waiting in the wings.

I won't tell you what I sang. It's not fair to songs, marking them like that. Because once marked, they remain glued to the moment and can never be free.

Tears streamed down Daddy's cheeks. His long Dorabjee nose turned red and watery. I cried a little too. Because of the story I was going to hear. Because of the peppermint fumes that came from the bedroom.

Mama-mon was on the bed. She didn't see us come in. The pink Heidi scarf lay next to her—on it was a pile of hair. Mama-mon was picking hair off her shoulders and her neck and her shirt. She just wouldn't stop—there were so many strands. She picked and piled up the hair in the scarf, which was already full. Thousands and thousands of strands, my Birbal mother, counting and counting to answer Emperor Akbar's question, 'How much hair do you have on your head?' If she didn't count it all, at dawn the emperor would say, off with your head.

Of all the things she talked to me about—black holes, singularity and what-not—Mama-mon never spoke to me about death. When death came up—and it often did—she looked the other way or said, 'End of conversation.' I remember asking her, when I was five, way before I met Anne Frank, what happened to children in gas chambers? Did they come out after being gassed? I also remember asking: if humans live to be ninety or a hundred, give or take a few, what happens to them afterwards? Mama-mon would insist we stop watching films midway or close to the end, ruining the climax, if death was around the corner.

I could have broken the news to her that I knew death like the back of my hand. But I reckoned I might wait for the right time.

That night Mama-mon talked to me about death. Called a spade a spade. Gave it a name. But not before she spent a long-muddled hour calling it the good fight, the cell-war, the conspiracy of the modern world, the orbit of disease.

That night I dreamt that Reba's crystal ball had swallowed me.

Cancer is a time machine. Life before the word lands its spacecraft in your life is BC, and life after it does is AC.

I felt the growing up growing inside.

The walls in the room kept shunting far away.

My heart galloped. An ocean in my tummy left me feeling seasick.

Growing up felt cold and stingy.

Side effects of biting into the apple of knowledge, according to Mama-mon.

I woke up the next day and asked myself if I had become a different person. My first instinct was to run to Kiran, who knew what it meant to be someone, a child-someone, whose mother was going to die. But there was no time for that. It was a usual enough day and I was soon packing my bag, stuffing in my lunch box, picking up the class register.

No one in class looked at me oddly. No one, not even Meera, asked if something had changed. I was, in everyone's eyes, Narois from the BC era. Who was not much different from the Narois of the AC era.

During recess, I told Meera. She opened her eyes wide and didn't know what to say. 'When?' she finally whispered.

'Daddy said we can't possibly put a date. It will happen when it happens.'

'And can't you stop it? Stop her from ... you know ...'

'They are trying very hard. And that's the dangerous thing apparently—trying very hard.'

Meera asked me if I wanted to buy anything special from the canteen. I asked for a choco-pie. Then I told her there was something else that I really wanted.

She was at her usual spot. Under the mulberry tree at the far end of the back field. That day she was alone, no one hovering around to have their tomorrows looked into. We picked up a heavy stone each from the gravel path circling the field. The idea was simple—to smash the imposter crystal. Reba sensed we were up to something, and I think she was getting ready to scream.

But what could we do; there was no crystal ball to smash.

On the lunch box that served as her table was a stack of cards.

'Where did you hide the crystal ball?' Meera demanded.

'It's gone. Whoosh! It went away last night. Crystal balls do that, didn't you know? They leave once they have done their job.'

And coyly-slyly she asked, 'Did you want anything? These cards here can go all the way down the road into your future. I don't need to do a thing—it's between you and the cards.'

'What are these?' we asked, unable to stop our curiosity.

'Ah, these aren't ordinary tarot cards. A real witch gifted the set to Mom, and with these she was able to find out that my dad has another farmhouse where he meets *her*. Come on, Narois, I snuck these cards out just for you ... do you want to see if your mum's boyfriend will take her overseas?'

Have you ever felt something pulling you towards itself? I did, at that moment. It was a force stronger than the gravity that gets you when you hurtle upside down on the Battlestar Galactica—that's a roller coaster on Sentosa Island, you know—a ride that, Mama-mon calculated before Daddy bought two tickets for me and him, could buy a whole month of food, water, electricity and medicines for a family of four, besides paying their rent.

I sat down with a thud before Meera could drag me away and pulled a card from the stack.

Reba said she had been bang on target—my mother was going to the Paris Fashion Week next year and she would wear what Gigi Hadid wore to the Met Gala. Then she made a sad face and said, 'The only downside is that your Mama is going to forget all about you and your poor Daddy.'

'Mama won't forget me, you fool! She is going to die,' I screamed at Reba and pinched her arms, because that's what I did best. My pinches could sting you and leave you bruised.

With a yelp, Reba ran off. The tarot cards lay scattered on the wet grass.

I felt as if a weight had lifted off my shoulders.

Reba took her revenge. And by the end of the day, our entire class knew that my mother was going to die. And now everyone looked at me as they should—they were seeing Narois from the AC era of her life.

11. Arabian Nights

School awards were announced by the headmistress. 'Your wordsmithing, your mathness, your getting-ahead-of-the-rest-ness will be cheered and medalled. But the things to look out for, the things you will be remembered for—these are the top two crowns—awards for RESPECTFULNESS and SINCERITY.'

My name was announced for the RESPECTFULNESS prize. Another girl in grade five was getting the SINCERITY prize.

I got hugs and hair ruffles from my English teacher, Nita Ma'am, and my class teacher from grade three, Miss Jenny. Meera said she would bring her autograph book for my signature. Zorawar came over with a sort of smile. He said, 'I hate awards but am glad you are getting one.'

Reba told everyone during lunch break that I was getting an award because my mother was dying. 'It's a consolation prize, dummies. Do you really think she deserved it?'

Armish put an arm around me. We bought coconut cake from the cafeteria to celebrate and walked over to the empty football field. The grass was wet and there were muddy patches on which we slipped. The sun was out, steaming away leftover rain. In the warm comfort of the net, Armish held my hand and said she had never met an orphan.

'Do you know by when you might become ... you know?'

I said I didn't. That there was a strong possibility I wouldn't be one, after all.

'Oh, we thought it's going to happen any day now!'

Later in the day, Jyoti Sharma banged a duster on the table. Through the cloud of dust motes, I saw her looking at me sternly. Her face as gloomy as the thunderclouds that were back in the sky, hovering over our football field. *Do you deserve it? Do you?* That face was asking.

At home we celebrated. Mama-mon debated whether we would be happier if it were a merit prize. Daddy said his heart was full. There couldn't have been a better triumph.

A prize for RESPECTFULNESS. What did it say about the person? I could have done with a Best Acrobat or Best Investigator.

We lived in a tent of rain. Toadstools appeared magically at night, shining white in the overgrown grass. Snails walked to and fro. The morning sun took them. Rain seeped into our shoes. We had puddle feet.

A nest of songbird fledglings fell into our garden. Blown in by a storm. Their little necks trembled. The mother bird stood guard. Swooping in with an insect or a worm or a broken fruit. One afternoon the mother bird disappeared. We panicked when she didn't reappear at sunset. Here was a nest full of orphans whose language we didn't speak, and there was a wicked cat prowling around. The birdlings were squeaking with hunger. They kept opening their mouths. Mama-mon looked up bird food on the Internet and asked Nago Didi to mash up some boiled rice and egg. We stuffed the gooey mash inside my toy syringes and managed to squeeze in tiny dollops down their red throats. I hoped I could give away my share of papaya next morning at breakfast if Mama-bird didn't come back.

At night we moved the birds into a cardboard box, punched holes all around it for air and set up a fortress with chairs and tables to keep the box safe from the cat.

'What if we bring them inside the house?'

'What if Mama-bird comes looking for them?'

We were up at 4 a.m., waiting for the first light of dawn. Mama-mon tottered and held on to the door. It was so weird to see her body hunched like an old woman's. I looked away.

The birdlings woke up, hungry and chirpy. Out of nowhere, Mama-bird appeared. She eyed us suspiciously and then dived in with a worm in her beak. She broke little pieces and fed all the mouths and went away to get more food. I kept a watch, just in case she went away and didn't come back.

In the days to come, I began to slide deeper and deeper into a swirl of musical notes. Water trickling, cake batter dripping, a bus horn, chalk screeching on the blackboard, friends whispering their not-sharing, their keeping-me-out. To the sound, words would add themselves and start a concert. Such as the word Orphan.

Orphan ran between octaves, shape-shifted from a flat to a sharp. I strung medleys using two or three notes—gloomy E minor, crybaby B sharp and their grave-note friends A minor and F.

Sometimes I hung it on the sad old peg of a Trivra Ma and tied the other end on a wind-whistling Komal Ni. On that wire it went to and fro—the word Orphan—marching on double beat.

Then one day I said, 'Let's hunt orphans!' I was a magnet that was pulling the entire world. 'Let's hunt for orphans to see if they are like the rest of us.'

Rishit signed up and demanded that we appoint him the leader. 'I am going to be a CEO one day, so better start leading right away.'

'But do you know an orphan? Are you on the way to becoming one?'

To that he had to say no.

Our network of orphan-hunters grew every day by leaps and bounds. We shared orphaning stories over recess. Our class bully, Prithvi, was an orphan. He had returned from school to find his mother hanging from the ceiling fan. Tina's dad died of a heart attack before she was born. He was a photographer. She scowled a lot and carried a bag, which made her hunch. It turned out that Abhimanyu, one of the orphan-hunters, was an orphan himself. A freshly minted one.

It had happened that summer—his mother had collapsed at the breakfast table while slicing a mango.

'Have you stopped eating mangoes? Have you stopped having breakfast?' Abhimanyu had glassy eyes and refused to volunteer as our test case. His elder sister came up to us the next day. Her face was as red as a beetroot, and it looked like she had cried all night. She threatened to take us to the principal.

'Break up this cruel game right now. You'll grow up to be murderers at this rate!'

Zorawar stepped right up and said this was no game at all. 'Narois's mother has cancer. We are helping her learn. You are the one who is being insensitive.'

We carried on a bit longer. There were no new cases to be found in school. Except Hansa Didi who was the head girl, played national-level badminton and got us gold medals every year. But she had moved on and could no longer testify as to how it felt to be an orphan.

Much to our surprise, Armish had the best story to tell. Nothing could beat the orphaning of her Abbu's cousin in Ahmedabad. He was orphaned standing in a ditch that was full of shit—like real shit, fresh human shit. Men with swords cut his mother in two halves. She stayed alive as two parts—one part tried crawling towards him. Then they sliced up her head, arms and legs—all parts kept moving and quivering until they couldn't anymore. His fireball father ran towards his sister, on whom there were black shadows pounding. But the fire went out and all that was left was smoking flesh and screams. Abbu's cousin's orphaning hasn't stopped. It is not something that ends. He can hear the screams and smell the flesh and the shit all day, every day.

Kiran cried her eyes out and clutched on to Mama-mon when we broke the news to her. It was communicated quite simply—the way bad news is usually conveyed and not through games and metaphors. 'Narois will need you to help her through this, my Kiran-bee,' Mama-mon said, her voice trembling for the very first time.

I tried to muster up a few tears as well. After all, I was Mama-mon's real daughter and Kiran was the other daughter. My eyes pained with the effort. I used my pinch on myself. I winced, but it got me no tears, while Kiran's T-shirt was already wet and she had snot all over her hands. The news affected her so much that

Kiran couldn't go to school the next day. I went over to her house in the evening. We sat on our perch after dinner. The forest was dark and still. A thin wisp of smoke rose from the trees. It curled up into the sky, rising far above the treetops.

I wondered if the smoke came from Velu's coal oven. He was probably cooking dinner for the Jugnus. Was he roasting a chicken or toasting rotis over the fire? A chilly gust swept through the forest and the smoke vanished.

Silver Samir came back from whatever weather-work he was attending to. Rani seemed very pleased and stayed next to him throughout. Our job with the Jugnus was far from over; we still had to find out who had framed poor, innocent Suraj. It made me so angry to think that someone would play such a horrid trick on him. When I asked Silver Samir about it, he said, have patience. I didn't mind if it took a bit longer. Kiran didn't mind either. She had a special bond with Velu. I hoped I would form a bond too, with one of the Jugnus.

That evening, after a particularly rainy spell, Velu lit a small fire over which he toasted pieces of malai chicken. Yoghurt marinade dribbled down on the flames; they started hissing and let out a smell that made my mouth water. Silver Samir said that we had not heard the best story of all—the story of Bhaiya Jugnu and Vinay Jugnu. They looked like brothers but were not. They were famous wrestlers, but their fathers beat them to a pulp. When they spoke, they finished each other's sentences.

'We were born on the same ...'

'Full-moon night but ...'

'Our mothers were not the same ...'

'One was a prima donna and ...'

'The other a saadhvi ....'

'We were born in a cruel town where ...'

'Fathers came and went and ...'

'Beat us black and blue....'

'One day at a kusti match, we ...'

'Fought and fought but could not fell each other ...'

'Since then, we have been a pair. We stay together, roam together and ...'

'Finish each other's sentences.'

When Silver Samir was done with his story and whistled, birds woke up from sleep and flew over to join our camp. A great coucal swooped in and spoke to no one. A purple sunbird, looking very sleepy, sat on his shoulder. At least half a dozen babblers flew in, making a racket, and paid no attention to the others. Then he let out a throaty sound and a nilgai appeared. It kept its distance. Velu went into his tent and came back with a dhol, which Silver Samir tucked under his legs and began a drum roll that could compete with the roar of an ocean. I flew and crashed and felt flips in my stomach as he kept up the drumbeat. Then he sang, and it was a song that I knew. When he saw me humming, he twirled his fingers, and I started singing too. That evening, I told them the story of NF and about his incredible music, which I am not allowed to discuss in front of Mama-mon.

'There is something fishy about a white rapper. Why would you usurp Blackness? It's not your history. Stay away from it.'

While I think I understand what she means, I really like NF and it made me happy to be able to sing a few lyrics with the Jugnus applauding me. The beats and the words bounced out of me, swinging from trees, teasing the leaves.

That Monday I found a note in my tiffin box. It was something she used to do when Daddy was a sailor. She left small notes in his luggage. They kept popping up until the end of his eight-month-long voyage. Inside his underpants, shirt pockets, taped to the luggage lining, sewed into his shoe or socks. Once, his ship sailed into the terrifying Typhoon Nida. It was the worst storm in maritime history. All the sailors prepared to die and said their prayers. As the ship pitched and rolled violently, Daddy ransacked his belongings and dug up every single note that was left to be found. He unglued them from shoes, ripped open the suitcase lining, played his favourite CD to get to the part over which she had recorded her message, dug into the clothes he had yet to use. It took him a whole hour to find six months' worth of messages.

Very soon the sea calmed down. The waves became gentle and there was no trace of a storm. Daddy felt foolish and disappointed. There were no more notes to look forward to.

On a pink origami bird stuck to my apple was a trick question: 'What comes after Mama-mon?'

I bit my cheeks, drawing blood, loosening the flesh. When I asked Mama-mon for an answer to the riddle, she said it was unlucky to give away a riddle's reply.

'What's more important than the answer is to remember there is such a question.'

The riddle of the pink bird drummed near my eardrum, beat with my heartbeat, and became quite a band. AEDAEDC on the piano—staccato legato staccato legato. It rode my tongue like a wave, pushed and prodded my tooth, uprooting it way before time. Spit and blood kept my mouth busy.

'In there is a little hell,' said Meera when I let her have a look. 'Worse than Azkaban.'

Hell is not a bit like Azkaban. It is a mountain, upside down, with many levels and challenges. At the Santa Maria railway station in Florence, a bookshop sold *The Divine Comedy* comics. Mama-mon bought me one and we read it together on the train to Rome.

'Dante had Virgil, which must have made hell quite a pleasant place to be in,' I observed. A friend at the Gate of it all. To see him through.

Mama-mon repeated this like a chant: 'You don't need friends. You are your best friend.'

The day of the award ceremony arrived. My tummy became a volcano crater. A non-stop tickle irritated the end of my spine. I was not afraid of the stage. I liked the stage. But something about the prize made me unwant the attention I was going to get.

We stood in the wings, peering at the stream of parents gushing in. They were much noisier than us, trying to grab seats closest to the stand fans. A burst of flowers and handmade festoons decorated the Hall of Grace. Rustle of cotton, shuffle of feet, whispers of pride. A cloud of flat notes rose.

The giving and taking of the award happened.

Afterwards, once the school anthem and a song of gratitude were sung, we mingled with the parents. Photos were taken and parent-words drifted around—which child which award? Merit is rote-learning. Why not one for music? The future of such awards or award-getters.

Mama-mon was throwing her head back and laughing, looking spectacular in a mint-green saree with white flowers on it, extremely short hair and unusual earrings. Prachi's mother, Rara Aunty, was there, and so was Aunty Rebecca in her full police uniform. They looked solid and their shadows were thick. Mama-mon looked wispy, like a mist settling, here now, gone soon.

At a joke she laughed again. Threw her head back and ran a hand through her hair. That's when it happened. Clumps of hair came loose, stuck to her fingers. She did it a second time, I think somewhat in disbelief or maybe she had forgotten what was happening to her, ran her hand once again through her hair. Another big clump came loose and there were tufts flying down like black ugly cobwebs and settling on her mint-green shoulders. Then another tuft flew further away and spun on the floor like a pinwheel. All eyes were on it and on her. Daddy held her around the waist, and they looked at each other. Mama-mon smiled and winked at me. Then she pulled out from her bag a soft peach cap with golden threads, glittering. She put it on, looking like someone from the *Arabian Nights*. Then she hugged me and walked away. Sharp notes, ascending, as her heels struck the floor.

12. Kubla-Eyed

A day before my tenth birthday party, we put up festoons and balloons, swaying to folk songs and B.B. King. On evenings like this I could really enjoy the music and not feel the pressure. Not be answerable for the musician or the song. It wasn't likely that suddenly, mid-song or pre-song, I would be asked to sing—a sort of test that I hated. The both-of-them—my parents when they talked about my music became the both-of-them—insisted it wasn't a test. Why was I thinking of it as one and it was disappointing that I should! Could I not have fun singing along? I must take a leaf out of the nightingale's book who sang not because she was asked to but because she couldn't help but sing.

'But that is one sad bird, Mama-mon—singing itself to death, heart-to-thorn. I don't want to be a sad bird.'

'Narois,' she would say, 'a nightingale sings. That's what it does.'

Birthday bargains were struck. My music or theirs, cake with food colour or not, books as return gifts or nail art and superhero merch. That my disappearing Mama-mon would let me have the creamiest cake with rainbow colours and let my friends play whatever music they wanted—Alan Walker, NF, Imagine Dragons, Taylor Swift, Billie Eilish or even, I dared hope, a few really feet-tapping Bollywood numbers—and give some importance to my waning popularity at birthday parties because I always gifted books was obviously not going to happen.

'What's wrong with gifting books?' she asked me. 'It's good for the world, don't you see?'

Daddy convinced her that because of the hardships that came with going away on Mondays, it would be easier to gift something in-the-box.

'Gifting books is the simplest thing. You pick it like fruit from the shelf.'

My heart sank to the bottom of the deep seas.

Finally, she agreed to Hogwarts keychains and Poppits of different colours.

She also let me have a cake of my choice.

But there would be no tattoo artists making roses, cobwebs or dragons on our cheeks. Nor would there be a magician pulling out white pigeons from a hat or coins from our ears.

'You are old enough to amuse yourselves.'

My friends wanted to know what to expect. Birthday parties were usually in an air-conditioned game park on top of a shopping mall—not in someone's house with nothing to do.

Zorawar asked if there would at least be gaming.

'I don't have a PS4. Or a gaming computer,' I whispered, my cheeks flaming when he rolled his eyes and shook his head and said he wasn't coming then.

Sanvi said she would die and go to heaven if the return gift wasn't a book.

'Invite the right set of friends, those who should be your friends, and not those who are your friends by chance, says Darwin.'

When Mama-mon ran out of things to say, she borrowed from other people.

I needed friends, or you could say I had a need for friends. Finding and keeping friends was a hobby. All types of them. I had hundreds of friends, even if some of them I had met only once and never again, at least not yet. Wherever I went, on the train, at hotels, by the seaside or trekking up mountains, I gathered friends.

For my tenth birthday, I was determined to call as many as possible. Fill up our house. Old friends, reluctant friends, barely friends, friends of friends. I hoped that Armish would agree to be my BFF. She asked what gift I would like. Glitter pens would be nice. I longed for a sprightly dozen. And some decorative tape. But I wanted her to choose. If we were to announce best friendship, the gift had to be special.

Kiran was excited and happy for me. She said she would be on top of the stairs all evening and watch us jive. She helped me stuff the piñata with eclairs and mints. She placed the 'Happy 10th' helium balloon outside the front door and said, 'The world must know!' I wanted to invite her. I knew which dress she would wear if I did ask her. Her hair would be done in space buns, and Choti Ma would let her use a coral lip gloss, some of which she would smudge on her cheeks and over her eyes.

At last, my birthday evening arrived. The house looked festive, and there were endless glasses of punch. Music of my parents' choice played—Harry Belafonte on shuffle, sounding way too old. I had managed to wriggle out a karaoke mike, two helium balloons and a disco light.

Armish came with her brother Goofy. The first one to arrive, she walked in with a fish inside a polythene bag. Never have I seen such a shade of striking red. Goofy stood behind her, peeping out. He was carrying a round fishbowl and a packet of brilliant stones.

'Happy birthday, Narois,' she said. 'Your first pet. Don't kill it, okay?'

A pet. My own fish. Only Armish could think of something as clever and kind. A red fish that came all the way from the rivers of Thailand. It had to be transferred right away or it could die. We hurried over to the dining table, assembling like knights around Daddy-King-Arthur, gentle, patient, the one who knew, the one who had a grip on things. Once the owner of a giant aquarium with fifty fish, he filled the bowl with water and invited us, with clean hands, to place a few colourful stones at the bottom.

'They will remind him of the riverbed. We are creating an ecosystem for him. Making him cozy,' he said.

We added plastic moss and Brazilian Micro Sword plants that Armish's Abba had bought from the fish shop. The Thai riverbed dazzled with colours. King Arthur of the fish ceremony carefully emptied the pouch—out poured the water and with it a bouncing red fish.

'How do you know it's a he?' Mama-mon hovered around, nervous and thrilled. She would have never approved of a pet, but here it was, and now she had no choice. We were responsible for another living creature.

'It's a betta,' Armish said. 'A male betta is always more colourful and grand. You have to give it a name.'

And before we could come up with one, Mama-mon called it—our little betta red—Kubla Khan.

'Named not after the warrior, but after the poem,' she warned. So Kubla-named-after-a-poem became our first ever pet, and Armish left no room for doubt that she was indeed my very best friend.

Soon, the party picked up. Daddy saved the day by playing Shakira. When we were shy on the dance floor, he jumped right in and grooved and shook with embarrassing energy. Then Nago Didi came in with piping hot cheese rolls and bacon wraps.

Meera could dance to anything that had a rhythm. Zorawar boasted about his latest PlayStation. Saanvi showed us photos of her pet—Doodles, a French terrier. When we ran out of things to say, I dimmed the lights and proposed a game of Chinese Whispers. Secrets spilled out. Zorawar's parents were getting divorced. Saanvi's elder sister had a boyfriend who was really old and carried a gun wherever he went. I forget what other secrets were shared, but I do remember feeling that secrets are overrated and exhausting.

Zorawar asked me why Rishit wasn't invited. 'Why would you leave him out? You're jealous that he is better than you in maths?'

'Stop it, Zorawar!' Meera, mid-way through her moves, came to my defence. 'It's her birthday. She gets to invite whoever she wants, and Rishit is horrid.'

Reba asked, 'Why does your mother have short hair? She looks like a punk.'

'You silly girl. Who says only punks have hair like that?' Zorawar replied.

Yes, who says—we wanted to know.

Meera whispered to me, 'Don't let them spoil your day.'

No one asked about Kiran. Not even Meera. No one had ever met her.

The cake was a fondant Sorting Hat that won claps of glee from everyone.

After the party, Armish and Goofy stayed back.

'Abba spent the entire morning looking for a perfect fish in pet shops. His boss will make him work extra.

If he doesn't, the boss will fire him. So, please, Aunty, he is going to be a bit late.'

Mama-mon nodded and said that all bosses are criminals, she who has never been a boss. Despite all her talents. What kind of boss would you have been, Mama-mon?

We sat amidst the confetti and watched Kubla swirl in his little glass bowl, swimming with all his might, on and on in circles, flapping his showy fins, doing little zigzags. It was close to half-past 9 in the evening when Armish's father came to pick her up on a bike.

We went to see her off at the gate. Armish put on her helmet. Sleepy Goofy sat squashed between Armish and Abba. Perfectly sandwiched, they rode off.

We stood for a while on the road, watching cars whoosh past. An ambulance screeched by. Kiran's house throbbed next door. The Chir-pine tree rustled.

The birthday gift from Kiran was a handmade broomstick made of flour dough—microwaved and painted gold. She had come to wish me in the morning. I put her gift on my desk.

Mama-mon hugged her and asked if she had decided what to wear for the party.

Kiran said, 'Oh Aunty, I can't come. I must go for my maths tuition today.'

When Mama-mon insisted and said there could possibly be no party without her, Kiran cooked up a perfect story. Her mother's sister who lives in Agra was going to be in town for an evening. 'Poor Masi, her heart will break if I don't meet her. She can't come that often, Aunty. You know how strict her in-laws are, and after she had another daughter, they don't let her go to her maika anymore.'

Clever Kiran. Mama-mon's other daughter. She knew how to distract my mother. Mama-mon ranted on and threatened to send the authorities to Masi's house in Agra, but I don't think she believed Kiran that day. She kept looking at me sideways, her face grim with disappointment. She knew. She knew I had deliberately missed inviting Kiran.

But what would Mama-mon know about making and keeping friends? She who had none. Kiran would have been such a misfit with my school friends. I was sparing her the awkwardness. Surely that meant something?

To bring the curtains down on the birthday, we went for a drive. Drives were our thing. And before I came along, drives were their thing. How that went with the whole climate-change worry, since that too was their thing, I couldn't tell. When I asked them-both, they said it was a sin, but we were allowed one flaw. Long drives made their eyes gleam like Aladdin and Jasmine on the magic carpet. They could be giddy and cringeworthy when they weren't fighting over their bombs and our bombs and Israel and Iran.

We sped through the night traffic, sightseeing, touristing, taking in the hundred lighted windows of the Taj Mahal hotel, the BMW Mini Cooper showroom,

Red Fort, the Ushnak Mal shop in South Extension, Prime Monster graffiti in an underpass for which the artist would surely be taken to the gallows, them-both said, while tsk-tsk-ing worriedly for that anon artist. We saw a cartwheeling girl whose braids could stand up straight, the UN offices where Mama-mon should-have-been, the tailor shop where Daddy's sailor coat had been lying unclaimed for nine years, the first ever skyscraper of Delhi and the hospital where I popped out of Mummy's tummy. Then finally, a real gift—two scoops of electric blue splish-splash ice cream balanced on top of a crispy cone. I fell asleep, hoping to show off my blue tongue at school on Monday and thinking of ways in which I could keep my tongue unwashed a whole weekend. Was that even possible?

Probably because of all the cake, I woke up in the middle of the night and heard worried voices outside.

Was Kubla hungry or dead? Had I failed my pet-duty the very first night? I scrambled out. All the lights in the living room were on. Mama-mon lay on the couch, her head resting on a pile of cushions. The air around her crackled. Daddy was talking on the phone with someone who was asking many questions.

He kept saying to her, 'Close your eyes, rest them, please.'

Her left eye was full of blood. The eyeball drowned in a black-red pool. I thought I was dreaming, and in that dream Kubla swam in her eyes, a giant red fish clouding the white ocean.

She turned her Kubla eye at me and held out a hand. 'Machu Picchu, did we wake you? Are you hungry?'

I floated into the soft lagoon of her skinny arms, the fluttering tent of her batik-print kaftan. If I am called Machu Picchu, which Mama-mon says is my nth name, it means I have done nothing wrong. Whatever was happening was not because I had tricked my dear friend and let her choose maths over me. I am still good. I am still loved. I am still a child.

13. Until the Fireflies

From that crisis of bloodied eye, Mama-mon could be rescued by none other than our Rani who came punctually at 11 in the morning, and our spirits lifted.

She puffed and huffed over Mama-mon's forehead, sprayed a blessing of Zamzam water, pressed a point on her foot and served her a spicy feast of the latest gossip. Mama-mon loved gossip—the other lives of people she only knew by name. And she laughed and sighed, and the eye looked less red.

'But still ...'

'Yes, still.'

'Still, there will be tests and doctors, just to be sure.'

'So, until we are back ...'

Yes, until then, and because Rani had a mystery gift for me—'a thing and a day,' she said—I was to spend the day with Rani.

'Call Kiran. We have lots to do.'

Kiran was already on her way. Today I was going to make up to her—that was the plan. Make up for not wanting her in the party where everyone talked about Air Jordans and Calvin Klein jeans and Victoria's Secret underwear, which would be worn 'the day boobs bloomed'.

Our house, smelling of presents and cake; Rani in her Eiffel Tower shoes; Kubla swimming non-stop, a swirl of red—I wanted to draw all of this with crayons and then to sniff those crayons and chew them up and taste the colours that the morning was made of.

From her tote bag Rani took out a tiny glass vial with a cork stopper, dark golden liquid sloshing inside. Carefully, as we watched, she sat the vial on her left palm and shone a light over it with her gold-painted nails.

'Meet the great and grand, the one and only khushboo of our times—Narois. Specially cooked from nargis flowers dried between pages of the *Arabian Nights*, washed in a flood of belladonna, blueberry and strawberry.'

Mama-mon clapped and cheered. I stepped forward to accept this wonderous gift—the smell of me, the memory and molecules of me—all capped in a bottle.

We took turns to take have a sniff. Mama-mon dabbed a few drops on her wrist and said she was in perfume heaven. Kiran and I rubbed it behind our ears and under our noses.

'That's enough,' Rani said possessively. 'Now keep it away in the northeasterly direction under the shade of wood. Attars must be kept that way for at least a month. Let it get comfortable, know your house, hear your voice.'

'Oh, that's so delightfully specific. Find us such a spot for Narois-the-attar,' said Mama-mon.

We tiptoed around the house with a compass. It was Rani who found the perfect spot, inside my parents' bedroom. 'Here it is,' she said, although I was quite sure the compass was pointing southeasterly and not northeasterly. On top of the quilt cabinet was an old wooden box where our house keys were kept. She asked me to raise the lid. 'Now keep it gently between the two most used keys. Keys are darwazahs to the other world. Spirits come and go in the vicinity of keys. Best place for the attar to come alive.'

I placed the attar between the single key for my mother's cupboard, which dangled from a blue Dutch shoe, and another key hanging from a tiger. There was confusion about the key that dangled from a tsunamika doll safety pin. No one knew which door this key opened. Probably a door through which we could no longer walk. There were many of those, keys to nothing, that shared the wooden box with the keys that were functional. Every time we locked up the house to go somewhere, keys were tried at locks frantically. Mama-mon swore she would organize the keys and put an end to this awful nail-biting misery of lockmatching. But that never happened. In our house we untangled nothing.

All we were clear about was the key with a shoe, which Mama-mon needed almost all through the day. That and a few others she was willing to mark—with a doll, a papier-mâché tiger, a string—until the keychains became a riddle themselves. Did the tiger lead to the box where she kept her jewellery? Was the key at the end of the string a spare one for the front door?

In her sky-blue kurta and dazzling white tights, Rani looked like the monsoon sky.

'I have arranged a perfect Saturday for you, Narois-jaan. Chinese lunch, the new *Lion King* and finally a dusk walk in the forest. We can stay to hear the first calls of the jackal and until the fireflies.'

Kiran and I wore matching outfits. Denims and whites. We hoped it would rain when we walked in the forest. Rani was jumpy and nervous. Kiran and I felt it but then focused on finishing up the delicious golden fried prawns. Rani let us order only appetizers. Without the burden of a main course, the tiresomely long noodles or the heavy-duty chomping of rice to bother about, we became creative and ordered dim sums and a side of French fries.

Mama-mon would have been disgusted, but she wasn't around that afternoon. It wasn't my fault that French fries were on the menu. All made in palm oil for sure, said the car horns and restaurant chatter in Mama-mon's voice. All in palm would sound more beatsy. Palm palm palm, all fried in palm.

We stuffed ourselves, and I wondered if the meal wasn't too expensive for Rani.

When the bill came, a long one really, Mum's voice came in through the clatter of fork and spoon—you put a hole in her wallet. That sounded like a perfect rhyme and could be immediately set to music. Rani asked me to check and calculate if it was all okay, down to the tip.

At the cinema hall, we felt hungry again and ordered a large tub of popcorn. Then we waited outside, in the hall of reflections. People looked at us, probably trying to guess our relationship, wondering how we were connected to Rani who was so dazzlingly beautiful.

We read posters. I told Kiran that I wasn't terribly keen about *The Lion King*. I'd much rather watch *Captain Marvel*. But I didn't want to disappoint Rani. 'Don't tell her a word,' I told Kiran.

Kiran said she was collecting coins for the release of *War*, Tiger Shroff's next film.

'My treat it will be,' she said.

The star of the day was neither Simba nor Brie Larson nor Tiger Shroff. In fact, the movie or the movie theatre was not about films at all that afternoon. It was about finding a tent—darkened, chilled, protected from the glare outside. It was about little things like putting a hand over someone's chest, slipping it in through the V of the shirt. I have seen my mother do it perfectly, thousands of times, wedging her hand inside Daddy's shirt and saying, 'If I don't wedge myself, I will run adrift.'

She made us watch the shipyard scene from Charlie Chaplin's film *Modern Times* to know the true meaning of wedge—the image on which her idea of Daddy rested.

'If the wedge is loosened, my ship will sail.'

It made no sense, I thought, even though Daddy was once a sailor and ship metaphors were a thing for my mother.

I mention the wedge because at some point between Simba's banishment and 'Hakuna Matata', Silver Samir joined us. He waved at us and slipped into the empty seat next to Rani who leaned into him, forming a wedge. He dipped into our popcorn tub and sipped from the large Coke Rani was clutching in her hands. Silver highlights in his hair, silver rings on both hands, silver bracelet, a silver chain—all that silvered up the dark movie hall. Rani was no longer jumpy or absent-minded. Silver Samir lowered his head down to kiss her. His mouth slightly open, he was scooping her up, sucking her in and his hand was on her monsoon-blue kurta, counting the buttons. Then it was slipping down and forming a wedge between her legs. Feeling dizzy, I gripped Kiran's hand as they made wet sounds with their tongues. I felt saliva pool in my mouth. Kiran and I dared not turn our heads fully. Our eyeballs ached from being parked at the corner of our eyes.

After the film got over, we climbed into Silver Samir's car. Rani sat in the front and kept sliding her hand under his on the shifting gear. We were heading towards the end of that day's excursion—to the forest.

Washed by a fresh spell of afternoon rain, the city was all smoke and mirrors—a blur of secret-burying haze and humid heat. Secrets could be of many types—they could refer to knowing something just as much as *not* knowing. Not knowing, for instance, what lymph nodes are. Whatever their type, secrets were the mystery ingredients that kept people interested in each other and made life worth a shot. Silver Samir was one such secret—a secret that Kiran and I held on to. A secret that even at the height of my friend-making project and at the peak of my mission to turn Armish into my BFF I wouldn't share. This secret kept me glued to Kiran. Mama-mon—who knew every tale Rani had to tell, every kick and slap that often featured in her life, including her break-up with that awful rajma-eating chap from New Zealand—even she wasn't privy to the secret of Silver Samir.

When I ask Rani why she hadn't told Mama-mon, she said she was going to.

'She hasn't been feeling tip-top lately, so I just want her to get sorted first before I, you know, talk about Silver Samir. I want her to focus on getting better.'

Sure enough, it was a lot to take in. Adults would find it hard to trust forest folk like the Jahanpanah Jugnus. They would explode into a thousand questions and promptly take away our forest rights. Even my parents—activist Imon, Friend-of-Jews Danish—would do that.

The film and Chinese made us sleepy. We stumbled more than we strolled. It was a cloudy day, the forest avenue was darker than usual. Insects talked in loud whispers, angry after the rain. Ant colonies scampered around their newly broken homes, bewildered and wondering how to avenge the loss. Babool trees shook themselves, drenching us with sprays of leftover rain. Thorny shrubs of kareel and ber trees closed in from both sides. An orange snake slithered past. Through this storm-tossed world we kept walking.

It was twilight already. Jackals were out. A nilgai stood by the hedges, looking at us sternly. The bird concert became deafening. We grew restless. It was late. Kiran said she couldn't miss maths tuition. We reached the oval clearing in the middle of the forest. Someone had strung up fairy lights, and there were songs on a stereo. It looked like a party, and sure enough it was—a surprise for me from Silver Samir.

'Surprise, surprise, surprise!' Jugnus came out of the shadows. Velu walked in carrying a brilliant blue cake with purple flowers that were melting in the heat. He put it on a plastic table, and we stood around in a circle.

'Happy Birthday, Narois!' Suraj was there too with Bittoo.

I turned towards Kiran, hoping she would be pleased to see Suraj. Now he could give her a ride to the maths tuition class on his bike. She wouldn't have to depend on Choti Ma.

'I don't like that Bittoo one bit,' she whispered.

The dragon on Bittoo's wrist seemed alive as he lit candles on the cake.

We stood around, and everyone sang and clapped.

There were packets of chicken and veg patties and cream rolls for us. I could die of the cream that I was eating that day.

Silver Samir handed me a packet and said, 'Specially for you from Wenger's.' I couldn't very well refuse. That would be rude. We ate the cake in silence. The stereo was loud. In the evening mist Rani and Silver Samir were shadows. I wanted her to come back, be close. Mosquitoes towered and buzzed over our heads. Mian Pagla sang a song from the river for us. Bhaiya and Vinay Jugnu picked up Kiran with one hand, balancing her on her stomach. She screamed with excitement. I wished they would lift me too; after all, I was the birthday girl.

Suraj gifted me a torch that also became a laser light. I could shine the laser at Kiran's window, and she would know I was out in the garden. It was the best gift ever, even better than Narois-the-attar.

It wasn't just Kiran I hadn't invited to my birthday. Suraj was not on my list either. My park-brother. Even though Mama-mon said she would never want to be a son-mother, I knew how much she loved him. The way she loved Kubla.

We sat on packing crates licking cream off our fingers. I wondered if I could offer the blue cake to a mother-bird for her birdling.

Bittoo included himself in our group, although he was much older.

'Suraj, come now, buzz your hair off, yaar. Just like me,' Bittoo teased.

Suraj grinned sheepishly.

'What next, bhaiya? A tattoo?' Kiran muttered under her breath. Suraj would eventually get a tattoo—every Jugnu got a special tattoo on his wrist.

Bittoo had bad apple written all over him. Yet he was evidently a Jugnu, and he was a friend of Velu who sauntered in and sat next to Kiran.

I could never get over the tiny ache that Velu preferred Kiran over me.

'Her eyes have been born. They are alive. This little child who reminds me of my daughter', was Velu's standard remark when I quizzed him about his preference.

'Eyes are born along with us. If they aren't, then you are blind all your life,' I argued.

'There are other blindnesses and other sights.'

Rich that, coming from Velu who, according to me, was as wonderful as he was disgusting. There was something about him, something surely more than the fact that he was the first murderer I had ever met in my entire life. How do I know this? Because he told us that story one day, and it was so wild! He spared us no detail about the murders he had committed. Velu's full name was T. Velu, the T being short for where he came from, the very place where his murders had taken place. He became a Jugnu two years ago, and unlike others who came and went, the forest was where he lived, under the blue tarp.

'That's my home, cheri,' he said scooping up gajar halwa with giant pieces of roti. Sitting cross-legged on the grass, he ate furiously, mostly in silence.

When it rained, the pelting of raindrops on the tarp reminded him of home where rain fell like bombs.

'I once had a little girl,' he told us.

'Did she go missing? Is that why you have left home, to look for her?'

'No, she died. The angels took her. I put her in the earth and left home, left my job.'

'You had a job, Velu?'

'Why, yes, I did, Miss Fancy. I used to work for a bank.'

No wonder, I thought. Banks, according to Mamamon, were thieves, murderers.

The party-in-my-name was breaking up, and I was ready to go home. Velu said he would walk us to the gate. I looked for Rani in the gathering dark. I thought I heard sobs.

Suraj came with us; Kiran and I slipped our hands through his, keeping him in the middle, keeping him safe and to ourselves. That was the best part of the day—the three of us walking together, children who have walked together since as long as they can remember. Velu followed us, mostly in the shadows, but we knew he was there looking out for us. The fireflies and crickets came alive and snakes hissed, wide awake, travelling alongside. Velu stopped when we neared the brightly lit gate.

We turned and waved at him, although he couldn't be seen.

Suraj came up to the gate of the Sharan House with us but refused to enter. Bittoo was hovering with the bike nearby. He had followed us. Suraj waved goodbye and they sped away.

Choti Ma was furious. She was angry with Kiran because she had missed her tuition class, because she was late for dinner, because Suraj was never home. Probably she was cross because they were not her children.

Kiran said Choti Ma was angry because her youth was wasted on Kiran's papa. An old man. Half dead. Who could no longer cook Chinese.

People are promises. Friends, relatives, parents, who come to you whole. Like a toy with all parts working splendidly. Or a car, revving. Or a book, every page intact. Then one day a wheel falls off. Or a mildewed page crumbles. A gall bladder, an appendix, an arm or a leg, lost on the operation table or in an accident. What do you have left then? This person that we continue to love but who is no longer what came to us at first.

Daddy was at the gate, smoking.

'You were next door all along?'

'Not really, Daddy. I was all over town.'

'So I see,' he said, eyeing the Wenger's cream rolls.

I gave him one and let him think we had been to Connaught Place. He did not ask me questions like a normal parent would. Did you take an auto or a metro? Did you get an Uber? Did you cross all roads safely?

Mama-mon couldn't have a cream roll. She could no longer taste food. Blisters and bleeding ulcers grew on her tongue, which had turned purplish-black and looked like it would wither and fall off. Daddy fed her bone broth, spoon by spoon, blowing on it, adding butter, whispering that one day, soon, she would be wolfing down super-spicy kakori kebabs. And that her tongue would dance again.

14. Meals without Borders

In the Age of Mondays, meals had no borders.

At home, you could eat up to a point and share the rest with a bird.

Mama-mon chose to stare at the food on the table. I often snuck out these forsaken meals for Velu.

I didn't want Daddy to eat leftovers stuffed in the fridge. Not just because I wanted to collect as much leftover as I could for the Jugnus, but because I felt sorry for Daddy who loved food. I would steer him to the piping hot bowls of daal or chicken stew arranged neatly on the dining table, sitting on mats with cross-stitched sceneries that Granny Dorabjee had sent for us, served in bone-china bowls with tiny cracks in them, giving off curvy smoke wisps. Around this would be tiny mounds of white rice and a tinier mound of black rice. Like a painting that no one ate.

On Saturdays, I had no trouble sneaking out several tiffin boxes of leftovers. Velu loved fish curry. He made a face at mushrooms. We always had loads of mushroom. Whenever I stole fish for him, he told us his story.

In his story, sometimes he was the murderer. Sometimes his father was. A murderer of people, to be specific, and not a murderer of this and that—a long list of which Mama-mon carried around. Murderer of our country. Murderer of literature.

Velu killed a clerk and an unknown person waiting at the bus stand hoping to catch the last bus home. Velu's father was more murderous, according to Velu, as if there is such a thing as more or less murder.

'My father killed his wife and younger son. That makes me a murderer's son. It's in my blood.'

We would stare at his yellow eyes, teeth rimmed with bloody gums.

'Do you have scurvy like Vasco da Gama's men? They had landed very close to where your original murder-ridden home is, hadn't they?'

'Nonsense. We don't care about Vasco in Kerala. And no, it's not scurvy, macha.'

'What about your bank job then?' Kiran asked him one day. 'You said you worked for a bank.'

In the story, his job didn't matter. Or his father's.

'He put a pillow on my mother's face. She kicked and struggled, and I tried to hold her legs, thinking that if I could just stop the kicking, she would breathe. He just kept sitting on her chest, his back to me, holding the pillow over her mouth and nose, pressing it down harder and harder.

'A few days later he came for my younger brother. My brother wouldn't stop screaming because Mother was dead and he was hungry. My brother was put inside a pail of water. I watched as he drowned, no longer screaming. He drowned in a pail. A pail. Not even a pond. Have you ever floated in a river? Or an ocean? Or a bucket?'

'Why didn't he kill you?' I asked.

'He couldn't,' Velu said.

'Why? The police came?'

Velu laughed and called me a rich girl asking silly questions.

'You have never studied a subject that we have—she and I,' Velu said, pointing at Kiran. 'You haven't. You never will. Police don't arrive just like that in a damp stinky shanty next to the sewage drain. They arrive in that house over the wall at midnight to join a loud party and drink free booze. And that house over by the khirni tree to investigate the theft of a tyre. They don't come to our houses. Unless they mean to put on a handcuff or kick our bellies.'

Velu could be mean. What was the use of stealing fish curry, lifting their slimy bodies carefully and placing them in the tiffin box, pouring out the turmeric gravy, only to hear that I hadn't studied a subject which, apparently, Velu and Kiran had?

And now Velu of all people, forest-dwelling Velu, who had one shirt exactly, was trying to steal away my old best friend.

The word steal is to be used carefully, please, Mama-mon warns.

Are friend-stealers way worse than, say, for example, history-stealers?

Soon after the incident of flying hair, Mama-mon said 'enough is enough' and made a date to meet her head. We greeted her head with bienvenido, as-salamu alaykum—the head that was now part of the face. There was more mother to see, more places to kiss.

'Best decision of my life,' she announced. We agreed.

I had never had my head shaved as a child. 'As if a foreign name weren't enough!' the Parsi side of my family fretted. A name that has no link to the parents. Poor child, what untold fears and enemies await her. On the sixth day after my birth—when angels should have been invited to visit and write my destiny on a piece of paper—Daddy's relatives mourned and prayed, apologized to Ahura Mazda. Granny Dorabjee, trembling like a leaf, asked Mama-mon if she could at least be allowed to carry away an imprint of my little foot.

'Just to kiss it every night. My little jewel. Kindly allow.'

'Why was she pleading with me?' Mama-mon grumbled when I was older. 'Was it not her right as a grandmother? Was I stopping her? Why treat me like a monster, someone who came between mother and son? I could have given her a piece of my mind … but I let her have a piece of you.'

Whenever Daddy became an Oblonsky or when she missed her United Nations job, Mama-mon remembered the sixth day after my birth and how Granny Dorabjee made her feel ashamed and misunderstood. She'd speak to me of the horror of it all, but really, as it began to dawn on me, she'd be speaking at Daddy.

When I was six days old, Mrs Ava Dorabjee, mother of Danish Dorabjee, took out a little box of red powder from her bag, mixed it in a bowl of water, dipped my tiny feet in it and carefully took imprints on a white sheet of paper. That was the last time she saw me. Poor Granny Dorabjee, who now no longer leaves her flat in Colaba. Daddy visits her when he goes to his ship-harbours in Bombay, but he never suggests to Mama-mon that we visit as a family. Whatever happened that day—the day of Chhathi Na Lekh—it took away a chunk of Daddy's and Mama-mon's love for each other. That day onwards, their ship was always leaking.

After Mama-mon went to meet her head, we returned home. Alone, feeling overstuffed with Nago Didi's treats, I decided to give Armish a call.

Armish was at her Nani's house. 'I am always at Nani's house on Saturdays.'

I imagined a house as old as the one in which my own DinDin lived.

'Who is squealing so? Are those pigeons?' I tried seeing with my ears.

'My cousins are over!' Armish turned on the video. 'And yes, there are hundreds of pigeons cooing on our windowsills. But now I must go. We are playing hide-and-seek.'

'Who is the denner?'

'Afroz, my cousin. He is lethal.'

'What's for lunch?'

'Obviously, Nani's biriyani.'

My mouth watered as I pictured Nani's biriyani—white, yellow, muttony, smelling like Sunday.

'Hope you will bring some of that biriyani to school. Pack extra for me.'

She hesitated. 'If there's any left over ...'

'But before you go ... share your location, drop your pin.'

'What? Why?'

'Just ... just want to see which part of town you are in. Look you up on Google Maps. Since we are learning maps in school ...'

What I wanted to really know but didn't tell her was this—whether her Nani's house was next to the river or near the old fort. Whether I could reach her by car or a metro ride. Would there be traffic?

Needy Narois, niggling Narois. Calling Armish over the weekend Narois. Needy, needy.

Kiran came at noon to check in on Kubla who was getting ready to be a daddy. All day he was hard at work inside his aquarium, blowing bubbles, making a bubble nest on the surface of the water.

Kiran had a valid question. 'If you don't give him a female mate, how will he make a baby?'

We stopped running the water pump. The bubble nest had to be saved, even if there would be no fish-babies rocking in them. It was what made Kubla happy. The aquarium water slowly turned a dirty grey. Festive banners of green moss fluttered around Kubla's cave. A fly buzzed around the aquarium. Kubla chased it.

Rain clouds scampered away. The sky was a sheet of origami, crinkling and rustling.

But it was still raining elsewhere. In Bombay, for example. Kiran showed me a terrifying video of a woman getting washed away into the Arabian Sea. I saw death with my own eyes. She wore an eggplant-coloured saree, a bright pop against the mad and angry sea. It was a good pose—you had to give her that—leaning against a big rock, right at the edge of the Bandstand breakwater. Her children filmed her from a safe distance as she hung onto the four-legged tetrapod. A gigantic wave landed on her, dunking her completely. Everyone clapped. When the froth and spray cleared, she was no longer sitting on the rock. Her children screamed but kept filming.

At first it was a bit of a shock. Someone who looked like Mama-mon stood at the door. She seemed distant, like an Avenger. Then she hugged me tight and let me touch her new friend—the head, the skull.

'We will give her a certificate of crossing. Blessings from the mighty Neptune and Poseidon!' Daddy said.

'What have you crossed, Mama-mon?'

'I am crossing a constellation, darling. An endless ocean of stars. I am walking on water.'

'Will you still come to school?'

'Why do you ask? Would you not want me to?'

Typical Mama-mon: question for question.

I shut my eyes. A crowd of friends whispering to me, is she a new mother? Is she a punk? Is she a monk?

Punk-monk mother: Jesus and a sailor. I dreamt of the star-studded ocean over which she walked. The dolphins have come and a school of yellow fish. A school of fish. A school for the fish. Why do words have two meanings? Is it possible to choose different meanings? Mondays I could be schooling with the fish. Tuesdays I could nip back to school at my school. Now that would be a top-notch life.

15. Austen

I was two years old when I caught the kiss-kiss disease. It gave me a weekly fever and made me say things way beyond my vocabulary of those years. My mother quit her job at the United Nations office because they made her travel non-stop, and parting with her would make me sicker. One day at dawn she had to catch a flight to Jakarta. When she crept out of the house with her suitcase, my fever was peaking again and Daddy was considering taking me to the hospital.

'Twenty thousand feet above the Java Sea, I resigned from my job with a poem,' Mama-mon said with pride and rage when I was old enough to know what jobs were about. She posted that poem to Gloria Steinem who never replied. Mama-mon believed Ms Steinem would have if the envelope had reached her. 'Cronies in the middle, middle-class middlemen.'

So, I am saving up the poem, just in case she dies before Ms Steinem does. Then I will re-post the poem and write in clear bold letters—From the Ghost of Imon:

I raised a memorial
To dawn,
Four years ago
When clouds trembled white and frail
Against the aeroplane window.
I peered down sightless
And prayed I would see her again.
Days and weeks at my desk of equal pay
Her fever crept in with the afternoon sun,
Warmed my busy fingers,
Lulled my words till I became mute and
People said there was a light in my eyes.

Chiba, a Japanese man who lived nearby and was Daddy's work friend, got mugged in the Jahanpanah Forest when he was out for his evening run. Daddy took him to the local police station. The police scolded Chiba for running in the forest at such an odd hour.

'Would you do such a thing in your Japan?'

'Yes, of course,' Chiba said. 'I run five miles every evening.'

'All you chowmein people, you don't understand. Make him understand, Danish-ji, that when our people see their skin they rob them because … because why? How much is the Japanese dollar today?'

Daddy, a great impersonator, opened his mouth wide and flat when he made the police voice. He narrowed his lips and moved his jaws when he became Chiba.

We ate a Japanese meal that night. It was expensive, and Mama-mon ooh-ed and aah-ed over the bill. Then she forgot about the expense and said she would binge-watch a Netflix series that was about a man who ran a diner in Tokyo. We ended up watching an American film in which a man with a pockmarked face found himself alone in a hotel with a brilliant-looking girl who came and went, and they barely spoke. Bright billboards of Tokyo twinkled, and people looked up at them from taxis on busy streets.

That evening Daddy said, 'Even though we are liberals, the time to return is dusk—the golden hour when cows come home and birds flock back.'

This come-home hour was the worst hour of the day, according to Mama-mon.

'If you have not gone anywhere in the day, you cannot come home, can you? So don't call it the come-home hour.'

To face this hour, she drew up several twilight battle plans.

Late afternoons the house would be quiet and, as you know, wrapped in an orange glow. I built Lego towers on the floor. Midway, mid-painting, mid-cartoon tiger, she would leave me alone.

'On your own, on your own. Learn to swim. Get sea legs, captain your own ship. Daughter of a sailor.'

But Daddy is no longer a sailor.

'Once a sailor, always a sailor.'

She sat stunned for hours, her back against the wall. The tiniest noise would startle her. I would startle her. In that icy cave, she didn't read books or write or work.

Sometimes, at 3 o'clock, she gave me a snack or a hot chocolate.

Then she took out her purple coffee mug and said, 'Having a drink is not a bad thing, but you have it when you are an adult, and it must be to some end. Your drink should listen to you. Not the other way round.'

One afternoon, when I was barely three, Mama-mon bundled me up against the grey cold, took a few hours' supply of milk, cheese sandwich, saline nose spray. I sat in the back seat. We sang for a while. She (I imagine) out of tune, following me with half words. Car picnics were part of her afternoon battle plans.

Mama-mon would drive me to where she used to work. There were photos of me on her desk. She had taught me to say UN, Ban Ki-moon and poverty before I could say many other things. We'd park. A guard would come rushing, waving his hand, whistling. Mama-mon would lower the window and smile. He'd smile back, say 'hello baby' to me and then tell my mother that she couldn't park there. We'd cross the road and park on the other side.

On one occasion, I recall her friend appearing after a really long time. She waved from across the street and got into the car. Sam, with her snow-white hair and long earrings, was disappointed to see me, a child, tucked in the back seat.

'Adorable to have her, but I won't be able to smoke. We have to sit outdoors.'

At the restaurant where we went, I remember being scared of the tall trees swaying in the harsh winter breeze. I wanted to go home. Sam's white hair glinted in the sun. Her burgundy scarf had something written on it, which I tried to read. Or that's how I imagine it now. That afternoon, whipped by the cold wind, Mama-mon parted ways forever with her UN friends—another day and story that she never tired of telling. 'The day I took Narois to meet Sam.'

Apparently, I ate carrots and spoke in alliterations.

'Cold carrot. Bored baby. Hurry home.'

October came, and the air became festive. We felt lonely and cut off. Chemo Mondays, as we called it now, carried on as usual. Daddy accompanied Mama-mon every week, now that we had a name for it. Nago Didi kicked up a fuss on Mondays. Made me pizzas and baked outrageous cakes. Kiran came over to spend time with me. It was tiresome. I wanted to be completely alone and read a book. Not say a word. I wanted to call Armish and plead with her to invite me over to her place, which sounded like a warm, merry space with a dozen cousins running around. I wanted to ask Meera if she was going on play dates to Reba's house without me. I wanted to dare myself to do embarrassing things and feel the raw shame cut through me.

Mama-mon came back with stories of her own from the hospital. She called her medicine a magical wonder from the yew tree. It was a silvery liquid and had a mind of its own. One day she found an air bubble in the IV tube. 'I shouted UFO and rang the call bell. Spies have used air bubbles to kill their enemies. It's dangerous. I simply held on to dear life.'

Thankfully, air bubbles didn't happen every Monday, and my mother was usually back by 5 o'clock. She'd drink a cup of tea but fail to keep it down. Tea and extracts of the yew tree would come tumbling out soon after. We'd count—Vomit 1. Vomit 2. Vomit 3. Vomit 3.5. I'd lose count. I'd forget. Daddy wouldn't. He'd keep his distance because she wouldn't allow anyone to watch her when she threw up (or when she painted her brows, which were becoming paler by the day). Daddy kept count. If the count would exceed five, he'd pound a few medicines to fine white powder, which she'd put under her tongue.

I learnt quite a bit about the human body in those weeks. That the bone marrow is a non-stop factory producing millions of red blood cells every second. That the factories are in the ribs, the pelvis, the spine, which are constantly churning out blood cells—more than five billion in a day.

These factories started shutting down in early October.

At first, we didn't realize there was a mutiny. Mama-mon went about her good days feeling top-notch, interviewing for a new job. That too was happening—a job hunt when, on some days, she swayed like a quaking aspen.

'I need to look for a job,' she'd announce at such times.

Instead of explaining to her that a job when she was so weak was a mad and dangerous idea, Daddy seemed to brighten up. He said to her with a twinkle in his eyes, 'Yes, my love, that would do you good.'

The day she got called for a job interview, Mama-mon laughed, 'Karma, willy-nilly karma. Now I am getting a job ... *now*?'

She spent hours watching YouTube videos to tie the perfect turban.

On the day of the interview, she tied a silk turban and wore heels.

But at the hotel, after the interview, she collapsed in the foyer. Daddy took her straight to the hospital where they ran tests.

'If blood were a country, hers has gone bankrupt,' Daddy explained.

The day before Diwali, she went to the hospital for a blood refill. Daddy donated to the blood bank.

From the blood transfusion she came back with rosy cheeks, and her chest no longer heaved. Her eyes shone like a cat's in the fog.

'But now I am part someone else.'

'Em, people receive blood all over the world. Be thankful that someone made it available and saved your life,' Daddy scolded Mama-mon. He was tired of her constant cleverness.

Strangely that little scold seemed to soothe her, and she no longer thought of the blood as someone else's.

In the last week of October, she got the job. She was going to be head of campaigns for a company that worked on rainfall. We celebrated. I drank pink lemonade. Daddy had a glass of whisky and Mama-mon raised an empty champagne glass. The room was smoky from the whisky smell and the autumn haze gathering outside. Our air purifier was already glowing dangerously red.

'Now I need a wig,' Mama-mon said, rubbing a hand over her velvety head. 'It will be winter soon. My head needs a cover.'

Later at night I heard Mama-mon and Daddy discussing the wig. Daddy was telling her how she looked so beautiful with her head bare. I agreed with him—she did look spectacular. But there was something exciting about a wig. Maybe she would get two or three types to wear as she pleased and sometimes I could wear them and stage a play.

'Are you worried about the new job, Em? What might they say when you go to meetings?' Daddy asked.

'Everyone judges, Danish.'

'But you scoff at those who judge. You teach them a lesson.'

'Maybe. But it is my duty to wear a wig at least once. To feel the full impact of this life ...'

After the blood that was not hers, she would have hair that was not hers.

Mama-mon and I went to different wig parlours around the city. She tried on a variety of wigs—curly, straight, blunt, windy, streaked. A wig parlour in Nizamuddin Market tried selling her wigs made for air hostesses. Nothing fitted her head, nor did she look herself in them.

We went across to the cake shop from where you could hear trains whistling by. I had a large slice of banana walnut cake, dripping with toffee sauce. Mama-mon sat across, making phone calls. She smiled a lot when she spoke to whoever was at the other end and before hanging up sent them kisses and hugs and prayers. Mama-mon never prayed. She never air-kissed anyone except me.

Who were these people? Why was she so sweet to them?

'Well, darling, can't I have friends too?'

'But you don't like friends.'

'Touché, my child. No, I don't. But these people are different. We are pilgrims of sorts—you know, people who tread and tread along a road and fight fascists together? Exactly how it is in that book I keep talking about.'

I didn't know exactly, what she was talking about. But I got the drift. Mama-mon had found friends who were once sick like her.

Someone from that group had an unused wig that she could lend. We drove for an hour to the other end of the city to meet the wig. But it turned out that the lady would need it again. The wig's job was not done ... not yet.

'We got to know just this morning, so I couldn't call and inform. It was a routine investigation. The reports have shocked us, you see,' a very polite and soft-spoken man said. 'You can understand that Raji-ji will not be able to meet. Kindly excuse her.'

Then he offered us tea, which we refused. He folded his hands and said he would ask his Wahe Guru to bless my mother and bless her family.

Mama-mon curled up on the back seat. Daddy drove with a face of stone.

Through the same network, Mama-mon found another wig parlour that specialized in wigs for 'people like her'. A few days later, the wigmaker called to say the wig was ready and could be picked up on Saturday. Mama-mon said I could come if I wanted to and to 'bring Kiran if you like'.

It was already November, and a grey smog hung low. The wig shop was inside a shopping mall at a busy crossing. Metro trains thundered past. Cars honked. Rickshaws, autos jostled for space. Kiran and I held hands. Mama-mon wore a pollution mask and covered her head with a cap and a scarf. She was tottering a bit. Kiran and Daddy held her at the elbow.

The mall was sleepy and damp, except for the wig parlour, which was spread across two floors and lit up like a circus. All other shops—the narrow feng shui shop with shelves full of smiling Buddhas and crystal trees, the one with salwar suits—were terribly dull. Shopkeepers sat on stools and stared at the wig parlour, which was bustling with activity, and at the people who came in needing wigs.

A tall man whose bald head sparkled in the bright lights welcomed Mama-mon. He made her sit on a chair and examined her head, feeling her skull like a potter. On shelves that ran across the length and breadth of the parlour were heads wearing wigs of different kinds.

'All original hair,' he said when he noticed that we were looking. 'Human hair sacrificed at temples. Nothing synthetic.'

Mama-mon's wig arrived placed on a head mould.

'See, exactly how your hair was before you began the treatment. No difference. Slight parting on the right, layers around the chin. It is you again, the face you lost, the *you* you lost,' he said in a chant.

Daddy grimaced and put a hand on Mama-mon's shoulder. She looked at Daddy and said, 'Would you mind looking away?'

She didn't say that to us, so we kept looking. She was now completely in the hands of the wigmaker.

I asked Kiran if he might be hypnotizing her.

'No, he is just helping her,' she said and put an arm around me.

The wig landed on her head, transforming her. It was perfect—how her hair fell over her eyes, a left parting, the slight curly lift of the ends. Her wiggy hair was an out-and-out replica of her hair as it was, but her face met the wig with cold vibes and together they failed to make sense. She looked lopsided.

I had a terrible urge to pull it off her head—wigged mother making me cold and sick.

'I want you to keep wearing it for ten minutes. See if it's too tight around your head,' the man told her. 'We don't want to block off your circulation, and yet we don't want the wig falling off.'

He left her side to attend to other clients, including a man who wanted to learn how to gel his wig hair and a woman who insisted that they sprinkle her wig with greys.

We stood around Mama-mon whose face looked like a broken mirror. Everything was at odd angle, the nostrils, left eye, the chin, her brows. I wanted to look away.

After ten minutes, Mama-mon said she had a wild headache. The main wig-man took off the wig, and we saw that it had left a deep red welt around her head. It ran from her forehead to the back of her head, which was sparkling white otherwise.

He loosened the elastic a bit.

'Can't stretch it anymore. You must get used to it. Make it a point to wear it for a few hours at least.'

A junior wigmaker came and took us to the sink. He was going to show Mama-mon how to take care of the wig.

'See, this is human hair, but it's not growing on anyone's head. It's without a root and has no blood supply. So, essentially this is dead hair and cannot look real if it's not taken care of regularly.'

He taught Mama-mon how to wet the hair under cold water, rinse it up to the last strand and then use shampoo and conditioner. When the wash was done, it had to be lightly wrapped in a towel. Once the water stopped dripping, she would have to comb it and curl the end and leave it to dry naturally on the bamboo head that came with it.

We left the wig parlour with the wet wig sitting on the bamboo head. It sat between me and Kiran in the back seat.

Daddy wanted to talk to Mama-mon about the new job, probably because he felt she needed a distraction, but he had no idea what it meant to save the rain. The car came out of the Okhla underpass and suddenly Mama-mon sat up, riding the crest of a brainwave. She turned to us happily and said, 'I am going call her Austen.'

We said 'hello Austen' to Austen who was sitting between us, still quite damp.

16. Khooni Jheel

The day Daddy and I spent at the Asola-Bhatti Sanctuary was bitterly cold and gloomy. Clumps of fog hung on leafless trees and shrubs. Trekking across the yellow plateau, we reached a small cliff. Below, us, surrounded by miles and miles of shrubland and sandy soil, was the feared lake: Khooni Jheel. Not bloody red, as promised. Not even a hint of red anywhere. Ripples of sapphire blue shot through with still depths of emerald green.

'Imagine, Narois, gallons of blood must have flowed that day, colouring the lake's waters.'

'Did the sepoys murder in hundreds or tens, Daddy?'

'Mutinied. Quite the opposite of murder. It is unclear who killed whom at this lake. Because history tells you, does it not, that the conquerors become the conquered swiftly enough … although,' said Daddy, handing me an egg sandwich and squinting through the binocs at a falcon flying by with a long echoing shriek, 'at the end, there is a lake of blood, which later becomes a tourist spot.'

Daddy was lonely and looked as if he desperately needed friends. How I longed to tell him about the Jugnus. He would love to befriend them. But I buried the secret yet again. A promise was a promise.

It was a day worth journalling about. I wrote a diary entry, not quite truthfully since truth is bland, and took it to school.

Meera caught me with it and said, enough being secretive. 'Come on, let people know.'

She told everyone she met, 'Come to the library during recess. I have something to show you.'

Zorawar, Armish, Saanvi, Reba and a few other kids turned up. Rishit came because he wanted to spy on us. Our librarian Mrs Kumar had gone for lunch. Suman Didi was at the counter, keeping an eye on book-stealing, kissing-in-corridors children.

We went over to the classics row by the window, which was naturally always deserted. We heard silver fish chomping up the pages of *Ivanhoe*.

I read out my diary entry about our trek to Khooni Jheel, spicing up sections, adding heads and tongues of sepoys floating in the lake. I claimed I had seen a little girl's hand imprinted on a stone.

What a hit it was! Zorawar and Meera slapped me on the back and called me the OG.

'You slay, Narois! Better than Naruto even!'—which coming from Zorawar was a huge compliment.

Meera said I had a stan following—fans were ready to ink in my name on their arms and kill for me. Although who they were she couldn't say. 'Stans don't reveal their identity.'

Meera typed out my story and took twenty printouts from Aunty Rebecca's office.

They flew off her shelf like hot cakes.

'That's so dope. We are totally vibing with your world where all parents and adults are dead and children can choose their kind of candy-flavoured death and there are mutinies and bloodied lakes.'

My journals were the newest horror, now that Annabelle the Doll was gone from our lives, haunting a new host. And my friends were done waiting for my mother to die or for Zorawar's parents to divorce.

Zorawar followed me around and said I was beginning to look famous.

'Kid's got a crush on you,' Meera observed.

Jyoti Sharma held me at her desk, her eyes glittering and dancing. 'Wait till I catch you red-handed. Wait till I get my hands on the rubbish you are writing.'

Armish was now firmly best friends with Reba. Meera said it was because I had overdone my possessiveness.

'Just let her be, okay?' she said.

Time glided. Days were short. Soon, I stopped writing that journal and got selected for a school play. Every day we rehearsed during lunch break.

One day, during the break, while we were rehearsing, Armish, who was the tallest kid in class and was playing the role of a tree, came up to me and said she regretted not being my best friend. What was I up to, she asked? How was Kubla?

Kubla had stopped making bubble nests. The nests needed warmth. The water was too cold.

'Come and see for yourself,' I said.

'Maybe one of these days,' Armish said in a preoccupied-with-other-thoughts voice. I waited for her to tell me more. Which she did, biting her lips down hard, 'Abba says there will be trouble. He is looking for a job in another city. Before we leave, you must come to my Nani's house in Jamia.'

'Oh, invite me,' I said.

Before she could, the music changed, and it was our cue to go dancing on to the stage.

Ustadji moved my singing lessons to Saturday afternoons. He had been invited to sing at a series of musical soirées every Sunday. Rani offered to pick me up from Ustadji's house. She came wearing a sari. I was so proud that someone who looked like her was my guardian. All the others—didis, parents waiting in the courtyard of the old mansion, Ustadji's neighbours peeping in from their balconies—stared.

Rani and I sat in a rickshaw. Through narrow alleys, waves of street chatter and the frying hiss of jalebis, we zigzagged. Kites shaped like lizards whooshed. Little girls, with their mothers buying rainbow-coloured scrunchies for their hair, chattered. Kiran would have seen so much more; I listened more than I saw. Our driver-uncle, Mohan Chacha, waited for us in the car parked on the main road. Rani messaged Silver Samir to tell him we were on the way. We told Mohan Chacha to take us to the mall.

Rani bought a bottle of patchouli oil for my mother. Silver Samir waited for us outside a bakery. We had a croissant and then strolled along the cheerful patio where a small fair was taking place. I went over to the pet corner; Mekhala Didi, our senior at school, volunteered at the centre that had set it up. An abandoned Labrador puppy looked up at me.

Mekhala Didi came by and said hello.

'What happened to him?'

'The owner died and then her husband couldn't keep them—the puppy's mom, siblings and him—because he was too heartbroken. Want to adopt?'

Guiltily I shook my head and said no, not yet.

'One day you will, cheer up.'

'Can I cuddle him?'

The other girl glared at me. The centre had a 'no adoption, no cuddle' policy. They are not cute, they need a home, a poster read.

I wondered where the mother was.

'I have a fish now,' I said aloud to Mekhala Didi. 'His name is Kubla Khan.'

She congratulated me and asked me how he was doing.

'Not so good, actually. Can you tell me how to make him better? He seems cold.'

'Oh, get a water warmer, Narois. You can't afford to let him suffer even for half a day. Pets can't speak. They need more attention from us.'

The other girl scoffed and guffawed. It was unbearable. She was mean.

Mekhala Didi said she had to go now and would see me later.

I said I wasn't sure if we would meet again.

'Oh why?' she asked. I had the other girl's attention now.

'My mother has cancer. She may die. That's why we don't have a pet.'

The rude girl's face became squelchy like splattering tomato. Mekhala Didi said oh! And then turned to fill up the forms that needed her attention.

I skipped away. Far away from the pet corner. A band had taken stage in the open amphitheatre. They were singing terribly out of tune, but it was festive.

Rani and Silver Samir sat on a bench shaped like a tiger. He had his hand around her waist, and when I came close I saw he was bizarrely caressing her waist where it was bare under the sari.

At first it was the matter of a timetable. In those weeks, fun outings with Silver Samir and Rani were always planned after my music lesson, and Kiran couldn't possibly miss her maths tuition, which was also always on Saturday—she was, quite frankly, terrible at maths. The maths teacher at her school was very sick and bedridden and would probably never be able to get up. Maths was going to be a free period for an eternity. The teacher's absence meant a future free of the subject. But Kiran wanted maths in her life. She wanted it so much that she gave up Silver Samir evenings. This wasn't my fault. Slowly, I started avoiding Kiran, glued as I was to the thrill of being with Rani and Silver Samir. He taught me many things about winter—how not to not be afraid of ice cream when it's bitterly cold; how to listen to lions roaring from one corner of the haunted Purana Qila.

When a friend of his got married, he took Rani and me along, and I pretended I was their daughter. Rani lied to Mama-mon when she took permission. I found it a terribly practical thing to do. 'My cousin is getting married. I don't feel like going all by myself. Please let me take Narois. She will have great fun, and it will be a distraction.'

Mama-mon helped me choose a dress and drew wings over my eyes. Rani tied my hair in a perfect French braid.

We bumped into Kiran at the gate. It wasn't a Saturday, and there was no maths tuition. I made an excuse about not being sure what Rani's plans were; Kiran couldn't tag along uninvited, could she? Kiran admired my dress, the wings over my eyes and said she was happy that Mama-mon was finally allowing a tad bit of make-up. Rani stood on her toes and peered at the far end of the road, over the endless stream of headlights. Where was our cab? We were late. Due to our lateness, we didn't look Kiran in the eye. Dressed to the nines, in silver-and-gold dresses, Rani and I dived into the cab and drove off. Kiran's face darkened and glowed in intervals in the passing traffic. I was sailing my boat away from the lighthouse face. I was going into the dark.

17. A Funeral

On 6 November, Kubla Khan died. We found his stiff body in the morning, lying on neon-coloured pebbles at the tank bottom. Mama-mon blamed herself. Daddy consoled her and said such things happen—fish die all the time. But I had a nagging hunch that the water warmer we got for his tank might have fried him to death.

'Should we take him to the vets for an autopsy?' I whispered to Daddy who replied it was out of the question.

'Plan his funeral. That might make you feel better.'

Kubla was officially mine. But I wasn't feeling the pang of his passing as much as I should have.

Kubla's death was the beginning of a November that I will never forget. Kubla's death was a sign of things to come.

Later, Mama-mon would say, 'We paid for the sin of letting Kubla die.'

Frying a little betta red in its own happy waters.

Kubla was to be buried in the garden, under the orange tree. We would make him a memorial headstone with the neon pebbles and plastic trees from his tank, and as service, read the poem after which he was named.

I was the hearse-bearer and singer. Kiran wanted to wrap Kubla in silk. Daddy said he should be returned to earth.

Armish was the first person I informed.

'I am sorry he has died, Narois. But fish die easily. It's not your fault.'

The soft wiseness of Armish calmed me. I often imagined that later, when I was an adult living in a grand city, somewhere far away, every Saturday, no matter how busy I would be doing important things, Armish and I would talk on the phone, catch up about our lives, and in that way never ever lose touch or be strangers who were cold to each other. In such flights of fancy, I always pictured Armish wearing a yellow kurta, sitting in the half darkness of her grandmother's old house. I never saw her anywhere else. I didn't see her on the beach, bright and sunny. Or standing on the top of a skyscraper. I was the one in these places. She was always an inhabitant of that tiny slice of her life I had seen once on a video call.

'I will ask Mohan Chacha to pick you up in our car. Please come for the funeral.'

'Don't depend on it, Narois. Naani needs me here. We don't leave her alone these days.'

'Is she sick? Is she dying? Is that why you are missing school so often?'

Clicking her tongue, Armish said Naani was hale and hearty. But the world wasn't safe anymore. If they left her alone, they would probably burn her to death. Fry her like Kubla.

After the funeral, to cheer me up, Kiran said she would arrange a special meal for me at her house.

The chandelier family was away on vacation, so Kiran's Papa had loads of time on his hands. He spent most of the vacation relaxing with the baby and soothing Choti Ma. One day, they went for a film. Kiran and Suraj took care of the baby. Another day, he took her shopping. The day he took her shopping, Papa came back truly happy, laughing a lot, carrying five shopping bags bursting at the seams. Kiran cried her eyes out. We sat next to Kubla's grave, and she let her tears flow.

'He bought her a peach kurta with silver flowers. That was my mother's colour. They went to the exact same shop and bought the exact same piece of cloth. How could Papa?'

'Yes indeed, how could he!' Mama-mon said when she heard.

One Saturday, not long after Kubla's funeral, when Daddy was out, we watched a film called *Stepmom*.

Mama-mon said, 'We are watching this because of Julia Roberts. Daddy and I are wild about her.'

Julia Roberts was the stepmom and Susan Sarandon was the mom who was dying of cancer. 'Stepmoms step in to fill a mom-shaped gap,' she slogan-ed to me at some point in the film.

I asked if Kiran could watch it with us because she had a real stepmom and could tell us if the film was showing stuff that really happened. 'Not this time, Narois,' she said.

Daddy turned red-faced angry when he heard we had watched the film. Mama-mon and Daddy fought and fought and kept fighting long after I slept, which was anyway post-midnight.

'Why did you show her that film? Why are you planting these thoughts in the poor child's mind?' Daddy went berserk. He said he was going to let himself loose, he was going to forget about the cancer that didn't allow him to feel sorry for himself. Beware, Daddy said, and overturned the coffee table in our living room, crushing underneath it the blue bowl with seashells from the Andamans and the ceramic butterflies from Pondicherry.

'I was preparing her,' Mama-mon said in a voice as unshaken as the pyramids of Giza in sandstorms.

I lay still in bed, wondering how such a violent battle could erupt over a film that I had found quite slow and depressing. I knew what stepmoms were. I wasn't an idiot. My friend Advita had a stepmom called Ginia. She was nice, wore silver jewellery and had a tattoo at the nape of her neck. Stepmoms were like a new friend.

The chandelier house was dark. Kiran and I crossed the driveway, squeezing past a fleet of cars, parked and covered to keep off the dust while the owners were away. A silver Jaguar peeped out from under a cover. The backyard was bursting with flowers. There were yellow, pink and red roses, hydrangeas and blood-red hibiscuses.

'Come, smell the herb garden,' Kiran said. We sniffed the oregano leaves.

Brilliant lights lit up the back wall. The top was turned into an electric fence when the owners were not at home. Stepping into a blind spot where the CCTV cameras couldn't see us, Kiran showed me the corpses of dead squirrels.

'Only two so far, thankfully,' she said.

Squirrels scampering on the wall got electrocuted when the high-voltage fence was turned on. Their bodies smoked, shuddered and fell with a thud. Their friends would smell murder and stop climbing the wall for a few days. The little bodies were lodged in the bush, looking almost charred. Was squirrel meat a delicacy anywhere in the world?

Uncle had made mutton curry and crispy lachha parathas for us. The mutton pieces were tiny and soft. Everyone, except me, munched on green chillies for extra hotness.

After dinner, Kiran and I sat outside, swinging our legs through the iron frame of the staircase. I could see our garden over the wall, looking sad and overgrown, with a few droopy pansies.

The electric fence quivered and snapped under our bare feet.

Suraj came out talking on the phone. He was leaving again. 'Don't wait up for me,' he told Kiran.

There was something different about him these days. He was taller and aloof, although he couldn't help being kind.

Kiran saw me looking and leant over to say, 'He has dyed his hair like that vile Bittoo. That's why he looks different. Now he is threatening to get ear studs and is driving Papa crazy about it.'

Choti Ma dimmed the lights, let the baby play and started watching make-up videos on Instagram. Papa had to go back to the chandelier house for some work. We sat alone, the forest watching us.

'Sometimes I see Velu's red eyes blazing in the dark. Looking up at me,' Kiran said

'Aren't you scared?' I asked, shuddering.

'No, why should I be? He is looking for his dead daughter. It's how I look for my mother.'

I had never asked—how do you look for the dead?

The squabble over Suraj grew worse as days passed. He snuck in every now and then for a change of clothes, a hot meal or to ask for money. Uncle lost his temper one evening when Suraj demanded a jaw-droppingly huge sum of money. He slapped Suraj. Angry fingers made marks on thin cheeks. Suraj stormed out and vowed never to come back. Kiran and Uncle stayed awake all night, waiting for him to return. Kiran said she must have called him two hundred times.

'I don't know what has come over my poor brother. He is being controlled by someone else. Choti-Ma says someone's done a black-magic spell on him.'

Over a week passed; there was no word from Suraj. His phone was switched off. There was no way to contact him, so on the eighth day, Uncle took a day off and went looking for him. We made a list of friends, meeting points, old tutors and gaming parlours.

Uncle said, 'Add as many names as you can think of. Who are his friends? Where all is he likely to spend time?'

Kiran and I looked at each other. I knew exactly what she was thinking—should the Jahanpanah Jugnus be on the list? But that wasn't our secret to tell. Even if it was our secret, we couldn't tell it. It was the telling that we couldn't, shouldn't—or was it wouldn't?—do. Mama-mon said there was a thin line of difference between the words, and usually people got it wrong.

At the end of a long day of searching, Uncle came back exhausted, without any news.

'We have to bring him home. Even if the police are looking for him, the boy must come home forever.'

'But Papa, won't Bhaiya be arrested then?'

'Why should he be? He is innocent. Those drugs were planted by someone else. I will prove his innocence. I will go to the police and plead for their help. One more day I'll wait. If he doesn't come back, I'll report him missing at the police station,' Uncle murmured to himself.

I waited eagerly for the day to pass. It hurt to see Kiran cry so much. Even though the Jugnus had led us to Suraj, they had not exactly proved his innocence. It was time now for the police to be involved.

At school I discussed Suraj's case with Meera. With great concentration and willpower, I made sure to leave out any mention of the Jugnus.

'So, Rani the great-solver couldn't help, could she? Yes, you are right. These things must be solved by the police. Not by little girls like you,' said Meera, very haughtily, forgetting altogether that she too was a little girl like me.

'No point lodging an FIR now,' she went on knowledgeably. 'Police won't do a thing because they will think Suraj was just angry and went off in a huff.'

'Should we inform Aunty Rebecca?'

'Oh, she doesn't do regular missing-persons cases. Easy-peasy ones are handled by her staff. Mummy does murder and other awfully violent crimes. But, of course, if a VIP were to go missing then she would have to swing in.'

Since this was my first real-life experience of a person going missing, I thought it was rather clever of me to plant the information with Meera—just in case Aunty Rebecca needed to intervene.

Anyway ... one more day became five more. We hadn't heard from Suraj for almost a fortnight. Uncle brooded all the time. But no, he was yet to file a police report.

Mama-mon said it was understandable that Uncle didn't want police trouble. His employers wouldn't want a police jeep in front of their house, making queries.

'You see, Narois, it may cost him his job.'

18. Magenta Mahatma

Mondays were less frequent now. Each Monday cost Mama-mon a fortnight of being sick. The week no longer had good days. She came back from the hospital with a white face and her body trembled. Then slowly, as the pain filled her up, she became as still as possible.

I would sit next to her. Sometimes she went so still that I had to remind her, 'Mama-mon, are you breathing?'

She would nod or just blink twice.

The new job was a breeze. It was not keeping her too busy because they were still figuring out how to help the rainfall of the world. It occurred to me: Mama-mon, too, was a Jugnu—weather-working as she was. Every evening, she joined forever-long meetings in which people from different countries dialled in. They talked about the rain in many different accents. On Tuesdays, she kept her camera switched off and dozed on the call. I did my homework next to her and kept watch.

One day, over a call, to distract herself from the humongous need to puke, she tried making a charcoal sketch of a boat floating in reeds. Mid-sketch, she fainted on the drawing book. The boat became a shadow on her left cheek.

I ended the call. Mama-mon woke up. 'I annoyed the cruel conqueror of good cells who demands full attention,' she said.

After that day, she sat like the Rock of Gibraltar, spine straight, head still. I kept a finger on her arm or her back, light as feather, not even fully touching. A hug could kill her.

The doctor prescribed a double dose of the strongest sleeping pill on earth. 'Let it rock her away,' he said on the phone. She hated floating away, letting go. So, she fought the pill.

When she slept, the cold clammy fist on my stomach eased up a bit.

Daddy fixed me dinner, and we sat outside in our dry, unkempt garden looking at the stars.

'Narois, we need a telescope. I will teach you to look at the stars.'

I was truly afraid, for the first time perhaps.

Daddy borrowed a telescope from his friend. The ladder rested quietly against the wall.

We looked up at Orion and the Seven Sisters.

Was she losing the fight then? Were the other cells winning? Is that why we were telescoping stars and watching stepmoms?

'Not at all,' Daddy would say and become very upbeat and scientific since he knew I was a logical person and liked to see an argument well arranged.

'You see, Narois, this is the most powerful medicine in the world. Naturally it will have side-effects.'

'Like the nuclear bomb, isn't it, Daddy? Kept killing long after it exploded,' I said.

Daddy winced. He pulled me into his solid embrace, the one that made you feel you were in a planet all to yourself, and said, 'What have we done! Fed you with too much, haven't we, my Vera Narois? No, my love, this war is different. The medicine is on your mother's side. Would you like to know what it's called?'

He told me, and I wrote it down, letter by letter—Doxorubicin, also known as the Red Devil. I preferred the earlier medicine, which came from the yew tree. The one that rhymed with Calpol.

After they switched medicines, a sloppiness descended on us. There was dust everywhere. An electrician fitted cold white bulbs instead of warm white ones, and we didn't care. Our house was cold without heaters. Clothes hung unwashed on the banister. Blankets, under which you could curl up any time of the day, were left on the sofa.

One evening, Daddy lugged in a black-and-red sports bag. He took it straight inside the bedroom and asked for the cupboard keys. Mama-mon stared blankly. She was in a fog, seeing but not seeing. Her grey cells were dying in the fight, along with her red blood cells. Her brain was becoming lighter. So light, she said, that she was afraid it would fly off with her words and memories and stories.

'I know where the key is,' I said and fished it out from the wooden box. When I opened the lid, a gust of Narois filled the room. My namesake attar was doing well. It had leaked a bit around the neck of the bottle.

Daddy plunged into the tangle of Mama-mon's sarees. He was making space—pushing aside a Superman doll, boxes full of baby hair, baby teeth, old letters, certificates. It was amazing to see how much she kept inside the cupboard. Part of one shelf held her jewellery collection. Daddy cleaned out the other side of that shelf.

Mama-mon's haze tended to lift as suddenly as it would descend. Her razor sharpness would be back, and her fingers would fly over the keyboard as she'd attend to her work emails.

Now she asked snappily, 'What's in the bag, Danish?'

Daddy hesitated. He was nervous. Instead of answering her directly, he looked at me and roped me in.

'Wanna see what's in the bag?' he asked.

I played along, providing Daddy the enthusiasm he needed.

'Come see money, Narois. You have never seen such a humongous sum of money.'

With a flourish, he opened the zipper on the bag. Halfway through he struggled as it got caught. I asked him to pull harder. After a bit of suspense, he parted the bag and said *voila!*

Heaps and heaps of notes lay in the bag. We peered in as though at a historical monument—thousands of magenta Mahatmas and stone-grey Red Forts stared back at us.

'Is this your money, Daddy?'

'Not quite, my love. This money is required for the project we are running in the Bombay port. You know all about it, don't you?'

I did know that the Kala Khatta outside Lion's Gate was better than the one at Juhu. I also knew that only Thums Up could help you belch after a bellyful of the most delicious mutton berry pulao at a Parsi restaurant. I have not tasted any of those delightful goodies because to Bombay we never go.

Mama-mon was frighteningly quiet. She didn't even glance at the bag. We waited for her to say something. After a while, she asked, 'Why does she need to see the money? Why do you have that kind of money? How much is it?'

'Money is a spectacle. Would she, as a matter of routine, see so much money in one place? It will give her a sense of quantity.'

The money was no longer spoken of. It fit nicely inside the cupboard, and I forgot about it. How money comes, how money is made—this was a mystery to me.

I had never seen so much money. I mean, who does? Other than a few odd notes inside parents' wallets. Money remains hidden, doesn't it? Until it cracks through the surface of our lives, like cake batter piercing through the cake crust when there is too much heat or too little.

Daddy started bringing home money regularly. Large chunks of it stashed in bags of all kinds.

Then one day I came back from school to find the bedroom door locked. My parents were inside. I thumped on the door with my elbow as my hands were sticky from the melting cola blast. Ice creams in winter was Silver Samir's thing. We had ice creams, even if my teeth felt like they would fall off, if Rani and he happened to meet me after school. And that day Rani and he had met me and treated me to a cola blast as a special treat. My lips stunned and my tongue frozen, I called for Mama-mon and Daddy. A tiny thrill was jumping on a trampoline in my stomach. On a weekday, Daddy was at home. Mama-mon opened the door slightly and smiled at me and Rani. But she didn't invite me in.

'Why don't you ask Nago Didi to fix you both lunch? We won't take long to finish what we are doing.'

The door remained open only slightly. Rani said that was a good idea and moved away immediately.

I was embarrassed with Mama-mon's coldness to her. But I was curious too.

We had lunch, and Rani left for her tailoring and saloning visits.

Mama-mon let me in and bolted the door. On the bed was a pile of jewellery—gold chokers, emerald lockets, the spotted deer locket she wore to parties, my grandmother's wedding set, my other grandmother's necklace set with rubies that came all the way from Burma, a string of pearls that Daddy had gifted. We played with the chains and the bangles. I strung the pearls on Mama-mon's white head. 'Now you are properly Cleopatra,' I said.

They made me wear all the chains and slid bracelets on my hand. The bangles went up all the way to my elbow. I put the ruby necklace around Daddy's neck. He looked at the mirror and wanted to wear more. I dangled two bangles from his ears. 'Now you are properly a Raja Bhoj,' said Mama-mon.

Rani came with terribly sad news. Bhaiya Jugnu had died and Kochi was missing.

A memorial was being held for Bhaiya at Ground Zero. Rani, Kiran and I attended. No one had a photo of him, not even Vinay Jugnu. So, they put garlands and flowers around the twenty-kilo mace that Bhaiya was inseparable from. He could lift it like one lifted a book. Vinay Jugnu was asked to say a few words. Unused to speaking in full sentences, he muttered a few words, jumped over the parts that Bhaiya would have filled in and ended up saying nothing but gibberish. It wouldn't be an exaggeration to say that he was now a man without meaning. Overnight his muscles had shrunk.

'I am retiring from ... Vrindavan which will shelter ... The colour of money is ... and fathers who ... Was not my companion, my friend but ...'

We gaped at Bhaiya Jugnu, trying to catch words that were invisible. Silver Samir put an arm around him and called him a gentle giant and swore revenge on the police.

'They shot him from the back and said, oops, we missed! May lightning strike them down. May the floods swallow their families!'

I whispered to Kiran, 'Why would the police come after the Jugnus? Should I warn Meera that the Jugnus are planning to release a flood? What if Aunty Rebecca had ordered the shootout?'

Kiran was sobbing and didn't hear a word of what I said. Was she really so fond of Bhaiya Jugnu?

Velu came and sat beside us. He patted her head and said, 'Poor girl, what she sees with her deep-seeing eyes breaks her heart. She knows that our time here is over. The Jugnus must find another forest.'

'You will leave Jahanpanah? But this is your home, isn't it?'

'You think this little blue tent is my home? Expand your heart, Narois Didi. See more than what you see.'

Well, I couldn't see all that Kiran could see. I have heard that repeatedly from Mama-mon and from Velu. It hurt. A lonely dark cave stared at me with its open mouth. I couldn't ask—you will leave us adventureless? You will abandon the forest?

Velu reached inside his shirt pocket and took out a ticket. He had a reserved berth on a train that would take him back to where his daughter was buried, his true home.

Mian Pagla said he had received good news. 'I don't want to sound too excited because our friend has just passed. But I am so happy, Didi-bhai. My family has followed the river and are now camping on the banks of the Yamuna. Wish me luck, pray to Allah that I find them in the crowds. That I reach before the dark waters have swallowed my little children and burnt their stomachs with those poisonous fumes.'

We sat around the garlanded mace and ate steaming dim sums. Silver Samir got up for another speech and said, 'Jugnus never end. We continue to light up forests. But we don't grow roots.'

'It's so sudden!' I cried out.

Don't go. Don't go. I am not ready to let you all go—I screamed in my head. Invisible sentences were real after all.

'Storms are not sudden. They gather for a reason, dear child. And once they do gather, they cannot be stopped.' Silver Samir argued, making no sense at all.

'Can't we share numbers and addresses? Can I call and write?'

'We will communicate with you in signs. That's what Jugnus do. And aren't you a Jugnu now?'

When did that happen? When did we get promoted to Jugnu-hood?

A blanket of hush fell over Ground Zero. No good-night bird-calls, no hissing mist, no fireflies punching holes in that blanket of hush. That's how silent goodbyes are then. Silent and ordinary. It was the first of many goodbyes for me, and I can vouch from experience that they are not the tear-spilling, gut-wrenching, tectonic events that one might expect.

A few dim sums were left over. Velu insisted that we finish those. He had to catch an early morning train, and there was some packing left to do even if he was living under a blue tarpaulin.

What would happen to the kettle that whistled non-stop? Would Velu carry it back with him? Or was it a Jugnu property? I kept the question to myself, fearing that it would sound more like a wince if I said it out loud.

We scattered after that. Rani stayed back with Silver Samir. I wasn't sure if he was going anywhere. But a nagging fear took hold of me that if he went, he would take Rani with him too.

Would she abandon her Abbu's library of attars for his sake? Would she abandon me?

Velu followed us to the edge of the forest. Kiran hugged him tight. He collected her tears in his palm and smeared them on his forehead. We walked away from him and the nilgai that had followed us.

That evening, Kiran and I tied a white handkerchief to the railing of our perch. If Velu was ever lost, he'd spot the fluttering napkin. He'd find us.

19. Will-o'-the-Wisp

November nights thickened, leaking blobs of Prussian blue. Inky-deep, exciting. I missed the Jugnus. Kiran and I met every evening.

'But Silver Samir is around. He can give us Velu's address. Narois, you ask him.'

'But it won't be the same, will it.'

'No, it won't be.'

The forest was empty now. No point gazing at it.

One evening, we were on our usual perch, staring out at the treetops. A thin wisp of smoke curled up from Ground Zero.

'Kiran, look! Is that from Velu's stove?'

A smell of chicken cutlet came travelling all the way. After a while the smoke died down.

My evening outings with Rani and Silver Samir stopped just as suddenly. Most days I was stuck at home.

Rara Aunty invited us to her Halloween Party. She was an old friend, so old that now it didn't matter if she was originally Mama-mon's friend or Daddy's. Our families were fused, like relatives. Rara Aunty's husband and Daddy were trying out various business ventures together and her daughter, Prachi, was my senior at school. On Halloween, Rara Aunty, who had lived in the US for many years, decked up her house with cobwebs, broken teeth and bloody footprints.

'This city has not one decent Halloween party, I am compensating for that sorry lack, you see. Bring more children. I am doing two dozen trick-or-treat bags this year.'

Mama-mon hated Halloween and called it an American parody.

'But it was originally Celtic, was it not?' Daddy asked.

'Yes, but the Americans have usurped it.'

Despite her hatred for Halloween, Mama-mon had no problem cooking up looks. One year she was Frida Kahlo, with flowers, a unibrow and a crêpe bandage wound around her chest like a corset. Another year she had a bullet hole the size of a 10-rupee coin painted on her forehead.

'Now I don't need to dress up. I can go as myself. Cancer Halloween.'

Daddy winced. Whiplash words.

'Oh, but I was being sarcastic,' she said.

Daddy nodded and smiled and said sure, if it was sarcasm then it couldn't hurt.

Waxing and waning, with slow hands and aching bones, she dressed me up as a vampire. I wanted to be Harley Quinn with space buns and purple-green eyes. I was a vampire every year. I hoped that this year would be the last as a vampire because the scary vampire collar of my costume barely came up to my ears and the long sleeves no longer hung in a loose frightening drop.

Mama-mon painted a trickle of blood—it drooled from my mouth—with her Elizabeth Arden lipstick. She generously added glitter on my cheeks. I was translucent.

Daddy dressed up too. First time ever. He wore a white mundu and a black turtleneck. The melmundu, which they had bought on a trip to Kerala years before I was born, was moth-eaten and musty. He draped it around his shoulders loosely. He looked beautiful. The mist of his perfume rose and filled the evening.

I looked at Mama-mon nervously. As her eyes flickered, my heart became a knot.

'Ah, you are Aleya, the will-o'-the-wisp ghost,' she told Daddy casually.

But I knew that voice. It shimmered with pain and betrayal.

'I don't know what that is.'

'No, you wouldn't, Danish. Despite your love for the marshy lands and for me! It is a ghost from the lands of paddy. This look that you have created ...'

'Come, why won't you come?' He held her hand.

'Dressed as what? Cancer?'

Lights were dimmed at Rara Aunty's house. It was another world, with spooky music, dark corners (where skulls and skeletons huddled) and adults who tried to look and behave scary and became ridiculous instead. As if that was the definition of being haunted.

'Why should we fear spirits?' Mama-mon's voice rang in my ears. She was resenting this already—she who could become one soon.

'Time to think of ghost rights, ghost identity,' she seemed to say with a laugh that sounded eerie. A laugh suited to the evening.

Although dressed to the nines—as witch, vampire, something unidentifiable, The Joker and (imagine my horror to find) Annabelle-the-Doll—we, the children, were calm and slightly bored.

Like every year, our mix remained the same. Meera was there, thankfully. Some seniors from school who were Prachi's classmates. And there was Ari whom I met only once a year at the Halloween party. He went to The British School and had an accent. When November came and the days became short, the thought of meeting Ari left little magnets in my spine. He was taller this year and his hair fell wildly over his eyes.

'Hullo, Narois! What are you up to?'

Ari did not game. He played the piano, and he had his own band in school, of which he was the lead singer. His long fingers were smooth with oval nails.

Rara Aunty was dressed as Tinker Bell. She wore a green costume with bells around her waist and ankles. She came jingling just as we were getting ready to watch *Stranger Things* on Netflix, which I felt guilty about since Mama-mon had forbidden the show. 'Parents around the whole world are letting their kids watch it,' I had argued. 'Parents around the whole world are mad,' she had replied.

Rara Aunty came to the rescue. 'Not happening, kids. Come on, come on. Out of the door and into the night! Right away!' She chased us out.

I told Prachi that her mother looked ravishing. Ravishing Rara. Compliments are best when they alliterate.

I went up to Aunty and told her so.

'Oh, thank you, darling. How observant of you. But nothing close to Imon, no? Your mother who is such an artist of looks. The party is so sad without her.'

Prachi whispered to me as we headed out that her mother had bought that dress from Amazon. They were delivering within a day.

Rara Aunty herded us to the front lawn where pumpkin lamps and trick-or-treat bags were lined up in neat rows. Kunal Bhaiya, Laal-ji and Mohan Chacha parked the cars they drove and waited to accompany us. That was their charge tonight. Rara Aunty would send dinner and hot tea later.

The cars looked on as we filed past. I heard the fuel knotting up and freezing in their pipes. Streets were empty. We walked as per the map Rara Aunty had provided. From one friend's house to another obliging neighbour to the Honduras Consulate. The Honduran first lady had moved in recently. She wanted to make friends, so Rara Aunty advised her to throw an open-house Halloween party.

No one was willing to be tricked. It was easier to give away treats. Soon we had an armload of candies. At the corner of Poorvi Marg, two girls and a boy wanted to join us. They were barefoot, they wore party hats.

'Don't you dare go all socialist now like Imon Aunty,' Prachi whispered to me. 'We are not giving them candies.'

'But why not?'

'Charity is bullshit. Will you end their hunger with a chocolate? Mummy says people who are constantly rolling down car windows and doling out stuff are actually ruining it for these luckless beggars.'

I hadn't thought about that. Usually, we just wanted to share.

They didn't want chocolates.

'Can we walk along with you?' one little girl asked. She just wanted to Halloween. To toast her feet in pumpkin lights. To be a part of a bigger crowd of children in the dark moonless streets.

Laal-ji shooed them away. 'Go, go. Don't irritate us. Go or I will call the police.'

The three kids went away, stung but not unhappy. That little girl, whose braids stuck out almost at a right angle, and I had an eye-to-eye moment, a long enough moment for me to hand over the big Bounty bar that was jostling for space in my paper bag. But the moment passed, and she became a shadow.

Back at Rara Aunty's place, Prachi's father, Hannibal the Cannibal, opened the door. He wore a white apron splashed with blood.

'Did you kill anyone yet? I just did.'

Prachi rolled her eyes at him, and we quickly took shelter in the hallway where a long table was packed with delicious refreshments. Ari poured himself a glass of eyeball mocktail and offered me another glass when I came along. I felt a tickle at my neck that crept down the spine to the back of my knees. Mama-mon, the children in the shadows, my guilt on account of my will-o'-the-wisp Daddy, all of this disappeared. It was Halloween. And though it was American and put together with Amazon merch, I was a vampire with a shimmering face, and Ari's mad tousled hair was exactly how musicians' hair should be. We stood there talking about bands and fantasy fiction.

Ari said he was growing out of *Shadowhunters* and *Percy Jacksons*. And that I would too.

'Best to rush through and then leave them behind you. I am going to study music, so I have to free up my mind for the real stuff very soon.'

Dana—whose mother was a translator at the Spanish Embassy and father a professor—scoffed at our reading habits.

'Then what do you read?' we asked her.

'I don't read at all. Books are passé.'

Not wanting to sound stupid, I pointed out that books would survive us.

'What a dodo this one is,' she said.

Outside, the party seemed to have really picked up. There was tremendous yelling and laughing. The grown-ups were blasting pop songs from their times. I liked some of the songs, but we failed to blast Imagine Dragons over the crushing volume of their music. I worried for my Daddy whose edges were anyway frayed. I stepped out for a slice of graveyard pizza. Ari said he wanted one too. Dana made eyes and grinned.

'Those two are a number,' I heard her say as we slipped out.

Daddy was on a newspaper folded into a tiny square, dancing with Rara Aunty. She was tall, taller than my Parsi Daddy, on her thin heels. She shimmered like a moon. Grooving to 'Mustang Sally'; the music lighting Daddy up like a rocket. He was a magician with his hips and his waist, which just pulsed with the saxophone and the drums. Rara Aunty moved her belly and held her arms high up in the air. The entire party cheered them on. As the song progressed, the newspaper square got folded smaller and smaller, making them tighter, closer, balancing on toes, keeping each other afloat. Then the song ended, and Daddy found me with his eyes. There were echoes of his laughter and the face muscles were still stretched from all the dancing. But those eyes!

We looked at each other and remembered what we had forgotten for a while.

When we were setting out for the party, Mama-mon had said that she wanted a photo. Daddy said, 'Let's do a selfie.' In the turned screen of the camera, we looked like a splash of colours—vampire red, ivory black, neonness of partygoers. But it was Mama-mon who was the true ghost, the soul who visits on All Saints' Day, vanishing eyebrows, sunken eyes.

'Tell them,' she told Daddy.

'What, sorry?'

'Tell them.'

'What is there to say? You are a private person. Why would you suddenly announce it, Em? Maybe a lot of them have already heard. Why make it an occasion? Don't do it. It's not what you do.'

'No, tell them. I want them to see you for what you are.'

At the doorstep, while I was still editing the selfie, brightening it up with a special filter I had developed for family photos, Mama-mon was reacting to my Daddy's Halloween costume, to his beauty.

Daddy was gulping, his nose barely above the water.

'See me for what? As what?'

'As a tragic hero. As someone with endless possibilities. As someone who will rebuild himself after I die.'

Even by Mama-mon's standard, this was brutal. She wasn't talking about what would happen to me. She never did because that needed a kind of courage she didn't have.

Mama-mon and Daddy had an agreement—the news of her illness could be shared only as she wanted it, with those she wanted to share it with and at a time of her choosing. Daddy had sworn to her. A promise he couldn't break.

Dancing to 'Mustang Sally', moments before announcing his wife's cancer? What was Daddy thinking?

After the dance was over, we sat on the chaise lounge in the hallway. He coiled up his dancer's body, and I sheltered him. Rara Aunty hovered around Daddy with her tinkle. She tried to make him wear a wig.

But he wouldn't. He threw it off and hid his sad eyes behind heart-shaped spectacles, a party prop that happened to be lying around.

When the crowds thinned and we were with a smaller group of friends, Daddy broke the news. There was silence and murmurs and a sudden sob. All of them looked at me and smiled deeply and called me brave.

Rara Aunty hugged Daddy. Uncle Madhav, painter-cum-musician and Mama-mon's old friend, asked if he might call Mama-mon. Ari's mother, Mehr, looked stricken, and her eyes seemed to lose focus. She was too moved to speak. They sipped their whiskies in a trance. They rolled their wines in a spell. Like fireflies, cancer stories gleamed and glowed. Every one of them knew at least one friend or relative who had had cancer and had died of it, died a horrible death. Madhav said it was a true Halloween night.

I said I too had a story. Of Marie Curie. Who discovered radiation and then died of the cancer it gave her.

And Rara Aunty wept till the bells on her dress jingled and jangled.

On the way out, Ari and I exchanged email addresses and promised to write to each other.

'I don't think I am coming next year,' Ari said.

'Same. I am going to skip it.'

'So let's …'

'Yeah, let's.'

A few days after the Halloween party, they came. With wire cutters, acid bottles, rope lassoes and bombs.

I woke up in the middle of the night, feeling thirsty. The house creaked. The wood shivered in the cold. A tired hammer of the piano key returned to its position. I waited, a cold dread in my heart.

The forest was coming in.

20. Magic Mountain

After Daddy's announcement, Mama-mon expected callers, a whirlwind of visitors.

'Bake muffins, Nago. Just in case they bring their children along. Keep a jar of lemonade and a bottle of infused water in the fridge. Just in case. Just in case.'

Mama-mon painted her brows with care—arched them and filled them in with a pencil.

'I am officially a spectacle. Must live the part.'

It was like a party. She used to love parties, even if she hated the people who came to the parties.

We had made guess-lists of guests—Rara Aunty, surely, along with Prachi, maybe Mehr Aunty (perhaps she would bring Ari, and we would break our record of not meeting more than once a year). Once news got around properly, there could be other friends. On that list were some people who had to be barred from entering.

'If they call to plan a visit, just tell them I am immuno-compromised. My blood factory is on strike.

At risk of infection! It will scare them off,' she said. 'Just like AIDS.'

'What's AIDS?'

'Ah, Narois! Your reading is slipping. AIDS is a game-changer disease. It changed how we think about each other.'

You are never too young to know. Swim, swim. Learn to float, hold your breath, breathe underwater—whether it's the pool or the middle of the salty ocean. Knowing about things, about the world, according to my mother, is a bit like that.

'Well, darling, AIDS was managed. But still, it's a deadly killer.'

'Has cancer been managed? Will you live? Even though it is cancer?'

'Of course I will. But as you know by now, living and dying are all in the head. If I die, do you think I won't be here? I will be, all the time. Around you, inside you.'

'That's semantics,' I said.

She told Daddy later, 'I must have done something right as a mother. Raised her well.'

'Semantics, huh?'

'Oh yes, and perfectly used.'

For a few days after the big reveal, she painted her face and wore a turban at home.

I longed for guests to come with their sympathies, goodbyes, gifts and prayers. To sit on the ladder again and drink their wine and fall off the sofa.

Their laughter versus ours from the children's room.

Punctually, as the first winter fog snarled and swelled around the city, my eczema flared up. Inner arm, at the elbow, on my shoulder blades, a constant itching ran through me like an underground train. Deep inside, rattling and scratching. Mama-mon applied a thick coat of steroids mixed with Vaseline over the bumps. What worked best was the oats milk she made at home, dripping it slowly over the angry skin.

Suraj turned up one evening at dinner time, hungry and penniless.

He wouldn't stay. He wouldn't finish school. School was an unfair demand, he said, one that was chaining him down.

'There is so much else happening in the world. How you survive on the streets is what matters. How you fight, how you snatch for yourself.'

He carried a photo of the prime minister in his threadbare wallet, the one that had not a penny to buy him food.

He ate and borrowed money from Choti Ma, who was kinder to him now that he was gone, and would rather part with the money just to keep him away from their stair-top home.

I missed Suraj, maybe not as much as Kiran did; after all, she was his own sister. And his going away was costing her, bringing on her poor head so many troubles. Choti Ma's headaches had become more frequent. She couldn't bear even the shift in air and dust when a person moved near her. Kiran did her homework outside the room, keeping an eye on the forest that was emptied of the Jugnus.

We dangled our legs through the rusty iron frame of the staircase and scanned the forest. Far away, through the trees, we saw Ground Zero silver the gathering dark. We spoke to Suraj who now had a phone and claimed that he was eating chicken every day.

'I will get some for you two, one of these days.'

My mouth watered thinking of the chicken he might get for us.

But Kiran could only weep. She hid her face and sobbed.

And then I cried too, thinking of our brother.

The guests never arrived. Messages came—long, poetic, teary, dull. Mama-mon's phone was often with me since she couldn't bear the Internet. Or being addicted to it. I wasn't allowed a phone yet, but friends called and messaged sometimes on Mama-mon's phone.

Sangeeta Aunty's message was the longest. I read it out to Mama-mon who gave a sideways smile.

Mehr Aunty shared a photo of her cousin who 'god rest her soul, fought so hard. Stage 3, exactly like you. Have you considered acupressure?'

Prachi's father offered to send her reports to his friend, a gene scientist at Duke University. 'Information is your best friend.'

We strung together these gifts and calls and graded them as silly, fake, kind, true, bizarre.

'If you will grade my cancer, why won't I grade you back?'

Daddy didn't like participating in such grading because he liked people. He liked hearing from friends and accepting whatever was their idea of friendship. I was like him—an exact replica, Mama-mon said. So we, the identical lot, often confused the grading.

A distant cousin sent news that she had just finishing running a marathon for the cause of cancer patients, posting at 7 a.m. a photo against the Sydney Harbour Bridge, her hair flying in the breeze, a glow as pink as dawn on her cheeks. Daddy and I were going to grade that 'true-blue', but Mama-mon said it had landed a punch in her stomach. It was making her hyperventilate.

There was only one message that was graded 'cruel' unanimously. It was a book from Madhav, with whom Mama-mon often had deep discussions and who always left her feeling sad for all the things she couldn't do. The one who reminded her of the life she would have had if Daddy and I had not been a part of it. He sent her an old copy of *The Magic Mountain*—a gloomy, depressing book in which, according to the blurb on the back cover, Hans Castorp trekked all the way up to the Alps to be among dying people and then got a disease and started preparing to die himself. 'Death is a story,' he wrote in curly letters, 'one that you could prepare to tell or leave as a legacy for Narois.'

Mama-mon sat stunned, the book open on her lap.

For the first time in many weeks, she held me tight with her cheesestick arms. The sea roared in my ears. Mama-mon was holding me afloat; the message from *The Magic Mountain* was making her do it.

The sea terrified me.

And then I knew. I graded it cruel.

'Who gifts *The Magic Mountain* to a dying woman?'

'Em, you aren't dying.'

'That's beside the point. All these people, they are the ones who will turn up at gladiator games. I don't blame them, I understand. The circus of someone else dying is what keeps us going. It is what tells us that death isn't coming for us, not yet.'

'He has always been soft on you, Em. Now he feels he has a right to shock you ... or ... I don't know what he is trying to do.'

'Don't digress. Don't just go off in any direction you feel like. I will not have you turn the tables on me. He may be soft on me or he may be experimenting with his feelings, but he doesn't appeal to me the way Rara appeals to you.'

'I don't care about Rara!'

'I do, oh, I do. I have no blood left! But I care. I care for every single person who is walking around, their blood banks jingling with platelets.'

'If it hadn't been for the money, I would have never seen their faces. Ever,' Daddy whimpered.

Bags filled with money kept appearing. Each time the size and make of the bags were different. One day Daddy carted in a full suitcase. I was no longer invited to have a peek. Cash looks repetitive anyway. Perhaps if he created piles of money, and let that pile rise high up, touching the ceiling, filling up the room, it would be dramatic enough to watch. The notes would rustle so:

Em CMaj7 G6 G6/F#

But you see it's not me, it's not my family

Em CMaj7 G6 G6/F#

In your head, in your head, they are fighting

I hummed the song non-stop. Played it on the piano; strummed it on the guitar until my fingers bled—'*with their tanks and their bombs and their bombs and their guns*'. Mama-mon said I was changing my fingerprint. An impossible feat, but there I was achieving it.

'Run', she said, 'Run run run. Far away from the rotten half of the double helix.'

Winter settled. There were flowers in the garden—early petunias and pansies. The air smelled of cigarettes, and our tongues felt grainy. A metallic taste started sharing space with the salt and the cumin and the drifty sweetness of candyfloss. Despite the cool relief of chilled oatmilk drips, the insides of my elbows and my shoulder blades were on fire.

One evening, when Mama-mon needed her most, Rani returned with suntanned cheeks and necklaces of shells.

But where she had gone she wouldn't say.

'Was Silver Samir with you?' I whispered.

'Perhaps. Samir is always with me, right here.' With her finger she made a hole in her chest.

She spent an hour calming Mama-mon with her lullaby voice and magic fingers. 'Every evening, when the sun set over the water, I floated a prayer for you,' Rani told her.

I was relieved that Rani was back.

But, as it happened, she had come only to say goodbye. She was going away with Silver Samir on a long trip. Far away.

'How far? Hawaii?'

'If that's far enough, then yes, Hawaii.'

But I knew she wasn't going to Hawaii or to any place where she would dance with flowers in her hair and drink piña colada. Mama-mon had once said, Rani has compulsions, and it isn't polite to ask what they are.

'Better we set her free and hope she comes back when she can,' Mama-mon told me once Rani disappeared.

21. Shadowhunters

Mama-mon and Daddy argued non-stop. I stayed awake listening to their raised voices, sobs and things breaking in the living room. They sounded ridiculous as they hopped, skipped and jumped from one topic to another. It became exhausting to listen in. What connection had Rara Aunty with gold jewellery, or Daddy's Parsi family with the Palestine conflict, or the poems Mama-mon wrote with Tokyo, or a ship called *Atlantic Leo* with graffiti on the walls of Chile? And how was all of this connected, like clues in a treasure hunt, to cancer?

Does cancer take an article? Is it 'A' cancer? Or just cancer? Is it a simile or a disease?

In songs and poems and chit-chat—it grows like 'a' cancer.

Strummable on guitar.

I laid my head on the pillow and listened to the forest to drown out their arguments.

A cold mist swirled over us. Jackals called out to themselves, and a breeze knocked on the windowpanes. In that blanket of muffled sounds, I drifted off to sleep.

At 3 a.m. I woke up thirsty. The house throbbed with echoes left over from the quarrel, with footsteps and a ghastly nail-scratching whirring. For a moment I thought I had entered Mama-mon's dream, that I was trapped in it.

The whirring sound was near, it was real. Only a few steps away.

What we have sometimes feared, talked about, laughed at was happening. There were people in our garden. The glass door of our living room slid open, ruffling the still air of our tightly shut house.

Probably this was Daddy going out for a late smoke. Or stepping back in from one.

But that couldn't be—because when I got up to investigate, he was right there on the bed, sleeping next to Mama-mon who was now stirring awake.

Yes, it was happening—there were others in our house.

Daddy woke up and scrambled out of bed. He tried to pull the chest of drawers across the door. It wouldn't budge. It was too heavy. He bolted the door. No point in that. We knew. A few kicks and the rickety bolt would fly off.

Footsteps crept up the stairs to my study room on the mezzanine floor. The creaky panel door of the main switch cabinet was yanked open, and almost instantly the tiny lights in our room from the mosquito repellant machine and oil heater went out. The house was darker, quieter.

Our hearts thudded, waiting for them to barge in.

Daddy frantically looked around for a phone to call 100 or speed-dial the security guard. But our phones were always kept outside—far away from our brains. Mama-mon would sleepwalk to those phones in her nightgown to look at Daddy's call logs and messages—dig into his day. I had seen her standing there, face and chin lit up with the green light from the phone. If we weren't worried about radiation reaching our brains, we would have been able to dial Aunty Rebecca, who could have sent across a team of robber-catching police.

But now there was nothing left to do. I scrambled across to my parents' bed. Mama-mon threw a blanket over me. To keep me hidden.

And they were in the room. I peeped through the folds.

Standing at the foot of our bed. Four of them with tight masks over their heads. Their burglary uniforms were all black as expected. One of them pointed a pistol at us. His aim didn't seem that good, and he couldn't decide who or what to shoot—it swung from Daddy to Mama-mon but came back to Daddy who sprang up and stood with his hands on hips that had swayed to 'Mustang Sally' on Halloween night. Now the man with a pistol had something to do. He promptly whacked Daddy on the head, and his fellow robbers pushed Daddy to the floor.

'On your knees, head down,' he said.

'Be quiet or we will shoot you,' said another one.

They were saying the usual things that are said when a robbery takes place. But they weren't saying, for example: 'If you call the police, we will murder your daughter who is hiding under the blanket.' At least not yet.

Blood trickled down Daddy's face. His curls were damp. They tied his hands with a wire and forced him to sit on the floor in one corner.

My eyes had adjusted to the dark, but I could barely breathe under the blanket. One of them shone a phone torch at the dresser. The 2.45 a.m. Lufthansa from Frankfurt roared past, flying low over the forest. A jackal howled. A neighbour coughed.

Mama-mon grunted. Then she spoke. Bizarrely at first, slurring, blurring. Then she spoke like thunder, and I was scared. Oh, here was the end. They would shoot her just for speaking. Then she spoke the way she does, Mama-mon—accusing, angry, calling Daddy Oblonsky. She flooded them with her talk about cancer, about tongue ulcers and blue fingernails and nausea, and about how the poison of chemo seeped out through her sweat and her urine and her tears, poisoning everything that she touched or sat on or ate from. Her breath could kill. Didn't they know that cancer was infectious? So very infectious.

Then one of them snapped and said enough. He took out a dirty blue cloth from his trouser pocket and stuffed it in her mouth. He tied her up.

I was next. They pulled off the blanket and stuffed another cloth inside my mouth. It smelled of puke and urine, and I gagged and vomited into it.

Mama-mon passed out.

I swallowed the dirt of my rag and my vomit and desperately flared my nostrils to keep breathing. Then I sank into a darkness.

And I was in front of our school, which was next to the sea, and there were chimeras running across the beach. Hundreds of them. You had to duck and dodge to avoid being crushed under their hooves. On the other side of the sea, which became as narrow as a road, parents stood, waiting for the children to cross over. They lifted their giant ID cards for the chimeras to see. I walked over the sea, which became calm and glassy, and I could see all the way to the bottom where the seahorses galloped and ugly blind fish swam. Halfway the glass floor shattered, and I sank into the darkness, and the chimeras, my parents, the students crossing with me, sounded like a howl far away as I sank right in.

A man was now sitting on Daddy's chest, eating a banana. At the cupboard, which was wide open, another man was rummaging through Mama-mon's sarees, draping her violet and silver silk around his shoulders. The pearl necklace was around his neck. Most of the cupboard was empty now, sarees lying in a heap on the floor. The ornaments were disappearing fast into their rucksacks. The latest money bag—which looked like a fat caterpillar—was on the floor.

They didn't seem to be in a hurry.

Mama-mon made retching sounds and passed out again.

Daddy requested them to open our gags.

'She will die if you don't. She is sick.'

'Tell us where your most expensive Scotch whisky is.'

He told them and pleaded, 'Take what you want, just release her … I mean, them.'

'What's the hurry? We are hungry. Let us have some of your rich-man food and daaru. Chhotu, go get the biriyani from the kitchen.'

'Should I heat it?' Chhotu asked. He had a thin raspy voice.

The other men laughed at him and called him a spoilt idiot.

Chhotu came back with a casserole and beer cans. They sat on the bed, next to where Mama-mon was lying, and ate from our plates, drank beer. They ate and drank very fast. When they were done, they used the bathroom, not even bothering to close the door properly, so I heard their pee plunging into the pot. One of them farted when he was done.

Now they were through, a few more minutes, I told myself.

My bladder was full. I could wet the bed and disgust them.

On their way out, one man kicked Daddy and rubbed his shoe over Daddy's cheek.

The man who had been trying on Mama-mon's silk sarees was struggling to take off the pearl necklace. The clasp was stuck in his long and frizzy hair, and he yelped because it kept getting more and more tangled.

'Ouch! Help me, help me, it hurts. Chhotu, come back.'

Chhotu returned to release the clasp from his hair. 'Here, shine the torch for me, I can't see,' Chhotu said.

The man to whom the pearl necklace now belonged shone the phone torch, pointed it at his neck. The pearls shone, brilliant in torchlight, scattering a halo and little rainbows on Chhotu's wrist as he struggled to release the clasp.

Then they were gone, with the gold, the cash, the pearl necklace, Nago Didi's casserole of biriyani, a few beers and two bottles of Scotch whisky.

The police, when they came, asked us to make a list of things that were taken.

But that was many hours away, and now the burglars were disappearing into the breaking dawn. I hoped they would fall off the wall, that the dawn birds, which were beginning to chirp, would create a ruckus and wake up the entire neighbourhood. I spat out the gag that was not really that tight; I had to puke before I could help Daddy. Then, I untied him.

Daddy and I thought Mama-mon had died. But her forehead was hot.

The early-morning Cathay Pacific flew in, then came the milkman who rang the bell once to say milk was here, better collect it before it goes bad. Newspapers were dropped at the front door. At 6.30 a.m. after Nago Didi let herself in with a key, Daddy made a call.

'Rebecca, we have been robbed. Will you come?'

Aunty Rebecca came quietly, sans uniform, in her white sedan. A fleet of police cars, with sirens-on-mute and flashing beacons switched off, waited nearby. 'I dropped Meera off at school and came right over,' she said.

Oh, school. On the sea beach, where chimeras ran. I floated back into the night and felt sick.

Aunty sat on the sofa and had tea like any other guest would. She comforted my parents, held their hands and said it would be okay.

'If only you had called. Don't you have me on speed dial?'

'Oh, we would never bother you like that,' said Mama-mon.

'What? When the DCP is your friend and there is a robbery happening? Don't be ridiculous, Imon. My question is: why didn't you try to call?'

They told her about phones being outside as we didn't want radiation to leak into the room.

'That's a thing in cancer treatment, is it?'

'Yes, sort of,' Mama-mon said hurriedly.

After finishing her tea, Aunty Rebecca walked around the house, looking intently at the forest wall where the wire mesh and iron grille had been pulled down. Then she studied the neat squares cut on the glass and mesh doors, walking carefully around the shards on the floor. She looked at the open cupboard and examined the empty spaces.

'Did they force you to give the cupboard key?'

'No, they seemed to know where to find it.'

'What do you mean? Where was the key?'

We showed her. The key's hiding place inside the wooden box, next to the vial of Narois.

With a big hmmp, Aunty sat back down on the sofa and beckoned me over, smiling kindly. She side-hugged me, said I was such a swift reader and asked me to fetch a book that Meera could read. 'She wants to borrow the latest book you have read.'

'*Us Against You*? Is she allowed to read that, Aunty?'

'Oh yes. Quite wild to read it, she is. Will you go fetch that and also perhaps your science copy? I think she missed some schoolwork.'

She never does. Meera never misses schoolwork. Why not say, okay, adult conversation coming up, kindly exit the room.

I went upstairs to get the book and science copy. Last night, the robbers had gone halfway up these very stairs to switch off the MCB. The door to my room was still shut. I flung it open, half-expecting someone inside. In the morning light, with a DCP in the house, I almost wished I could find someone hiding behind the yellow blinds.

I crept halfway down the stairs. Aunty Rebecca was asking for a full download of the things that were taken. She said she knew from experience that people who got robbed were often embarrassed about the things that got robbed. Would there be any such thing? She wanted them to tell her before her police force descended for a full investigation.

Daddy and Mama-mon hesitated. After a few awkward minutes, Daddy told Aunty Rebecca about the bag of cash that wasn't supposed to be there.

'How much?' Aunty Rebecca asked, her face now stern, police-like.

Daddy muttered an amount that made her grimace.

'Is it black? Well, of course it is. But is it yours?'

Daddy nodded and said he was ferrying it for a company that sound like Impeximus to me. A Roman company? But the money wasn't black at all. It was magenta and had monuments on it.

Mama-mon was silent all through. Aunty Rebecca told Daddy sternly he would have to deal with the people whose money it was all by himself. About that she couldn't do anything.

'But can you bring back the money?'

'Depends. Money spends itself fast. The gold and the pearls I can bring back for you if we act swiftly.

But money ... that changes hands, and once it is used to buy something I can hardly reverse it.'

I walked slowly into the room. Daddy was droopy. His straight spine became an archer's bow. Mamamon sat staring at him, her eyes on fire, sparkling with tears.

Something worse than robbery had happened just now.

Aunty Rebecca excused herself and gave Mamamon a hug. 'All will be well.' She was the only person who could say such things to my mother and get away with it.

Then she turned to me and said, 'Narois, would you like to spend the day somewhere else? Take a break from all this?'

Of course I wouldn't. Who would want to miss the police cars and the detective work? I said my hands were still hurting from being tied and twisted, so I'd rather rest and be at home.

The police came with their sirens. It was such a sight. They cordoned off the parking lot with yellow tape, roped off our little garden. Mohan Chacha, Nago Didi, Parvati Aunty who was a cook for our Scientologist neighbour Mr Bharot—they were all nervous and jittery.

Boots trampled over our old worn carpets and measuring tapes measured everything—from the face of the green Buddha to the distance between the door and the piano.

Flashes of last night kept coming back. Details that were always there but dawned on me now. Such as erratic notes—a messy string of sharps with a final three-fingered slamming of the C-sharp scale. Someone in the gang had had an urge to have a go at the piano.

The Inspector sat next to me and said he knew me very well.

'I took you to a game park at the mall when you and Meera were babies. Don't you remember me?'

I nodded yes, not wanting to be impolite.

He asked me a few questions and then said I could go.

Free at last, I asked my mother if I could run over to Kiran's.

'Call and check first if she is home. It's a school day.'

I called Choti Ma who sounded different. 'Beta, why have the police come? I was so worried, I thought someone has died. Is your mother okay?'

'But police don't come when people die.'

'Oh, they do if they are murdered, no?'

'My mother is more likely to die of cancer than be murdered.'

She seemed offended that I hadn't given a straight answer to her questions, and then said that Kiran was at school and I shouldn't hold her up. She had to bathe the baby.

Late evening, after her maths tuition class, Kiran came home. I had napped in the afternoon so I felt rested. Mama-mon had given me paracetamol for the pain. Nago Didi had put a cold compress on my wrists and shoulders, all the while sobbing. She sobbed right through the khichdi she cooked for us, forgetting to put salt.

'Poor girl, she didn't deserve those questions.'

Mama-mon hugged her and asked her to go home. 'Go, take rest.'

Nago Didi said she didn't want her sister and brother-in-law, with whom she lived, to doubt that anything was amiss. She was crying so much.

'Oh, just tell them. Come, let me call you an Uber. Don't take the RV today.'

'No, no,' Nago Didi said. 'When I start crying, I can't stop, and now my eyes are swollen and puffy. I don't want their ridiculous questions.'

Finally, she stayed back with us, and I felt warm.

I re-enacted every detail for Kiran. Showed her how my arms were twisted and how a man sat on Daddy's chest.

'Are you sure his ribcage is not broken? Uncle is too thin.'

'Yes, I feared that too. Parsis have fragile bones, but Daddy is different because he was a sailor once upon a time.'

Thank god, said Kiran; she asked me if Mama-mon's pearl necklace would ever be found. 'After all, her initials are inscribed on the clasp.'

I hugged Kiran for reminding me of that. We had all forgotten about it—this valuable clue. It had been

Daddy's gift to Mama-mon on her birthday. Kiran and I had gone with him to choose the pearls and had sat next to the jeweller when he inscribed her name on the clasp.

'You would make a better detective than me,' I told her when I saw her off at the door.

'Come, walk with me to the gate.'

It was cold, and the air was soupy. Although Kiran was shorter than me, I bent my head to rest it on her shoulder as we walked side by side.

'Kiran-bee, remember the day a wasp stung you?'

'Would I ever forget!' she said. 'One day we will go back to that field and look for the coconut tree under which I was stung.'

That's when I told her about the mountain of cash. If Daddy had to pay back every penny, would we ever have money to buy flight tickets or stay in a hotel? By that logic, then, we could never take a plane to go to Goa where the coconut tree was.

22. Latin Sounding

I went to school with a bruised wrist. Mama-mon went for her next chemo. Life went on as usual. Except Daddy's didn't. His days changed, and finally I could see him lead that other life—the one that Mama-mon had talked about for as long as I could remember.

One day, Mama-mon said, 'Bunk school. Go with Daddy wherever he is going. Life is evidently a bigger learning experience.'

'How can you even suggest that, Em? You know what the conversation will be like. How can I even ... Narois darling, step out, will you?'

I was doing this too often these days—taking a pause. Sentences and meanings were broken, they hung around me like half-drawn washing—three-quarters of a trouser, a shirt without a sleeve, a skirt lost on the way to its hem. 'Financial' and 'ruin' were two words said over and over again. But always together. Never broken.

Heirloom jewels were competing with trashy money owed to a ganglord who lived in a place called Shamli. Which would be found? Which should be found?

Mama-mon called DinDin to give her the news of the robbery. After so many years, she was calling her mother to tell her that the ruby necklace from Burma was no longer with us. When she blurted it out, it sounded like the news of someone's death. All these years of not talking, and they were now talking about the most unimportant of things—like the house in Burma that no longer existed and my great-grandmother's frail neck around which the ruby necklace had spent close to half a century. How it cast red shadows on her glistening brown skin; how my eczema was improving with the oats milk drips. The most important news, the news of her cancer, she did not convey.

'Why wouldn't you tell your own mother that you are sick?'

'It's unhealthy to do so.'

'But it's a lie.'

'Don't be so black and white, Vera Narois. Have I not taught you better?'

But to Daddy she said, 'It's what it is, and she must see it without a tint. She will go with you. Witness you paying for your faults. Maybe the rabbi will say a prayer for her. Maybe she will be healed.'

'She may be healed at the Kali temple. The priest will say a prayer as easily. Why go all the way to a Chabad House for a blessing?'

'Easy won't do, Danish. We must walk the hardest part and seek every single prayer we can find.'

'Since when do you believe in prayers, Imon?'

Mama-mon turned her face to Daddy and the answer came hurtling at him like a million suns.

Mean Mama-mon—winning every argument using your cancer.

Daddy gave in and said, 'Let's take the metro. Parking at the Main Bazar is a nightmare.'

We caterpillared through the foggy afternoon. Nehru Place to Hauz Khas to Central Secretariat. Over the ground, under the ground. Empty carriages rattled and echoed. A flash mob greeted us at the Central Secretariat station. They were dancing to warn us: VAPING IS SMOKING IN DISGUISE!

Daddy bought me an Oreo McFlurry from McDonald's. 'Don't tell Mom!'

We walked around for a while to kill time.

'Are we going to the Chabad House, Daddy?'

'No, no. I changed the venue. No one goes to the Chabad House for such meetings. '

'But Mama-mon said the Chabad House.' I was disappointed.

'Mama-mon is ... you know. She says things, Narois. You have to understand. She says things.'

'Don't we have to reach by 3, Daddy?'

'Yes, my love. We do.'

He sounded like he was on the verge of tears. I knew he didn't want me to see whatever it was that he was going to be part of. We were standing at the foot of an unclimbable mountain, and somehow I had to make him hit the summit. I was his sherpa, with the mule and the oxygen and the flag too. We stood rooted in the middle of Connaught Place's hot bustle. Daddy's feet were stuck to the ground, his legs were buckling. He stared at the passing traffic, swaying dangerously towards it. A beggar called out to us and asked for alms. He held up an empty Starbucks cup.

'I could sit next to him, Narois. I am tired,' Daddy said longingly.

So, I took him aside and we found a park tucked in a dirty lane. We sat in the shade for a while, and I told him that I was ready to leave if he was.

'Let's go, Daddy. We should eat. My tummy is grumbling a bit.'

'Just now you had an ice cream. How can you be hungry so soon?'

'But I am, Daddy,' I said, and we flagged down an auto that took us to Paharganj where the lanes narrowed, and there were tight crowds of people who looked happy and full of adventure. They walked by slowly with backpacks, guitars and colourful vests. Lively music and the warm smell of something being fried greeted us as we climbed the steep stairs to a rooftop restaurant.

Daddy ordered fries and then forgot to order lunch. The waiter hovered around impatiently. He seemed full of airs. I knew exactly what I wanted.

'We would like to have chicken drumsticks and pork momos, PLEASE,' I told him and also pointed those items out on the menu. Since Daddy's eyes were darting across the terrace and he was paying no attention to lunch, I took a chance and ordered a can of Coke for myself.

'Bring it with two ice cubes, please,' I made sure to add.

Daddy sat upright on his chair. He looked taller.

I scanned the other tables for interesting food. Someone was having eggs swimming in red sauce. On another table I spotted an ice cream on fire.

The momos arrived. I broke one and let the cold winter air swallow its steam.

Two men came to our table. They were fat and strong-looking, but they didn't look scary. Daddy didn't even get up to greet them. One of them was a round oldish man. Could be anyone's grandfather. Mine, for instance. He wasn't exactly smiling, but his eyes twinkled.

'I am Eitan,' he said and offered to shake my hand.

Then he frowned and asked Daddy, 'Why did you bring this young guest? Shouldn't she be in school?'

The other man didn't introduce himself, but later I learnt that his name was Vikas, and he was from a place called Shamli.

'I have to attend a prayer at the Chabad House. We need to wrap up quickly,' Eitan said. But then he went on talking, and his face became redder than ever.

Daddy tried arguing back at first, but then he gave up and sat with his head bowed.

The lofty waiter was at our table again. With Mr Eitan, he was sweet as cake, saying sorry many times for not having 'kosher' falafel on the menu. Looking at the situation as Mama-mon would, I could tell that it was because of Eitan's white skin.

'It wasn't my fault,' Daddy said, and then he used a Latin-sounding word which irked Eitan beyond anything. He exploded and said he would take strong action and cause ruin. Eitan's face was ancient when you looked at it closely. He had deep furrows around his eyes and his cheeks were rough as sand.

As Daddy grew increasingly agitated and his voice rose, far from being scared or worried, Eitan sounded more and more like Daddy's father whom I have never seen—Behram Dorabjee died many years before I was born. People were staring at our odd table.

Eitan said he couldn't stay any longer and that he hoped Daddy would do the right thing. He got up, squeezed Daddy's hand, ruffled my hair, and walked away.

Vikas from Shamli was busy eating a roll. With his mouth full, he said something to Daddy in a drawl, which pushed Daddy off the cliff-edge he was hanging on to.

He took my hand and said, 'Let's leave, Narois. Now.'

We stormed out, climbing down the stairs.

At the metro station, I realized I was still holding on to a chicken drumstick. I was tempted to bite into it, but that would be so weird now that we had left, so I threw it in the dustbin. Daddy kept holding my other hand. Vibrations from his thudding heart rippled all the way down to his fingers, rattling in turn my carpels and phalanges. We sat inside a crowded compartment. As the metro screeched and coiled along dark tunnels, Daddy took out a paper napkin and pen. The napkin had that restaurant's name on it and smelt of momos. He spread it out on his shaky knee and drew arrows, speech bubbles and stick people. Then he drew bags of cash and a ship and hearts. In that ear-splitting noise of the underground, Daddy was telling me wordlessly the story of how he gave up the life of a sailor because he couldn't bear to be apart from Mama-mon. How he was now a partial sailor, one without a ship but connected to ships and harbours. How the money was simply a risk he was taking—people did that all the time—and how it belonged to many different people who had trusted him with it. Eitan was one such person—a stick human in the circle of things, along with Rara Aunty, her husband, the goon from Shamli. On one corner of the napkin, there was Daddy with a suitcase in hand. And all around there were many hearts breaking.

Mama-mon's tongue blisters bled. She sucked on ice lollies to numb the pain. Her nails were black and her fingers seemed shrivelled up. The rest of her glowed. White and purple. Like a reflection.

Then one evening she said, 'I am opting out of treatment.'

'I knew you would say it,' Daddy said. 'Is it because of the money?'

'Yes, what else? You took a risk, and now it's gone. We are done for.'

'But I didn't touch the money for treatment. There is no connection. It was meant to be an investment for something unconnected to you.'

'The cancer made you do this, Danish. You were keeping money aside for the "in case", for the "what if", for a flimsy, unforeseen future.'

'Give me a few days,' Daddy said. He was saying that to everyone these days. 'I will sort it out.'

And Mama-mon crossed her arms and sat up like a tree.

When Mama-mon did that, it was best to float away.

Deep winter had descended swiftly. The garden door remained firmly shut. One day, Mohan Chacha took away the ladder. We had just discovered that along with gold, the robbers had taken the small tin box in which Mama-mon kept my milk teeth. The box jingled, so they thought it held valuables.

Aunty Rebecca said the jewellery would be found one day or the other.

'Usually, these things get solved quickly, but this gang left no footprint. There was a terrible newness to the way they did everything. Pulling down the grille and barbed wire with a car! Can you imagine? What artfulness and confidence! How could they smuggle a car inside the forest? That's a matter I am yet to solve. They drove the car right up to the wall, then tied one end of the rope to the grille and another to the fender. Stepping on the pedal, they drove off into the sloping brambles on the other side till the whole thing came off,' Aunty Rebecca stood up to explain with gestures. She told us that the robbery was going to be featured in the 'best cases of the year' and get included in the book of 'top burglary tips'.

Apparently, the police were most foxed by how the thieves knew there was biriyani in our fridge and how they knew exactly where to find the key.

'No fumbling, no hurry to leave. It's as if they were walking in the park,' the Inspector had said that morning.

Daddy went around town having conversations about the bag of money. Wherever he went, I went with him. I was missing school, and no one seemed to care.

'Maybe they don't have any money left and can't pay my school fees,' I told Meera one day.

I hardly saw Kiran that week since I was out with Daddy almost all the time. One evening, when we returned, I found her waiting for me. Her face was beaming with a tremendous happiness.

'What is it?' I asked.

'Suraj has come back. He returned last night and said he was tired of roaming around and being hungry and that he wants to go back to school if Papa will allow it and if the school will take him back.'

Mama-mon and Daddy celebrated with us. We called for a chocolate cake, which Kiran took home to share with Suraj.

I wanted to go with her but thought better of it as Papa was giving Suraj a very long lecture on the phone.

Some people I encountered with Daddy were nice; they seemed embarrassed to see me, and they claimed they understood Daddy's compulsions. 'Mrs Dorabjee is too sick to take care of poor baby, so you have to bring her along,' they said.

I winced and wondered what Mama-mon would think of being called sick and Mrs D. Sick Mrs D.

There were other people I met with Daddy who were nasty. A few were a bit scary. Daddy's speech to all these people was now something I had learnt by rote: 'Yes, it was in my house, and it got stolen on my watch. But agree, will you not, that it was an act of force ... (Once again, the Latin-sounding word cropped up, which I made a point to note down when it was spoken next). Give me time, and I will return every penny. But I need time, a lot of it, actually.'

One day, Daddy and I went to Rara Aunty's house. She was wearing a white bodycon dress, her hips flaring like Kim Kardashian's. Prachi and I were in the balcony, warmed by the late afternoon sun. When the door opened for the popcorn and cold coffee to enter, we heard bits of adult conversation.

Prachi said, 'The loss of money has greatly upset my parents, but they are being kind to your dad because your mother has cancer. That's what friends are for, you know.'

Wanting to change the topic, I proposed listening to Taylor Swift songs.

Prachi dimmed the lights in her room and took out her projector. 'Let's do this properly!'

We lay down on her bed and watched Tay-Tay climb over hundreds of Tay-Tays on the ceiling above us.

'This one is for you,' said Prachi and played a song called 'Soon You'll Get Better'. It was a soft croony number with terrible lyrics about holy orange bottles and doctors' chambers and nurses. Prachi hugged me and said, 'Did you know that Tay-Tay's mother had cancer and that it has come back again?'

'It's okay,' I said. 'I am not thinking about that all the time. And I know my mum will get better. She says it's just like having diabetes or getting a heart attack.'

'The truth is—the scientific truth, mind you, coming from my dad who has many cancer-geneticist friends in the US—that once you have cancer you can never be rid of it fully, totally. Tiny cells float around your body only to wake up at their own sweet will. They come back bigger and stronger.'

Once we returned from Rara Aunty's, I found Mama-mon playing a singing bowl. Notes floated and sat like owls on the fan, on the curly C of the wall lights, then whirled below, touching my nose, weaving through Daddy's hair.

I was looking for clues. Clues that would help solve the robbery case once and for all.

We sat around the bowl and closed our eyes.

Kiran came in mid-way through our experiment. 'What were you doing around the bowl?' she asked.

'Listening to the singing bowl for clues that we may have forgotten. Mama-mon says vibrations can churn up lost memories. Just trying.'

It was cold outside, so once the singing-bowl-experiment was done, we stayed indoors, making slime. I had an unopened Nat Geo kit of glow-in-the-dark slime. We rolled and kneaded and watched as the mixture hardened. The slime, which is usually hit-or-miss, turned out perfectly that day—just the right mix of stretchy and gooey. We divided it up—equal halves—and switched off the lights. In total darkness, the two orbs slowly glowed with a light that seemed to come from under the sea. The slime did what we would make it do—it became strands, it dropped to the floor, it jumped up, it stayed stuck on the ceiling, it wound around our necks like a living snake. We kept kneading and pulsing and rubbing.

It was hard to let go. Kiran said she would stay for dinner just to give me company. We ate tomato soup and fried rice.

'My other daughter,' Mama-mon said and hugged Kiran who wrapped herself around Mama-mon's thin hairless body.

Kiran and I painted our toenails; they matched.

Then Kiran went home. With her half of the slime.

At night, I dreamt of a dragon. Lit by a green, fluorescent glow. The dragon was tiny and wore pearls.

I woke up in the morning with a dream to tell. A dream that I telephoned to share with Aunty Rebecca. The singing bowl had worked.

23. Consequence

Our science teacher stubbed her toe and went limping to the staffroom.

'Prefects, mind the class,' she ordered.

I stood at one end of the classroom and Meera at the other. A fight broke out over who was the best Avenger.

Paper missiles rained. People shouted. We gave up the minding and Meera came over for a chat. We talked about Suraj.

'Meera, do you think the police are still looking for Suraj?'

'Quite possible. It's not what you'd call a cold case,' Meera mumbled.

'When they come for him, if they do, will he be tortured?'

'Maybe. Electric shocks are common. They also dunk heads in the toilet pot, although on paper that's only for adult criminals. Children face far worse torture apparently.'

The smell of that cloth with which the robbers gagged me came back, and I felt like puking.

'What's that? Oh, Narois, look. What's Reba up to now?'

Reba was creeping up to the blackboard slowly, crouching a little and moving as close to the far wall as possible.

'Why on earth does that girl have to move like that? As if she is on a secret mission.'

I was about to ask Reba to return to her seat when Meera stopped me. 'Let's see what she is up to. Could be fun,' she chuckled.

Reba took a coloured chalk from the teacher's desk and started writing in big yellow letters on the blackboard—S, then E, then X. She turned towards the class, her skirt flaring like a ballerina's tutu, and said, 'Ta-da!'

No one noticed except us, and we were too dumbstruck to react. Meera grasped my hand, and she squeezed it so hard, I winced.

Reba took out a paper rocket and hurled it towards Rishit.

The rocket hit Nivaan's eye, and he yelped and scrambled up. He headed straight for Reba and gave her a pinch.

Seeing how things were getting out of hand, and unwilling to be seen wiping that word off the blackboard, Meera and I banged the prefect's gavel as hard as we could.

For a moment the class was startled. We pointed at the blackboard and asked Reba what on earth she meant by scribbling that word. Did she want to be suspended from school? Or did she want all of us to be made to stand in the corridor for an entire day?

The others had now noticed, and there were loud waves of oohs and aahs and giggles and well-dones.

I ordered Reba as strictly as I could to wipe the word off the board. Reba smirked. She had achieved the commotion she wanted to. Slowly, taking her own sweet time, she wiped off the three letters. Just as the X was vanishing, our science teacher hobbled back into the classroom.

It was during recess that things really got out of hand.

Rishit and a few other kids booed Armish and called her a Paki. 'Ungrateful lot. Go back, go back. Stop ruining our country.'

Meera, Zorawar and I rushed over to Armish to comfort her. 'Let's just go to the newspapers and tell them how nasty people have become,' I said.

'Let's first complain to the class teacher,' said Meera.

We decided to write out a proper complaint and passed it around for signatures so it wouldn't be as if we were the only ones standing up for Armish.

'Let's have it out—a test of who is who,' Meera said, thumping her fist on the desk.

Armish said she didn't want any attention on herself just now. 'My family wants to focus on saving Nani's house from being torched and bulldozed. And what's new? These days I often get called Paki and whatnot. Shouts that can break the glass on our windows. I hear them in my dreams. I may stop coming to school one of these days if they barricade our lane as well.' Then she quietly added something that sounded wise and also very sad: 'No point changing one person. Will his mother or father start thinking differently if you complain?'

'Why are they barricading your lane?' Zorawar asked, noisily munching on a carrot stick.

Meera rolled her eyes. 'Do you know anything about life beyond boxing and gaming? Do you even know that there is big trouble brewing in one part of the city? Thousands of police officers, drones and whatnot are being deployed. Mom says she has never seen anything like this.'

I tore a page from my rough copy and drew arrows and fences and countries like Daddy had drawn a few days ago to explain what cannot be explained in simple words. I stencilled Hitler, Mussolini and You-Know-Who in big print. Then I drew tears and a crowd of stick people, a peace dove and wrote SECULAR on one side and CAA on another side, fencing off all stick people behind barbed wires. I think I did a great job because Armish cried and hugged me and said no one had ever done so much for her.

Zorawar looked very impressed, and I hoped it wasn't simply because he had a crush on me.

Meera prophesied that things were only going to get worse. Rowdy thugs, armed with guns and acid bottles, were being shipped in from neighbouring places.

We told Armish not to worry. When her neighbourhood got entirely shut off with barbed wires, and she could no longer come to school for, as she feared, who-knows-how-many-days, we would send her all the homework and classwork on WhatsApp daily. She wouldn't fall behind in her studies.

'There is no Internet in our area any longer. How many times must I remind you all?'

Feeling quite hopeless, we headed back to class. Zorawar piped up brightly, 'If riots do break out, we can always hide in the Forest of J, under the cover of Fog Phitkari—eh, Narois?'

The class was unusually quiet for the rest of the day. Two words had been spoken that day—two off-limit words. We were running them in our head and tasting them with our tongues.

After school got over, Meera and I put the desks in order, cleaned the blackboard, shut the windows, turned off the fan.

Meera looked at the blackboard where the wiped-off word seemed to shine like a snail's trail. 'Why should it be off-limits? What do you think, Narois?'

'I'd rather not think about it right now. There are other words making me queasy.'

A police car was parked diagonally right outside our house. The Inspector who was working our case leaned against it, talking on the phone. He didn't even glance at me, even though I was the one who had furnished the first clue.

Would he ever have received such a tip-off in his entire policing life—one that came in dreams?

Mama-mon said I was growing up in the tradition of Blake–Coleridge–Ginsberg—finding poems and solutions in my dreams.

'However much we believe in the power of our inner thoughts, the police are unimaginative, you see, and unlikely to believe in clues that come in dreams. Strictly speaking, you dreamt of the dragon because you had seen it. So, let's just say that—without mentioning the dream at all.'

When we rang Aunty Rebecca, she said long hmmms and then a terse, 'Let me look into it.' She asked in a graver voice—the conversation was happening on the speaker phone, and I was rightfully a part of it, having done a big piece of sleuthing while asleep—'Hope you know the consequences, Em and Danish?'

Consequences?

'Yes, this is a solid clue. We are bound to find something when we follow the dragon. The house of cards will fall ... and when it does, others may be hurt.'

I think Mama-mon and Daddy understood exactly what she was saying at that moment. Although when the harm was done, and we went mad with grief, they said it was collateral damage beyond their imagination. Neither Mama-mon nor Daddy ever thought the consequences would be so dear. That day, the lesson I learnt was that cleverness came at a cost. And that betrayal had many colours.

A police car parked sideways and a police officer casually leaning against it revealed nothing of what could be happening a few metres away, that side of the pine tree. My parents were at home; Mama-mon was cooking, laying the table and attending a conference call. The stranger-blood seemed to have made itself home. Daddy looked like a two-dimensional cutout without his meetings and companies to run. Lunch was a big bowl of spaghetti bolognese, a rare treat bang in the middle of a weekday afternoon, despite our troubles with money and Mama-mon's general aversion to cooking.

'Let's watch a film.'

We drew the curtains and ran the heater on full to chase out the late afternoon chill. It was the coziest time I had spent ever since the Age of Mondays had begun. I finished my homework and sat down with a piano piece that had been playing itself in my head since the morning. I had to have it out.

Mid-way through the piece, Mama-mon walked in, speaking agitatedly with Aunty Rebecca on the phone. Startled to find me there—although my piano was loud enough to rattle the windowpanes and I don't know how she could have missed me making that sound—she immediately walked away.

Then she came back in haste and said, 'Let's go. Come, quickly.'

While racing to the front gate, Mama-mon panting and falling back but urging me to run faster, I came to know that because of the dreamt-up-clue, which I had packaged a little differently, as a spotted-and-observed-clue, Suraj was being taken away by the police. The seemingly laidback police car had all the while been hunting out my friend, my Suraj. Inspector and his deputies were ransacking their tiny room, trampling over our lookout, scaring the baby, roughing up Suraj—all this while we had been watching *Spider-Man: Far from Home*.

'Narois, we thought they would only question him about Bittoo. Like you told Rebecca, Bittoo was the one with the dragon tattoo. Now the police feel Suraj is more involved with the robbery, and so they are taking him away. But it's not true, we know it's not. We won't let any of this happen. They won't take him away for good.' Over-optimistic, Mama-mon. As always.

It was my worst fear coming true. And it was my fault.

Now I know why I dreamt of chimeras galloping outside our school. It was a portent, a sign.

I ran pell-mell across the slim stretch of our tiled driveway, spilling on to the broken sidewalk, horse-fast, hooves thundering, raising dust. My brother, my friend, my other family. It did not occur to me yet what I had done. That came later. Right then, I was simply running.

What if the police discovered that I too was a member of the Jahanpanah Jugnus? What if Bittoo gave away the secret hideout of the magical men?

At the gate of the chandelier house, the guard stopped us. Mama-mon screamed at him. Cars slowed down to see this woman, bald as Thanos, creating a ruckus in the middle of the road.

Mr Sharan, the owner of this house and all those cinema halls, half-hung from the balcony overlooking the front garden. He was a short man, so he had to lean over. Why he could never, like his children, come down and stand at the gate, I could not fathom. He was squealing instructions to the guards, urging them to stop us. Two bodyguards sprang out of nowhere, joined by two hefty men who had abandoned their driver posts by the Jaguar and Mercedes. All of them—this crowd of sumo warriors—ran at us. Daddy tried reasoning with them, looking ridiculous as he moved his hands about.

Mama-mon stepped away from the knot and addressed Sharan-at-the-balcony. 'Mr Sharan, if you let us in, we can talk to the police. The DCP is our friend. I think there may be some misunderstanding.'

Mr Sharan looked shocked that this bald woman with big shining eyes would speak to him. He stepped back and disappeared instantly.

At the far end of the driveway, we heard a howl. Perplexed, we stood still.

Another police car drove up, and the policemen spoke into their walkie-talkies.

The Inspector walked out and said, 'Hello!'

'Why are you frightening the poor child? I have known the poor motherless boy since he was eight. He is my daughter's elder brother. Will you just take whatever information he can offer about the real culprit and let him go?'

'Madam, are you really this naïve? Or are you just trying to be an ostrich? When you called in with the clue, you should have considered the consequences.'

'We had to share the clue, Inspector. Anyway, it was Bittoo who was spoiling Suraj, blackmailing him and forcing him to keep bad company.'

Suraj appeared at the other end of the driveway, pushed forward by three constables. Kiran followed him, holding on to the tail of his shirt. Uncle clasped him around the waist. My head reeled, my eyes stung.

At the gate, Suraj bowed his head low. Why was he being so obedient? Why could he not just argue back the way he did with Uncle? People had gathered to see. They were standing in a semi-circle, leaving space for the stage where we stood. Chola-kulcha-wallah from the T-point, Rohtash the medicine delivery boy, Nago Didi—they were all saying farewell. Mama-mon sobbed. Daddy stood next to Uncle and said something to the police—

something that I believed was stern because the Inspector looked annoyed and said, 'Don't worry. We know the rules.'

It wasn't enough. Nothing was working. A haze over my eyes and a ringing in my ears. In the blur, I thought I saw Rani in the crowd, standing tall in her heels, the yellow coat belted tight around her waist, her white-tipped nails, her frosty pink lips.

The police car drove off with Suraj in it.

Uncle said he had to follow the police. Daddy offered to drive him in our car, but Uncle refused in his quiet gentle way; with folded hands, he said it would be better if he went alone, with his people.

I noticed for the first time an older man who looked exactly like Uncle and his wife who was hugging Kiran. There were other people, too, who looked like relatives. One of them drove up in a white taxi and all the men climbed in. I ran over to Kiran and asked her to come home for dinner. 'Sleep over with me. You don't have to spend the night alone with Choti Ma. Don't even think about it.'

But the lady whom I had never seen before answered for Kiran and said it wouldn't be the right thing to do.

Kiran kept looking at her feet. She looked at them so intently that I looked down too. Her toes were still painted blue and purple, with little yellow polka dots on the big toes. I had the same nail paint on my toes, mirroring Kiran's. But I was wearing socks and covered shoes. Her feet were cold and shoeless. She had run out in a hurry. Keeping her lips glued close, she did not look at me even once. If I had known I was looking at my friend this close, touching-close, for the last time, I would have remembered her nose, her chin, her eyelashes. But as usual I found myself diving into her eyes, and the rest of the face did not matter.

A full moon rose over the forest. A blood moon. I sat out in the cold, staring over the wall at Kiran's room atop the iron stairs.

The forest buzzed. The forest with jackals and child-killing mist, a forest sans Jugnus and Velu's red velvet eyes.

Without the ladder I could see nothing.

Daddy came to call me away. I packed my school bag and got ready to go to bed. Wondering what message tonight's dream would bring. And whether that too would have consequences.

24. The End

On Wednesday, Mama-mon picked me up from school.

'We are going to meet a friend. Have lunch at IIC. See the peacocks of Lodi Garden.'

I saw peacocks every day. They perched on our classroom window.

'Can I have a burger?'

'Narois, you know my opinion about burgers. I don't trust the cheese.'

She ordered fish fingers for me. They were delicious.

We waited for the friend to arrive in the large dining hall. Huge windows opened out into a lily pond and giant swaying trees. A few lunchers gazed at my mother. Insolent starers, Mama-mon called them, and stared back with a sneer and 'shame on you for being curious' head-nods.

The friend who was an elephant lover walked in wearing cargo pants. I watched the lunchers as they smiled in recognition. Some waved at him.

His name is a bit of a blur to me, sounding like Achhoo Main-On, and because it suited the tall wiry person that he was, I didn't ask for a clarification. Achhoo Main-On ordered a steak, which appeared almost as soon as he asked for it—sizzling and steaming on a wooden board.

For an hour Achhoo spoke at a frantic pace. He asked if I was interested in wildlife conservation, and Mama-mon replied on my behalf, conversing rapidly to pack in as much information as she could.

'Won't you mentor her? She is so passionate about wildlife, aren't you, Narois?'

Achoo wasn't startled to see my mother's shining head. If he was, he didn't let on that he was startled and whistled in admiration instead. 'Go, girl,' he said to her at some point. 'Well done.'

Mama-mon made a face and said this wasn't an achievement really. It was cancer, etc. Then she shrugged. 'I am still me, aren't I?'

Elephant-carer Achoo nodded and said it was okay. 'Happens a lot. You are you!'

He reached over and squeezed her hand and asked me once again if I was a wildlife fan.

I ate another helping of fish fingers.

Mama-mon said she was only allowed home-cooked food and took out her lunch bag.

A white liveried waiter appeared magically and said that wasn't allowed.

Her eyes blazed, and I thought for a moment she would do what she did with the traffic police who caught her without a seatbelt a few days ago—she opened the top button of her shirt and showed him the bluish bulge under her collar bone—'This, what you see here, is a chemo port. I am undergoing chemotherapy. You understand? I have cancer. I can't wear a seat belt over this. It hurts.' The policeman fumbled and stammered and looked like he wanted to dissolve. He strummed his hand on the baton and managed to say, 'Ah, sorry, madam. For your own safety only ...'

With Achoo Main-On, there was another battle to focus on.

'I will have a cup of green tea,' she said primly and tucked the lunch box back in her large tote bag.

Achoo Main-On had been in Cambodia recently. 'Do you know where that is?' he asked me.

I nodded. It didn't matter if I said yes or no. It was a rhetorical question, a fine orator engaging the audience.

'Spent a month there teaching them how to care for their elephants who are no longer hauling logs. But worse situation back home if you ask me. Richie-rich of grotesque house has smuggled in a seahorse, and we have reports of a red-bearded dragon flown in under the radar all the way from Australia. Imagine, my dear'—he was doing it again, looking at me, drawing me in; clearly my name escaped him—'would you want to tie a dragon to your apron strings?'

He talked nonstop about basilisk lizards, macaws, pangolin scales and star tortoises.

A bagful of nocturnal geckos were found at the airport.

'Are they really a possible cure for cancer?' Mama-mon suddenly asked.

'Afraid not. Well, even if it they are, that is no reason to smuggle the poor lot. There were pregnant and baby geckos too.'

Mama-mon had her second cup of green tea, by which time Achoo Main-On was on his post-steak coffee. He was looking at me once more. 'Have you ever had bulletproof coffee, my dear?'

I had never, so I gestured no.

'Ah, worth a try. It's my boon and saviour inside a cold, wet forest.'

Finding her cue, Mama-mon said, 'Speaking of forests, we live next to one. And, ah, hear what happens next—a robbery. At gunpoint.'

Achoo Main-on was distracted enough to hear her story of Suraj and his troubles, and said finally, 'How can I help?'

He knew the Inspector General, but the Inspector General who was a top boss (and boss of Aunty Rebecca too) had told him specifically many years ago when he sought help for the elephant that had won him a conservators' award, 'My door is open if it's a tiger or an elephant problem. Don't come to me for anything else. Not even if you have a murder threat hanging on your head. I have too many favours to dish out, and you aren't even a politician.'

'Perhaps you would know an activist? Child rights? Juvenile justice?'

'Kahan yaar? Those days of activism are gone. I am no longer a bacchha with a jhola, no? Sadly, as you gain a name in the trade, you become the establishment.'

'He is like a brother to Narois. Isn't he, Narois?'

Now she was doing it too, drawing me in. I nodded.

Achoo Main-On said it was sad what the world had come to. Then he said, clicking his fingers at the waiter and signing in air, 'Narois dear, I am conducting a butterfly audit in the forest next to your home. Did you know Jahanpanah has a hundred different species of these winged lovelies? Do they come to your garden?'

Mama-mon looked away. Achoo Main-on had broken her spirit.

'Goodness and kindness are over,' she told me later. 'I can stick a pin in each one of them and watch them die. These unfeeling, selfish people.'

Don't give up so easily! I wanted to scream.

Exhausted and nauseous, Mama-mon fell asleep. I took her phone and dialled Choti Ma's number.

'What is it? Why are you calling? What do you want?' she almost yelled.

I asked if I could speak to Kiran.

In the background a familiar drumroll came from the TV. I knew it was a music talent show which came on at 8.30 every night. Choti Ma and Kiran never missed an episode. It was the only thing they had in common. Sometimes I watched with them. I could make out from the cheers that a contestant on the music show was being awarded the golden guitar; it would appear in a cloud of tinsel and glitter.

'No, you can't speak to Kiran. Go to the police if you have anything to say.'

She banged the phone down.

Why was she so angry? Why was she suddenly protecting Kiran like a real mother? Did she have something to hide?

Lying in bed, the story came to me. Choti Ma had stunned Kiran with a spell. Her soul was now trapped in the golden guitar that dangled in a Bombay studio. What we saw of Kiran—what went to school, behaved rudely with me—was a bare shell. Suraj and I, the true ones, would free her. But first we had to go looking for proof that Choti Ma was actually a drug mafia lord and she was the one who planted packets of Meow Meow in Suraj's school bag.

I made a little hamper of goodies for Kiran. Stuffed in chocolates, cakes and a few Geronimo Stilton books. Nago Didi added two egg rolls wrapped in foil. I made a card where I basically drew and wrote in code language that Choti Ma was somehow involved with Suraj's problems. Watch out!

The neighbour's guard stopped us. He said to Nago Didi that the Sharans had left specific instructions: 'That girl is not to be allowed inside.'

I would have to report the Sharans, too, to the police. They were holding Kiran against her will and not letting her one true friend through. Surely they could be arrested.

Mama-mon said she thought so too.

Then Daddy came back and heard about our lunch with Achoo Main-On. His heart broke, and I heard sea waves crashing. He said he was shocked that Mama-mon had sought out Achoo Main-On's help. Daddy called him a fraud and asked how she didn't care that he might consider her with pity. What about her resolve to keep *it* private?

'You told the world. While swinging to "Mustang Sally".'

Daddy looked stung. He watched me helplessly, not quite remembering if he had told Mama-mon about this little piece of dancing. Thankfully the moment was swiftly gone. It was no longer important who had told Mama-mon.

'Listen, Em. The police are investigating the robbery that happened in our place. If they succeed, the money will be returned. And your jewellery, your grandmother's ruby necklace, my mother's signet ring, the pearls I gave you. Don't you care? Don't you want all that back? I want my name cleared, Em … and I want to be free of Rara and Eitan and the others chasing me. Suraj is innocent, and the police will release him soon. We have Rebecca's word. But at least don't try to derail their investigation or accuse them. You won't help Suraj by doing that. Or us.'

That night I had a terrible leg ache. Daddy stayed up and massaged my knees and feet with a massage oil that had a sweet scent but left yellow stains on the bedsheet. Long terrible hours later, I slept.

The next day, a cold settled in my chest. I wheezed. The eczema got worse. Mama-mon made me lie on my stomach, laid an ear on my back and listened—breathe deep, hold, breathe out. She rubbed my shoulders.

Three times a day I was plugged on to the nebulizer. Lunch and dinner were soup, only soup—all kinds of soup.

On Monday I skipped school and stayed home, all alone. Nago Didi cooked for me, dusted the sofa, ran the washing machine and then left to see a doctor for her swollen feet. On such days, in the past, Rani would come over to keep me company. Kiran and I would do our schoolwork together. On one such day, my first ever visit to the forest took place. The sound of crickets welcoming us never quite left me. I can still hear it deep in my ear on quiet winter nights. It gets louder and louder.

There is no way to contact the Jugnus who are not allowed to carry mobile phones.

Velu said phones were a nuisance. 'Mobiles spoil our ears that are trained to be sensitive to the natural frequencies around us.'

The irony didn't miss me. Just when I needed the Jugnus—this situation was perfect for Jugnu-healing—they had vanished from my life.

That week, a stream of unexpected visitors came—two men from a bank and a police officer who had nothing to do with the robbery. Rara Aunty sent a lady who had a doctorate in prophecies. She held Daddy's hand and said she could see the boundless sky. The lady refused to tell us her name as that would cast a veil on her seeing of the unseen.

'I cannot betray the whispering women of the cave.'

Outside, a breeze picked up, swinging the chimes; the filament heater flickered. Giant shadows of the nameless woman danced on the wall. Had it not been for the long strawberry-coloured coat she wore, I would have been terrified—this strange person who promised she saw more than what we saw.

Rara Aunty remained on a video call all along: 'Trust me, for your own good. To help you tide over.'

Mama-mon drank her tea and rubbed her wrists, quelling the nausea.

The lady said she could see in the tea leaves the sun setting over Sydney Harbour and a young woman with short hair.

Mama-mon excused herself and went inside the toilet where she sobbed for an hour.

'I am sick of the police,' I told Meera the next day at school. She took it personally.

'You are bad-mouthing my mother.'

'She is a police officer, but she is not THE police. I spoke of them in general.'

'You are rude and selfish.'

That didn't change the fact that I was sick of them, and they kept crawling out of planks and walls like earthworms and centipedes during the rainy season.

One day the police came with Mr Kapoor, the landlord.

Our neighbours from the first and second floor, Angelika Aunty and Mr Bharot, argued with Mr Kapoor that the wire fencing should be fixed.

'Put up an electric fence like the Sharans.'

'The Sharans are, well, the Sharans. This house doesn't need an electric fence,' Mr Kapoor insisted.

'Why?' asked Angelika Aunty. 'Because we are not industrialists and smugglers? They won't expect us to have diamonds and money bags in our house? But look how wrong you are, Mr Kapoor! Danish had crores in his house! They struck with precision.'

Daddy winced. Mr Bharot noticed and patted his arm—sort of. He didn't touch anyone usually as that was not allowed in Scientology.

Angelika Aunty's little daughter Margot ran into Mr Kapoor's shin with her scooty. He groaned, and the police officer clicked his tongue in disapproval. That sure didn't help the cause of wire fence. On my part, I was glad for the sake of squirrels and the orange trumpet creeper, which had wound itself tightly around the wires. Come spring, it would burst into green shoots and brilliant orange flowers from which entire families of purple sun birds would drink nectar all day long.

A few days later Mohan Chacha rang the bell in a flurry to say Suraj had been let off. He was free. He had come home in an auto with his Papa and Tauji, and they went straight in. According to Mohan Chacha, Suraj looked like a little boy. His hair had lost its gelled firmness.

'It was a rough nest, just how a young boy's hair should be. Beta-ji has lost weight too and maybe some height.'

'Don't be irrational, Mohan-ji,' Mama-mon chided him. 'The poor boy is just exhausted and scared.'

Can you grow shorter and shorter? What if betrayals turn the clock backwards?

I scurried around to put together a bag of comfort. In went the scrapbook I had been building ever since Suraj had got arrested, page after page of coloured sheets on which I had stuck photos of our time together—the vacation in Goa, Kiran's sobby face after the bee-sting, visits to the railway museum, having ice cream at the Turkish ice-cream-wallah's stall, a camel ride in Jaipur, and an ever-so-rare photo of the three of us sitting with

DinDin. I had printed so many that the cyan cartridge ran out, and in the last few photos our faces were Martian red. I set aside a charms bracelet for Kiran, a box of After Eight chocolates and a dozen packets of Polo mints. In went my American President and First Lady cards and the flamenco dancer fridge magnet. I considered getting Suraj a fish, but Mama-mon said, 'Stop. Let us give them some time to forget all this. What's more important is that we help them forget.'

The constant whirring in my tummy got a bit better. Perhaps I wasn't at fault. Perhaps no one would know that I had passed on that little clue about the dragon. Wasn't it Kiran who said I ought to think hard and find clues? And clues can be like that—a loose rock that brings down the mountain. Who can you blame after the avalanche is over? The first rock that sends gallons of snow crashing, or the second rock, bigger in size, but a follower, not a leader?

I grabbed some more bits and bobs for the basket and got ready to visit.

Daddy said he would find a way to get me in.

Part the sea, Daddy. Knock down the Egyptian guards.

'Let me go first and have a word,' Daddy said.

I stood in the garden on tiptoe, trying to see over the wall.

The chandelier house was bright as ever with a thousand bulbs. On the top floor a masseuse seemed to be arranging bottles of oil. Then he went back and forth like the bow of a violin, strumming across a Sharan body.

'Narois, do you want a KFC burger?'

'Really Daddy? They won't let us in, you mean?'

'Not today, no.'

'Tomorrow they will?'

'Probably not. It's ... umm ... more complicated. Leave it for now, Narois. Let's just give it some time.'

I started crying. For the first time it seemed like a possibility that Kiran would be lost to me. For years we have simply glided into one another. The Sharans didn't matter. Their big house with hideous paintings and ugly statues was just something we had to walk past to get to the back where the garden was. And in that garden, amidst herbs and winter flowers, was the spiral staircase at the top of which lived Kiran, and always nearby and always keeping aside extra chilli chicken pieces for us was my other friend Suraj.

I fell into a deep, tired sleep. Mama-mon woke me up gently. She put a hand on my heart, the weight and warmth of which seeped through my dreams and pulled me back. Dawn was breaking but it was still dark outside.

'Machu Picchu, my little Bella, wake up, please.'

She rocked me up from sleep. Her waking words were as lilting as her lullabies.

'Kiran is leaving, my love. She is going away forever.'

I looked at her through the fog of my sleep. It would be better to go back to my dream. I turned back into my pillow. She pulled me again; this time she shook me gently but surely.

'No, no, Narois. It will hurt, but you must not sleep. Wake up, wake up. Kiran is leaving forever.'

She pulled me up, not so gently anymore.

'Let her be, Em. The poor child ...' Daddy was saying. Our bedroom was as bright as a cricket stadium. Like the chandelier house, burning every bit of electricity there was to burn.

Mama-mon was shaking her head and saying, 'She must not sleep through this, Danish. Or she will never get over not saying goodbye.'

I knew I had to run. The cold seeped in through my thin slippers and shawl which Mama-mon had wrapped around me.

An eerie blue light fell on the world. The birds of Jahanpanah gave a full concert. Car doors beeped, and brooms swept the streets.

I stood on the road as Kiran, Suraj and Papa loaded their bags and belongings into the waiting auto. Choti Ma held the baby whose tiny head peeped out of a blanket. They stepped back from the auto as the security guards counted the bags that had been loaded. One of the guards pulled out a plastic shopping bag and said it wasn't on the list. 'Open it!'

Choti Ma handed the baby to Papa who stood there, stunned and immobile. She grabbed the bag and wrestled with the tight knot. When it wouldn't open, Kiran stepped up to her and gently took the thin plastic bag. She tore open the bag from the side and showed the guards what it contained.

A bunch of papers that I recognized so well—the board game we had created last summer, a few puppets, our Uno cards, the Tiger Shroff collage I had made for her, a loofah from the Seville Hotel, her half of the glow-in-the-dark slime.

'You can't take it,' the guard seemed to say.

Kiran tore the bag open completely and let all our playthings fall on the road.

They got into the auto. Kiran and Choti Ma urged Papa and Suraj to climb in first. Baby was handed in. Choti Ma sat next to the driver, and Kiran balanced herself on the rod to the right. The auto swayed and groaned, moving like a beetle. We could, if we wanted, jump in front of the auto and stop them. Time was moving slowly enough. I could see myself jogging alongside and easily balancing myself, next to Kiran, on the rod.

But it went by, the auto and the world inside the auto.

We stood there as it picked up speed and turned a corner at the W-block park where we had met for the first time six years ago. I followed the yellow roof of the auto and a thin hand sticking out like a twig. For a moment I thought she was going to wave. I waved. But that hand didn't wave back. It grasped the side of the auto to hold on tight.

25. Mare Tranquillitatis

You see things that you aren't meant to see. A dead pope's wax-coated hand. Blink-and-you-miss-it naked men and women on TV. The words PET MRI CANCER TREATMENT. People kicked out of houses, their belongings in plastic bags.

These change you deeply, but you don't let on. You appear blissful and untouched, eating cotton-candy ice cream, watching the cute neon owls on your wall, playing morning games in school. The dull repetitions of childhood.

Two weeks had passed. Maybe three. I prayed to the God of Garlic for Kiran to be found. Slept with seven mustard seeds under the pillow. Woke up in the morning to find there were only five. Two were missing. Floating in the ether probably. Doing what the police were clearly not doing well enough. I poured nightmares into a tumbler half full of cold water and emptied the water down the sink. I held cardamom over the gas flame with a tong and watched it burn, burn. I buried the charred cardamom the garden. When a blood moon rose over the forest and we saw in the TV news—stargazers looked at it with their giant telescopes—I turned my back to it and drank half a glass of turmeric milk. I threw up the milk, a sign that it had curdled inside me.

Small gestures, a wink, a sigh—this is all he seemed to demand, Fakir Baba, the magician-cum-doctor Nago Didi trusted blindly; after all, he had cured her swollen feet with spit and elaichi. So immense was his power that he could pull strings over the phone.

One day Fakir Baba said, 'I need a strand of hair.'

'Not possible,' we told him.

'Find something. On a comb. Strands on a pillow. In the wastepaper basket.'

I found no traces of Kiran anywhere. So, I plucked my own hair, its wet bulb intact, dipped it in coconut oil, dunked it in water. Then I left it in the sun till it was dry but not bone dry.

Seventy-two hours passed, ticking slowly. Fakir Baba did not call. I became restless and I doubted. This angered Nago Didi, and she said that if I was going to be disrespectful, I could switch to a different method since I wasn't really a believer.

'Is that why it won't work? Or is it because I cheated with the hair?'

She added more salt to the fries. 'Why didn't you tell me so before?'

The fries went soggy at the table.

In due course, we cut all ties with Phone Fakir and began looking for a suitable private eye.

I googled a list of them—Noble, First, X-Eye, Bond and Brilliant.

Nago Didi sat at the table, a card of words propped up in front of her. She was nervous, but surely private investigators wouldn't care to talk to children.

Noble Detectives saw through Nago Didi and sensed she wasn't real. That it wasn't *her* problem. She was speaking on behalf of someone, and apparently that wasn't something they encouraged.

Nago Didi gave her name and address to First Detective Agency. To sound more authentic. That didn't work either. Sleuth on the phone said, 'Hold on, hold it. Say no more. No names. We don't want to know. Why are you giving us names? Who are you working for?'

I was listening in, expecting a warm and inviting voice to say, 'Come, we will find her.' Someone who sat at a table, drove a van, drank tea. Someone like Mma Ramotswe of the No. 1 Ladies' Detective Agency—books from Mama-mon's shelves I read secretly. What was the point of hiring a detective who judged and made you feel nervous?

I considered drones. They could be an option. I could fly them over the city, with banners saying CALL ME and I AM SORRY hanging from each robotic arm.

I wished I had followed the auto. Found a solution in situ. Mama-mon and I could have jumped into our car and gone after Kiran & Co., zipping-zapping, weaving in and out of traffic, keeping a respectful distance. Followed them to the other end of the world.

Better than hiring a private eye, surer than worshipping Garlic God.

In the other house, chandeliers blazed. A kirtan evening took place in which a tent was set up around the pine tree and singers sang tunelessly. One day, I saw a Zomato delivery person, balancing a massive pizza, gingerly walking through the gate. He was worried about people-mauling dogs. I didn't see much else.

Without the ladder, and banished from our perch, I had lost my perspective, the vertigo of all-seeingness. How I longed for my legs to be jelly with height. How I craved to walk through the forest, blurry and grey.

Only sounds wafted in. Of crying foxes. Of crickets. Echoes of fog.

A blind person's dream.

Bharot Uncle was getting a divorce.

'Such things happen,' Mama-mon said. 'Such things are expected,' she added.

Bharot Uncle's sons were in college. Their bicycles were parked alongside mine, gathering dust. I wheeled them into another alley since they were at their mother's; they weren't coming back soon.

Bharot Uncle surrounded himself with plants. Hearing them breathe calmed him. He bought a truck full of winter flowers. One hundred and two. I counted. He lined the staircase with pots. Placed them in his broad balcony that received full sun and blocked the sun from Mama-mon's garden.

'A veritable Nebuchadnezzar,' she called him.

We sent up plates of food to cheer up Bharot Uncle. Fish baked with mustard and poppy seeds. Or bone-marrow soup—magic remedy for cancer and broken hearts.

One evening I offered to deliver the carrot cake that Nago Didi had baked. Bharot Uncle, glad to see me, asked if I wanted a mug of hot chocolate. He invited me to see the garden in his balcony while I waited.

In Nebuchadnezzar's Babylon, there were hundreds of winter flowers blooming, nodding after a full day in the sun. Below us: the forest. I could see as far as the other end. Bharot Uncle pointed out the parapet of Tughlakabad Fort on one side and the Qutab Minar towering over the western horizon on the other.

A boy dangled from the minaret of the dargah inside the forest. He fiddled with the wires of speakers, which faced all four directions. Soon the sound boxes would come alive, pouring out long strains of azaan into the evening. Calling people. Telling them it was time for prayer. I stood there feeling cold, afraid of looking left—looking at the perch I once shared with Kiran. The desire to look had been my only reason for accepting the hot-chocolate offer and the delivery of the food-meant-to-cheer.

Corners, when left alone, speak. They speak volumes. The aloe vera plant, the handmade Tibetan prayer flags, the white handkerchief we had tied on the iron railing of our perch—a message of comfort for Velu whenever he decided to come looking for us—she had taken nothing. She no longer needed any of it. And now they were saying to me, did we never matter?

The sun went down swiftly, streaking our perch with its apricot glow. Soon it became a silhouette—the forest and the room in the forest. Speaker fixed and upright, the muezzin's call came gushing over the treetops. Bharot Uncle, forgetting the hot chocolate, stood next to me. He and I listened.

One day, Daddy came home with a fat brown file and a blue booklet.

I knew them well. Those were his seagoing papers, which were kept stashed deep inside Mama-mon's memorabilia shelves. They were there, and we lived with them, but they were not to be used, only to be kept as a remembrance.

So, what were they doing in Daddy's hand, demanding attention?

His eyes were swollen—I should have known.

He was smiling and humming—I should have known.

Typical Daddy. Whenever he had something difficult to say, he became a clown.

With a fake smile and ridiculous enthusiasm, Daddy said, 'I am leaving on a ship called *Sichem Ruby*.' And he hummed terribly off-tune: 'My heart is down, my head is turning around …'

I wasn't listening anymore. Not to how Daddy was a sailor at heart. Not to how he would show the world that he was best at what he did.

Once a sailor, always a sailor.

He no longer had to fight the banks or stave off the goons from Shamli. The sea would welcome him back and keep him safe.

'The sailor will earn back the money he has lost, un-tarnish his name. But yes, he will not be warm for a long, long time.'

Daddy's throat choked up and tears clouded his eyes. What kind of seafarer would he be, I wondered, if he was going to cry so much about leaving us behind.

One chemo short, nudged by Garlic God and whatelse, he was going to be ocean-traveller again.

'If ever the sea calls me once more, I'll take you with me, Narois!' This was a promise I had heard ever since I was young enough to ask questions and extract promises. So now what—now that the time had come for him to go back to the sea?

That night, we watched the half-moon with our binoculars. A large suitcase stood packed and ready by the door. Daddy and I sat in the garden, rubbing our feet in the grass, wet with evening dew. Mamamon was in the bedroom, scribbling notes for him, like she used to many years ago. I stole a look at a few of those.

And then I knew, love was dead.

- Thyroxine 75 on Sundays and Tuesdays.
- A box of Earl Grey tea bags to perk up your morning.
- See, I told you so.
- *House of Cards* Season 7, whimpers and drowns—what to do with the art of Kevin Spacey.

Not a single kiss. Or words that sounded like caresses across a locked door.

It was possible, on a clear night such as that one, to spot a few lunar maria. Daddy adjusted the lens to focus on Mare Tranquillitatis. I saw waves that weren't really waves. I saw an old lady spinning her wheel. Useless trivia, all this information.

Astronauts would circle the earth and see a ship called *Sichem Ruby* bobbing on the Atlantic—pointless little speck.

'The best view is when you are far away, isn't it, Daddy?'

'Distance and time. When you glance back from cold Hebrides, the song is sweeter so.'

Kiran was that song. Sweeter by the day. Now Daddy would join the orchestra.

I was numb. Overnight I became a sailor's daughter.

Daddy reminded me of the saying that the sea called its seafarers at her own will.

'*Sichem Ruby* is a fine ship. Sturdy, old. It has travelled from Chile to France and back, hundreds of times. The water remembers it like an old friend.'

'Does the water remember you, Daddy?'

His lips quivered and his long nose turned red.

'Letters, Narois, a-letter-a-day if you can, please. Send them flying with news and views.'

I nodded, unable to quite open my mouth. How does one speak?

Inside my throat was a moon-sized lump. It was eating my words with its strange gravity.

After Daddy, we shrank. Mama-mon ate nothing but bone broth and beetroot. I ate comfort food, day in and day out, swimming in the soft starch of potato and rice.

Then, one day, Rani came back to us, walked in with her tote bag of pedicure and manicure, nail art and chocolate wax. We hugged for a long time. Our news and grief had travelled by osmosis. No words needed.

Mama-mon said, 'Now that Rani is here, I would like to take a nap.'

Rani lit a lamp of lavender and chamomile and asked me to bring the Tibetan singing bowl, which she played expertly with one hand. With the other, she traced rivers on Mama-mon's forehead, around her eyes. After she slept, we crept out of the sleep chamber and left Nago Didi to guard the door.

Rani and I went out for a walk. A cold chill tickled my face. The breeze strummed my hair.

'Do you have any appointments today?'

Rani said no and I noticed that her tote bag, full of all kinds of wizardry, was no longer with her. She had left it at home, with Nago Didi. I felt glad and hopeful. She would be mine that entire evening. We would have a long chat. I had so much to share. Wasn't she shocked by how Daddy had left?

'Not really,' she said. 'He needed to go away for a while. Loving someone like Imon Di is not a cakewalk. I am sure he needs rest. A love like theirs ...' she sighed.

'Oh, but there is no love. I saw those notes. And there is no rest on board a ship. They have to work like galley slaves to keep the ship afloat and safe. Daddy told me so.'

We walked through the winter evening in silence, wrapped in our own going-away thoughts.

'Where were you, Rani?'

'Went to the Himalayas this time.'

'You and Silver Samir?'

She nodded. A nod that could mean anything.

'Are we going to the forest then? We haven't been for such a long time.'

'Not today, no. It's too cold, jaan. Let's just walk across to the market. It's so jolly there. We can have fish fries and then get on the swings at the I-Block park. I haven't been in the city for so long. I am dying to be in a crowd.'

The market dazzled. The smell of oil and deep frying kept us warm. Rani bought me a packet of prawn fritters. We watched as our greasy wraps were fried in the large pan. Dark brown chicken pieces were arranged in a neat row, then sprinkled with onions. Chillies if you asked for them. The temple bells rang, signalling the start of evening puja.

Rani showed me the ring on her finger. A thousand diamonds glinted. Then she parted her hair and showed me the streak of red, which made me queasy. Bending low, her perfume filling up my nose, she whispered her new name in my ear, her cheeks on fire.

'Say hello to Rani Srivastav. Wife of Samir Srivastav.'

'What will Abba say?' I blurted out; she wasn't pleased.

'His ghost, you mean? I can't forever listen to dead people, can I, Narois? We must move on.'

'Does it mean you will abandon the library of smells?'

She laid a hand on my wrist and said softly but firmly, 'I want to.'

Rani, no longer sparkling or rockstar-ish, held me close and said, 'For him, I can do anything. And I need to keep him close, and I need to keep him away.'

The market is also a forest. Squint your eyes, close them until they are open only as slits.

If you look carefully, you will see the woods, the brambly ber and kher trees, the overgrowth making a canopy, people who are foxy, a lone nilgai and a host of Jugnus, glimmering and glittering.

26. The Good Fight

On his second voyage, the ship circling Mt Fujiyama, young Daddy had pencil-sketched Mama-mon's side profile from memory—thin nose, cloud of hair, little hills of her collarbone, dark eyelashes, a pimple on the cheek. In the ocean, artists bloom like planktons. Sailors will draw, eyes shut, perfect portraits of their pets, wonders of the world, the trees growing outside their homes, faces of those they love. This artistry is short-lived. When ships berth, art disappears. All those years, after hanging his sea boots, Daddy had produced not a single drawing—not even a sketch of people with stick arms and round heads. Mysteriously, though, art came back in the Age of Mondays. He pen-sketched lovers, Florentino Ariza and Fermina Daza, sitting under a tree, copied from the cover of a novel. Mama-mon found it tucked inside his daily planner, the blue book in which he made list after list. 'How did you do it? You are not an artist,' she said. 'I don't believe this ... THIS!'

What she meant was, 'I don't believe you!'

Now Daddy was at sea, and his art kept popping up in my dreams. He was a Banksy setting banks on fire, putting notes to flames and painting wall murals that the world could see.

'Wake up, Narois, you are sleep-seeing, sleep-crying.'

'It was so hot, Mama-mon. My hair was on fire.'

'Not real, Narois,' Mama-mon said, placing a hand on my heaving chest. 'Just a dream. Nothing but a nasty n'mare.'

'But Daddy was there, and he was setting a bank on fire.'

'Just a mare, Narois, just a mare.'

To help me cope, to help me self-analyse, Mama-mon put together a folder titled 'Famous Arsonists in History: Acts that Made the World a Better Place'.

Arson can be a protest; it can be the good fight.

'Even though Daddy is fighting the good fight against people who wronged him, he did not actually set a bank on fire. It's just an idiom, Narois, an idiom we may have used many times. You, my idiom-conjurer, should know what it means. Should be the last one to worry.'

So, I read about the Naxal movement, about Emily Davison who set postboxes on fire, about letters that caught fire in transit. Mama-mon added chapters to the folder, and I expanded my world view about arson.

The condition of our purses was also an idiom—empty as a pauper's. Mama-mon's job as Head of Campaigns, Rainfall, was more of an idea than a job. She got half-salary because the other half had to be returned for the cause of rains. Seeing the condition of our purses and banks, I seriously considered introducing Head of Campaigns, Rainfall, to the Jugnus. Maybe it was time for them to meet. On account of our new state of 'being poorer than before', it was no longer possible to live in the house by the forest. Mama-mon said she didn't care where she lived and went house-hunting with gusto. Within days she had found a small apartment.

'It's perfect for us, Narois. We will move by the end of the month.'

But not before we had shed weight of our big-but-not-rich household. An auction would be held, in which we would put a price for most things that we owned. On the day of the auction, Mama-mon and Nago Didi dressed up the house, cleaned every corner, placed flowers, dragged in pots of areca palm. We all dressed up as well. I put on my Tommy Hilfiger dress, burgundy stockings and my Chelsea boots. Mama-mon tied a neat turban and wore an oversized silk kaftan in which she looked like a bird about to fly away.

Everything was to be auctioned—furniture, books, LPs, our oven, the dishwasher, Mama-mon's Don Quixote figurine from Consuegra, her cubism cushions, teapots, unused bathing salts from the Dead Sea. The auction manager arrived early with an armload of stickers and stuck a price on all the objects. We were giving away the piano, too. To discourage buyers, I slipped in a note under the lid. *'To whom it may concern: Please be aware that the piano is haunted day and night by the ghost of its former owner, Mr Perez Dorabjee. It plays itself at night, mostly "Clair de Lune". Whoever owns the piano, except for its rightful current owner (Vera Narois), will be driven to madness.'*

Auction manager went around inspecting the goods. He lifted the piano lid and threw away my note. I pocketed it, hoping to slip it in again.

My piano fetched the highest price and was the last item to be sold. I had hoped that this old friend of mine would stay, that Uncle Perez had tricks up his sleeves. It was too old to go away and be on its own. The buyer was a Korean lady who seemed to know what a Kriebel Upright was and asked me to play for her after she heard that I was the pianist. They lifted the piano on a moving wedge and pulled it away. At the door, an F and an A and the haughty, rarely played E from the lowest octave cried out. A few nights ago, soon after I had learnt about the auction, I had opened the wooden casing and inscribed a secret message deep inside, between the hammers. Many years later, when I would go looking for the piano, I would know exactly how to recognize it amongst the few hundred Kriebel relics across the world.

The last Monday in the Age of Mondays arrived.

'Why not come with me tomorrow? You deserve to see how I fight. It's your fight too.'

We packed sandwiches and I took books, drawing material, my iPad in my picnic satchel.

Mama-mon called her doctor and explained how I couldn't be left alone at home or be sent to school. Her doctor offered a solution, which elated Mama-mon and she sent phone-kisses.

The solution was to land me on the couch of Dr Ambrita.

'If they won't let a child visit, let the child be a patient,' the doctor said. Thankfully, the treatment she proposed wouldn't require needles or tunnels.

At the hospital, which resembled a busy railway station, we parted ways at the elevator. Mama-mon handed me over to a kind lady who wore a badge that said: 'Say Yes to Life'.

'I am your mother's friend. Trust me?'

I do, I said, why wouldn't I?

The lady with the badge led me to Dr Ambrita, who welcomed me and handed me a test that involved deciphering shapes, the sort of thing I am brilliant at, followed by an IQ test, the result of which she said was confidential. How my IQ could be a secret that had to be guarded from me I couldn't fathom. Later we chatted and I told her about my arson nightmares, about Reba's Annabelle fascination, about Armish and the barricaded lane in which she lived. I told her nothing about Kiran or the piano. It hurt too much.

When our hour was up, the lady with a badge came back to get me.

'Let's stop by the onco ward for a minute, okay? I need to pick up your visit permit.'

In a waiting room for patients—how many of those waiting their turn would actually have cancer?—there were exactly two people with heads as bare as Mama-mon's. Almost no one had a new crop of hair, and one person wore a cap because it was winter. When he removed it, I saw that he had masses of wiry hair.

Up on the fifth floor, Mama-mon was sitting up cheerfully on the bed.

'Come, Narois, the treatment is a bit delayed today. There is a long queue at the medicine-mixing lab downstairs.'

A nurse who Mama-mon introduced as Nurse Philomela came and checked the flow of a transparent liquid in the drip bag.

'Is this …?' I asked.

'Not yet. This is a steroid, preparing my body … getting me ready.'

Mama-mon ordered noodles for me. I ate and feeling upbeat, settled on the sofa next to a round window.

'That looks like the port hole of a ship, doesn't it?' Mama-mon said in a cracked voice.

Outside the hospital window, crowded carriages of the city metro rattled by.

The next medicine was an anti-allergic agent.

'Nothing to be afraid of. Somewhat like the cetirizine I give you when you get a cold. Another layer of protection.'

It made her delirious. She stared at the wall. One minute she was dozing off, the next moment she seemed ready to launch into space.

After a long wait, two nurses and a doctor wheeled in a trolley on which was a steel box with a small lock and papers that Mama-mon had to sign. This was it—the medicine.

They took out a little pouch jostling with red liquid and connected it to the chemo port under her collar bone. The medicine started flowing. They stood by on red alert, checking her pulse. I curled up next to her on the bed. She read a book, answered emails. Her boss from the rain campaign company called from Washington DC. Mama-mon put her on speaker phone, and I listened to her lush accent.

'Just thought of ringing you before I check out for my year-end vacation. Merry Christmas, Imon.'

It was Christmas Eve. We had forgotten Christmas.

Sister Philomela walked in with a kidney-shaped tray.

Mama-mon's treatment was over. The last drops of the medicine entered her body. The fat Huber needle which was stuck inside the port was taken out. We asked for a wheelchair because Mama-mon felt dizzy.

At home we sang a few carols, which echoed through the empty, furniture-less house. I lit a candle that made long shadows with its trembling flame.

Later at night, when the stomach pain hit her, I crushed eight steroid pills and made her swallow the powder without water. Then, after thirty minutes, I gave her one Ativan, which she held in her hand and stared at for a long time. I was simply following Daddy, how he did things on Monday night.

On Tuesday, I got a fever. Mama-mon and I lay next to each other, humming, telling stories. It was impossibly funny how we were now. Robbed, sick, lonely, dying. When the fever rose and I started speaking in another language, Mama-mon dragged me to the bathroom and sat me under the shower. What would it be to die in the shower, I wondered.

When people asked me, in the Age of Mondays, what it was like to be the daughter of a mother who was dying, I would tell them: 'First of all, it isn't 100 per cent certain that she will die. And if she were to do so, I am not exactly aware of any silver lining.'

'Do you cry all the time?' they would ask me helpfully.

'Does she hug you all night and never let you go?'

'Do you have a date?'

I wonder why I didn't feel the punch. Why the idea of Mama-mon dying was like standing in the shower. The water kept sliding off. Water has memory. But it ends up in the drain. Does it remember me when it evaporates and comes back as rain? A bit far-fetched, the idea seems to me.

Gravity is a dog leash, if you think about it. Keeps us from exodus-ing out of Earth.

'I prefer to think of us as people on a boat, mooring in new places as we float along,' said Mama-mon.

She was at last free of Mondays.

'Soon I will have coffee, and it won't burn my tongue.'

27. Last Leaf

Our last day at the house, we had woken up at dawn and listened to the chirping of birds. When our hearts were full of it and there was nothing else left to do, we had closed the main door behind us and taken our boat to the next stop. Which was a flat on the second floor, with a little terrace that overlooked a gurdwara.

The windows of our new home didn't shut properly, so December flowed in freely through the cracks. Our hearts were too heavy to unpack. We found a patch of sun in one room and sat there huddled for as long as the sun remained. From one of the windows, you had a full view of the gurdwara courtyard where people cooked in large vessels. Water leaked in a constant dribble from a broken pipe in the bathroom. Mamamon stuck a carrot inside the hole.

'I'll call a plumber tomorrow. Let's hope the house doesn't get flooded at night.'

Next day, I went back to school in our car, which we had kept, driven by Mohan Chacha, whose salary we were somehow managing to pay. Because of dizzy spells Mama-mon wasn't allowed to drive and I was years away from a licence. Daddy could return and take us everywhere.

Did she miss his wild screechy turns? Did she regret calling him an Oblonsky?

Rani came to help Mama-mon shift. They put up curtains; cheered up the sooty kitchen with photos from a travel magazine—the Bridge of Sighs, the Kettuvallams of Kerala, the misty mountains of Shillong. Places we have been to. On the bathroom window, which had a crack, we taped gift-wrapping paper left over from my tenth birthday. At noon, if the sun was out bright and sharp, the bears and unicorns looked alive. Mama-mon said the word for when light became silk was gossamer.

After we moved to the flat, Rara Aunty no longer called or messaged. Mama-mon said it was all for the best. She didn't want people walking all over the house in their winter boots, spreading germs. I think she enjoyed running a scissor through friendships.

With Mama-mon's half-salary, we had enough money to give back Nago Didi her job, if she still wanted it.

'Will you come back, Nago?'

'I was never gone,' she said and came over the next day. This new kitchen, according to her, was a hot mess.

Having a job suited Mama-mon. She switched on her computer and sat down to be part of her virtual office by 9 in the morning. Sometimes, in the evening, she asked Nago Didi to stay back and mind me while she went out, wearing her warmest clothes and a big woolly hat.

Revolution simmered in our city. Mama-mon went when she could to be a part of it. Lanes were curfewed, houses became prisons, shots were fired as people sat on hunger strikes throughout cold nights and days. Mama-mon came back and told me all about the singing, the love and hope that was shared, the crowds of people who turned up from all corners of the earth. She brought back pamphlets written in Urdu and English. One day she returned with a delicious packet of biriyani, which tasted exactly like the biriyani Armish would bring in her tiffin box.

'Remember, Narois, this is our Tiananmen Square.'

I imagined Shaheen Bagh as a big open space where tanks had rolled in or would eventually. To help me with my mind sketch, Mama-mon showed me photos and videos of the colourful tent in the narrow field where thousands sang songs all day long. I knew then what Armish had meant when she said that her city was not our city. Armish was the true Marjane, and her city was Persepolis.

Velu, Silver Samir under the blue tent of Jahanpanah Jugnus—I saw them in my dreams, which always ended with a fire. I was now a regular at Dr Ambrita's private chamber which, unlike her sparse chamber in the hospital, had the most beautiful yellow chair. I sat on it with my feet up. One afternoon she covered me with a soft shawl and spoke in whispers. I closed my eyes and drowned in her soft voice. When I woke up, it was evening. Mama-mon was sitting opposite her, by the table.

'Ambrita, I don't think I can afford regular sessions. Would once a month suffice? Just to let the steam out. Maybe you can warn me if you see something serious?'

Mama-mon liked being poor. 'It's the natural state,' she would say. 'Nothing to be afraid of.'

Dr Ambrita said that was okay. 'But have you thought of seeking some counselling support for yourself? Or signing up for a cancer support network?' she asked.

'I don't like labels,' Mama-mon said in a miffed voice.

'Think about it,' Dr Ambrita insisted. She took Mama-mon to a corner, thinking I couldn't hear. 'A significant chunk of Narois's anxiety is because she sees you suffering and she also blames you for sending her Daddy away. Those arson dreams ...'

'Yes, ever since Danish went away. Is it because she worries about him?'

'You see, Imon, and there is no easy way for me to say it, your relationship with Danish may have tipped Narois over. She carries so much she can't make sense of. Why did you call Danish an Oblonsky, for instance? Was he really having affairs? Who is Shani? Who is that busker in Port Haifa? What happened in the misty city of Durban, or for that matter in Japan?'

Yes, Mama-mon, I still want to know. Why was Daddy an Obsolnsky? What is an Oblonsky?

After many moments of pin-drop silence, Mama-mon spoke in a quivering voice, 'I imagined much of it, don't you see? It was easy to imagine. You see, there are layers, always, so I added what I was seeing to what he was seeing or feeling.'

'But that's your fantasy, Imon. Not Danish's reality. You cannot impose it on him.'

'Can't I? Our dreams have always collided, and I think he and I had come to share thoughts too.'

Ever so softly, so softly that I could barely hear, Dr A told her, 'I think the love the two of you shared was bordering on … something not quite pleasant or real.'

'But can love be contained? Can we not love unrealistically?'

'Yes, but at what cost, Imon? Would you consider seeking my support?'

I kept my eyes shut as their words waxed and waned. Daddy, tossed about, flung away from us.

Was I hypnotized?

Dozing, half dreaming, I heard Dr A ask the question I have dreaded for a long time. I wanted to pretend I was still out of reach, floating somewhere far away and it was Dr A's fault that I couldn't be awakened.

'Imon, who is Silver Samir? A friend of Narois's? A relative?'

'I have no idea. Who are you talking about?'

I went back home with my heart thudding. At a furious pace I tried to think of answers. It was so stupid of me to not have already prepared myself in case the secret of Jugnus was revealed.

'I must have made it up,' I said when Mama-mon asked me.

'You don't trick your subconscious, Narois. You can't. It came from deep down in your head. Must have meant something. Must be someone. He threw a birthday party for you? How is that even possible?'

Later at night, as Mama-mon slept, I counted the number of times I had met Silver Samir. Thirteen times in all. Twice we went to a film, five times to the mall. Six times when I smuggled food for Velu and the Jugnus (but mostly Velu since he lived in the forest and had no one to give him food).

The next day, on the way back from school, I told Rani that the question had been asked.

I expected her to get all flustered and say, 'So what? Jahapanah Jugnus are working for the good of this world.' Together we would tell Mama-mon the whole story, and she would invite the Jugnus over for dinner and take them with her to Shaheen Bagh.

Rani said nothing.

'Come on, Rani, let's tell her everything. Bring Silver Samir over and introduce him. He is your husband, after all. Won't that be terrific? Plus, maybe, maybe, there is a clue somewhere that will help the police find Kiran. It's all connected, isn't it?'

Rani stood still, her lips turning white; she couldn't or wouldn't meet my gaze. My plan to 'mainstream the Jugnus', as Mama-mon would say, was going up in smoke.

Festivities began in the gurdwara. Strings of lights were put up. Songs and drums were blasted over a loudspeaker. Streams of merriment washed over our cold flat.

'It's Lohri, darling,' Mama-mon said. 'The coldest day of the year.'

It wasn't the festival of grains that had put a skip in her step, nor the upbeatsy gurdwara. Mama-mon was ecstatic because finally, finally her poems—which had for all these years bounced around like a football in a deserted afternoon field, heard by only me and poor Daddy to whom they were knives and not poems—had an audience. That audience had an audience spread across the world. In the field where Shaheen Bagh-ers were protesting, there was a stage where poets and actors and singers from all over the world came to perform. It was open-mic, anyone could have their say.

One evening, Mama-mon went up and recited a poem. Someone filmed her, and now it was on YouTube where hundreds of people were tuning in to watch, rewatch. We played the video over and over again, clocking up the views. Maybe she would win a Grammy for it.

Mama-mon's poem, titled 'Shaheen Bagh':

I'd like a bomb in my mouth today:
A Kabbalah, a Syria, a wail,
Words, Faizi, words wistful.
I seek a janaaza of my tongue
To bury the grammar of so long.
From seeds of blood, bone and lost Babylon
Let my tongue resprout,
Ushering a spring of screams;
Craft towers, spears, valleys,
The aleph, the nastaliq—
My jihad al-nafs, my suffrage, my lutte finale …
Tonight when I go to where the wires are,
Where babies sleep, rocked by a revolution
lullaby.

To celebrate, we lit a small fire on the terrace with torn cartons and leftover packing stuff, and flung popcorn into the dancing flames. Rani stayed while our little bonfire lasted. Soon outdone by the gurdwara's giant bonfire with sky-licking flames, we went indoors.

Mama-mon was so cheerful, she forgot all about Silver Samir.

'Another two months, and I will have enough kept aside to buy you a keyboard. Dr Ambrita says it is very important for you stay engaged.'

I slept soundly. For the first time I did not dream of Daddy setting the bank on fire. Instead, I dreamt of Rani and Silver Samir—kissing as trees fell all around them, sandwiching between them a giant bottle of Narois perfume. Narois became the mist that covered the forest. I woke up feeling complete.

Without the piano or singing lessons, my days were lighter. I pored over the piano sheets and played the pieces in my head.

Without the forest humming next to us, Mama-mon seemed calmer. She planted wheat in an earthen pot. We watched tiny shoots break through the soil. When the saplings were a few inches tall, she cut them with tiny scissors and made a green juice which she drank every morning.

Little things, little rules, guided us through the day.

One day, she borrowed my blackboard and placed it next to the dining table. With coloured chalk she wrote on it: 'The Last Leaf.'

'Narois, as you know, my blood factory is ailing. We need to keep a track of how it's doing so that I can be safe. Latest reports tell me that my WBCs are very few. Whenever I test my blood, I'll tell you the values and you can plot it yourself. Red-coloured chalk for RBCs. White for the total number of WBCs. Blue and magenta for neutrophils and lymphocytes. There are no basophils left, so we don't need a chalk for that. But green, yes, green, for platelets.'

Her blood was tested every week. Because her veins were now thinner than a baby's, Mr Vikas from the lab used a butterfly to draw blood—letting it out slowly, drop by drop. When the blood report came, I plotted it out, like Mama-mon told me to, with multicoloured chalk. We had to keep track of the WBC Exodus—it's what Mama-mon called it. Was it happening too fast? My job was to ensure that the plotting did not get erased. Twice a day I darkened the red of RBCs, made sure the number of platelets I had drawn remained exact, watched carefully the blue neutrophils.

I drew and redrew Mama-mon's blood map every day.

And every day she read out stories that had hidden meanings, helping me make sense of our days with those meanings. When I asked her why she had named the blood map 'Last Leaf', Mama-mon read out to me Mr O. Henry's story and I understood, better than ever before.

> *'Six,' said Johnsy, in a voice still lower. 'They're falling faster now. Three days ago there were almost a hundred. It hurt my head to count them. But now it's easy. There goes another one. There are only five now.'*
>
> *'Five what, dear? Tell your Sue.'*

*'Leaves. On the tree. When the last one falls,
I must go, too...'*

Dr A wrote me a prescription.

'To help you concentrate better at school—this yellow pill. To mend your little worries and sorrows—this blue pill.'

Those pills made me sleepy, but my grades were better. When I sat with books, my mind did not drift, and I thought of Daddy and Kiran less and less. Except when I thought of not thinking about them.

'Are there side effects?' Mama-mon asked with a quiver in her voice.

'Gentle ones,' Dr Amrita said. 'Such as vivid dreams.'

Now I was confused. Wasn't I at Dr A's precisely to cure myself of those dreams?

For the upcoming science fair at school, Reba and I were made to work together on a board depicting the five senses. We made our peace with one another, which I thought was odd because we were meant to be enemies for life.

On a Saturday in February, Rani and I walked to the nearby market. It was still bitterly cold, and the oranges were the sweetest I had ever had. Outside the market a large and buzzing crowd had gathered around something. Since everyone was flocking to whatever it was, we thought of checking it out. A man was helpfully ushering people in and crying out in a singsong voice,

'Come, come, a thief has been caught.' We went closer. There was one more layer of people between us and the thief. I saw him on the phone screens around me before I could actually see him—the thief in a red shirt. An eye-popping red. Not grey or some other colour that could have helped him camouflage. He wasn't bleeding yet. Not in gushes. There were some bruises on his face.

A man who was recording the incident on his phone pointed out how the thief was drooling.

'It means his organs are probably exploding. Will they let him off alive? Surely they will unless, yes, unless he has stolen a cow. Then they will finish him off, bit by bit, right here,' he said.

The hitters had a rhythm. I counted every beat and step. Yes, it could be set to music. Do they rehearse, I wondered. Practice? But on whom? Five blows on the cheekbone, chin, followed by twelve quick slaps on the temple, between the eye and hairline. Then a break, which ended with the epic blow—a football kick on his ribs and sides. And with that blow the thief fainted and crumbled forward. The rope with which he had been tied to the lamp post pulled him back.

I nudged Rani, whispered to her that we should leave. But she stood there like a statue, breathing only when the kicking stopped, and the man blinked or groaned or moved, giving a sign that he was alive.

The police were standing at a distance, waiting for the beating to end. We drifted away, leaving the thief to his fate.

That night, the folder of arson grew. I added death to it—ways in which people died. I started off, as expected, with Anne Frank.

Anne was helping me, she was reaching from way back in history with hidden messages in her book. She got her period one day and called it a sweet secret. I got my period a few weeks later, halfway between age ten and eleven. One morning, there was a red blob on the toilet seat.

I was thrilled, not scared or spooked out. Anne had prepared me for this moment.

I yelled out for Mama-mon. She stared at the red blob, as if trying to understand what had happened, and I told her I had the 'sweet secret' inside me. She blinked, and I was scared she would cry. I felt like saying, 'Mama-mon, don't make it difficult for me. Just let it go.'

But she hugged me, and we made our peace with the arrival of my period well before time.

'Hang on,' she said. 'We must make a little ceremony out of it. Solemnize this rite of passage.'

We went to the bedroom. She opened her white cupboard. It was as neatly arranged as the wooden almirah that had been robbed, but it was devoid of keepsakes.

'Hoarding caused my cancer,' I had heard her say one day, a rare day when she had found a friend she could talk to on the phone.

Opening that cupboard, she reached inside the sparse shelves and took out a green square.

'My last ST. I was saving it for you. This I hand over to you, my Vera Narois. I knight you a wondrous woman.'

'Captain Marvel,' I said with a grin.

'Well, why not! She was something before they Marvelled her.'

'Mama, will you never have your period?'

'No, never,' she said.

I knew it was so because of the treatment, and I had heard her cry when they told her it would stop. How she clung to Daddy and said she felt empty.

'Now to give it a name,' she said, after showing me how to clean up and get all fitted with the ST. 'It's like Band-Aid. You can't go wrong with the way you rip off the plastic cover for the glue. That done, the rest is simple.' I failed to understand what the hue and cry was about. Except, of course, for the blood that seemed to flow like a river.

We called the period Hecate, after the goddess of magic and witches.

That night of Hecate's arrival, I slept with a hot water bag tucked between my legs. Mama-mon rubbed some lavender oil on my belly button in circles with her finger. I drifted off into a sleep cloud. Someone was beating a drum on my body. From every tap in the world, blood flowed. I kept saying, 'Look out, there is blood.' We were at a fast-flowing mountain stream, our feet in the cold water—Daddy and I. Mama-mon stood watching us, making videos. A blob of red fell into the water, and the water became blood. Daddy said he would stop it, the seepage of red, but he slipped on the stone and was washed downstream. I ran to the riverbank and grabbed a towel hanging from a shop. A warm, white towel. Grasshopper at the cash counter was counting out notes and coins. It looked up and cried out, 'Catch her, thief, thief!' A host of grasshoppers came after me. I ran, but they caught up with me. Then, ignoring me altogether, they went past, their gigantic legs and hands thumping the sandy bank. They crowded around a thin man tied to a giant pine tree from which pine-cone-shaped chandeliers hung. The grasshoppers started beating him up. At the bottom of the pine tree, a puddle of blood formed and trickled down to meet the mountain stream. Each time one round of blows ended, a pine-cone chandelier swooped down and lit up the face of the thief who was being beaten for the towel I had stolen unknowingly.

I saw his face, it was the face of Silver Samir.

28. Rip Van Winkle

Aunty Rebecca summoned us to the police station. 'There is something nagging us a bit. Come for a chat, won't you? Bring Narois,' she told Mama-mon.

At school, I got all my sums wrong and couldn't eat a morsel of my lunch. Mama-mon and I reached the police station early. The sun was nice and toasty, so we stood outside gazing at the grey building and its glossy tiled walls. Pots of brilliantly blooming petunias and pansies perked up the driveway and porch. Lights flashing, a police car was parked at the main entrance. Aunty Rebecca came out in a great hurry and was about to dive into the waiting car when she saw us.

'Horrible murder. A mother microwaved her baby. Must be off. My staff will take you in and have a chat. Not to worry,' she said and blew me a kiss.

We sat in her office. I had an ice cream, and Mama-mon leafed through magazines. But mostly she sighed and had deep thoughts that she kept to herself.

The Inspector came to meet us.

'Why was your daughter visiting the forest?'

'It's too vague a question, Inspector. Kindly clarify. We live next to the forest, and sometimes we go for walks. Why is that a problem?'

'Well, beta, you tell me and your mother. Why am I asking you this question?'

The thing about a trick question is that in order for it to work, it should be disguised perfectly as one that is innocent. The Inspector's question had TRAP written all over, and I had no trouble skirting around it.

'You are asking me because you are worried that I could have been kidnapped? Because the city is not safe for children?'

'Clever answer, beta. But my question is, why did you visit the forest, and whom did you meet there? Friends of Suraj?'

Now that it was unavoidable—the Inspector wouldn't take his eyes off me, which gave me limited opportunity and space to school my face while I thought of something—I said yes, I had met someone called Bittoo.

A curt truth, its main parts chopped off, serves better than a lie. It makes you feel confident and gives limited information to the person demanding an answer.

'Interesting coincidence. Because Bittoo is the possessor of the dragon tattoo—the wonderous clue that came to you. Were there others?'

'Oh no,' I said, just that once in the forest had I met Suraj's one and only friend, Bittoo. 'When I met him, there was no reason whatsoever for me to pull up his sleeves and check for tattoos on wrists.'

As expected, it was not only the Inspector who was asking questions now, but Mama-mon too, with her eyes, looking shocked and hurt, and her unusual silence.

The Inspector let us go and said they were making astounding progress with the case. Then he thanked us for coming in and seemed to stare right through my skull when we parted.

Mama-mon was quiet during the entire car ride back home. I think she wanted to be extra careful about saying anything in front of Mohan Chacha who was at the wheel. Once we had shut the door of our flat and were safely inside our four walls, Mama-mon erupted.

'Silver Samir has something to do with the forest, does he not? Who is he, Narois? If you don't tell me the whole truth, how will we ever catch the robbers? How will Daddy ever come back? Who were you with when you went to the forest? Did Rani take you? Was Kiran with you as well?'

Were the Jugnus, followers of the forest djinn, real? Can we be certain that it was Rani who took me to the forest? Maybe it was I who took her, dragged her there to fulfil my need for adventure and new friends—and, of course, to help Suraj.

The blue pill made me cry at times. Which is what I did, and Mama-mon felt it would do me no good to be questioned.

'Tell me about you,' I asked Dr Ambrita, noticing, for the first time, her golden-brown eyes.

Taken aback a bit I think she was, unused to being asked questions.

But it's only fair. You want my secrets? Tell me yours first.

Her pretty room was sweetly scented and had dreamy low lights. Very helpful setting if you wanted to hypnotize patients and dupe them into saying things they wouldn't otherwise. But I had a few tricks up my sleeves that would help me resist her spell. I could clench my fists and dig my nails deep and keep my mouth closed. I could think of something terrible whenever the sweet smell tickled my nose.

Dr Ambrita realized she had no option but to share a few of her own uncomfortable truths. We sat facing each other.

'Have you heard of Alexander McQueen?'

I told her I hadn't; that one must sieve what one knows, seeing that space in the head is limited.

Dr Ambrita nodded and said, 'Clever of you. But a stray nugget here and there won't harm. He was a rather brilliant and quirky fashion designer who lived in London. I worked in his studio as an assistant designer for five years. Then he died, and it wasn't the same anymore. So, I quit and took a tour of the world. My marriage broke, fell to pieces—you know like how glass shatters or a pillow bursts into feathers …'

That was the last thing I remembered. Feathers.

Duck feathers inside my down jacket. The cold forest. Nilgais silently walking along, their blue breath showing the way. Silver Samir kissing Rani. Velu feeding Kiran with his own hands inside the blue tent. Hands going to her throat and strangling her.

My birthday party in the forest, a cake with purple flowers.

Dr Ambrita stole my sleep thoughts and handed them over to Mama-mon, announcing with great satisfaction: 'All knots have been untied.'

'How can you be party to something like this?' I screamed.

'It's a crime, Narois … and we must always report a crime.'

'Which one?'

'What Samir did to Rani and to you. What Velu could have done to Kiran.'

'Velu misses his dead daughter. Inside the tent they pretend that she is not dead anymore. And Rani? You don't know half of it … she was his wife. What's the crime you are talking about?'

'Rani made you steal food, you spent time with a gang of outlaws. Narois, what have I always told you about strangers and boundaries?'

Mama-mon said no more to me but kept on muttering to herself—'Silver Samir, name like a hoodwinker. Threatening her, yes, forcing her hand, Rani's secret oppressor. Must be that ... why else, why else?'

Mama-mon called Aunty Rebecca and told her about my visit to the forests. She told the story badly, leaving out parts in the middle, dropping characters, missing links. She was upset that Rani had a secret life, a secret that was never shared with her. How could she—Mama-mon kept repeating.

That evening, Rani came over to cook us a special dinner. She turned up the heater in the living room, warming the flat. 'I am cooking a pulao tonight.'

The house smelt sweet and muttony. I was hungry, but also terribly nervous about Mama-mon demanding answers and a fight breaking out. Nothing happened. Except that Mama-mon kept throwing glances at Rani, deep stares that seemed to have the power to bore a hole and fish out all secrets.

At the table, Mama-mon told Rani about our visit to the police station and their questions about the forest. She did it with such slyness—not once asking Rani if she knew anything about it—that I stopped chewing.

Rani overturned a bowl of saffron curd. She just couldn't sit still. A yellow patch formed on the tablecloth. Mama-mon noticed, and having noticed, fell into deep thought.

'I am very exhausted, Rani,' she said after dinner.

'Let me give you a healing massage,' Rani said.

'I was hoping you would offer me one.'

As Rani put away the dishes, Mama-mon drew my nose on my nose, and traced my eyes on my eyes, and felt my eyelashes on her cheeks.

Rani prepared the bedroom for Mama-mon's healing sleep. She lit a lavender candle, which flickered and struggled to stay lit in the cold February night. They went inside, and I heard faint echoes of the singing bowl. In the living room I played with giant shadows on the wall. The filament heater glowed like a fireplace. I played 'Musette in D' on the table. After the 'Musette', I played 'River Flows in You' and finished off with the cheery 'Devil's March'. My fingers ached. Out of the shadows I conjured up Daddy's profile—his curls, his thin nose, his long arms.

I had almost dozed off when Rani kissed me on the forehead. I woke up with a start.

'She is asleep, Narois. Let her rest well. Do you need a snack? Can you sleep on your own?'

I was sleeping on my own a lot these days. So, I nodded and said it was all fine.

'There is bread, cheese, peanut butter, fruit. Whatever you need is in the fridge.'

I took out the homework from my bag and traced rivers on the map. Rani sat next to me for a while. 'I better go,' she said at last. I wanted to be alone with the shadows, so I didn't stop her.

She waited in the stairwell as I locked the outside gate.

'Don't forget to bolt the door, Narois.'

When I shut the door, she was still there. I stood at the door listening as she climbed down the stairs slowly.

Then, I was alone. With a deeply resting Mama-mon, shadow piano, maps of rivers.

Shall I recreate Kiran in the shadows?

Would it be the same—if she came and sat next to me in a shadowy body and spoke to me in a voice made of shadows?

By that logic, no one ever will be gone. There will always be shadows. Like an unlimited supply of Play-Doh—make, remake.

I went to check on Mama-mon—her eyeballs were still. She slept straight as a rod. The way people sleep a hundred-year-long sleep. But she was warm, she was breathing. Her room was cold, so I took a blanket to the living room and lay down there in the warmth and light of the filament heater.

I stayed huddled long after sunrise, clinging to the snug blanket. When I felt hungry, I ate a packet of Oreo biscuits. When I had to go pee, I tiptoed into the bedroom, and there she was ... a Rip Van Winkle. I watched episodes of *Just Add Magic* on the iPad. Could I cook a recipe to wake her up? I thought of going to the police—they were the closest thing on earth I had at that time. Should I report the healing massage? Did it break her neck or injure a nerve?

I had missed school. It was noon. At the gurdwara, a groom came on horseback to get married. I watched the drums and the dancing for a while, standing in a patch of sun. I toasted bread and ate it with cheese. The cheese gave me courage to make a list:

1. Try to wake Mama-mon at 1 p.m.
2. If she doesn't wake, ring Nago Didi/Rani ?? for advice
3. Try to wake Mama-mon at 1.30 p.m.
4. If she doesn't wake, ring Armish or Meera, and talk to them for courage
5. Try to wake Mama-mon at 2.00 p.m.
6. If she doesn't wake, call 102, and if truly desperate call 100.

I dreamt of the Inspector with a fish face. He made hot idlis for me. Daddy anchored his ship in the chessboard courtyard of the gurdwara. He and I ate idlis while Mama-mon slept on. Then the phone rang. And Mama-mon answered it.

'I was so worried, Narois, to see you sleeping like that.'

I gaped back at her, groggy-eyed. It was evening. I had slept through my hourly plan, which lay crumpled next to me. Mama-mon cried over the sheet of paper. She would save it in her box of memorabilia.

We ate real food—hot and starchy. Then we watched *Little Women*, and the day closed.

We never saw Rani again.

All along, I knew we had to let her vanish. But it was hard for Mama-mon to accept the idea that Rani would never come back. She missed her terribly and looked for excuses to call her. 'I am sure there is some explanation. She was coerced. Oh, why didn't she confide in us? Maybe she was in danger.'

Sometimes Mama-mon felt let down. 'Where is her humanity? How could she lie? How could she betray us?'

For days, she dialled Rani's number at random. Rani's phone would keep ringing, becoming the sound of sea waves crashing on the shore for an eternity.

29. March Has Come

Rara Aunty threw a party to which we were not invited. Prachi said she felt terrible, but it couldn't be helped.

'Ari will be there, and he is sure to ask about you. Should I tell him about your troubles?'

I said it didn't matter. Then I said: 'Could you tell him that he is my Butterfly Lion?'

Prachi made a big O with her mouth and her eyebrows shot up.

'You do have a crush on Ari! What code language is that you both are speaking in?'

I shrugged and said I wasn't thinking about such things yet. Although Anne was falling in love with Peter van Pels. They sat at the attic window and watched the chestnut tree sway in the breeze. I could have sat at a window with Ari, watching the trees of the world sway.

'If you had a phone, I could have passed on your number to him.'

'Not a chance that was going to happen.'

One morning, Meera came running to me, forgetting all about our fight.

'Narois, she is back! She is alive!'

We hugged each other in joy and rushed down to the Hall of Grace where Armish was back at her usual post as the prefect of the morning assembly. She looked taller and thinner, and her eyes did not twinkle as much.

At lunch, she shared masala pasta with us, just like old times.

Her Nani's house had been blocked by fences from all sides. They couldn't take her to the hospital when she had a heart attack last month.

'She lived, Inshallah, just because she is strong. Not because we could take her to the hospital, which is ten minutes away from where she lives.'

'Can't you just climb over those fences or tear them down? What fences are these?'

'If you climb over these fences, you will get a bullet.'

That night I asked Mama-mon about the fences. She had stopped going to Shaheen Bagh because clearly her poems or the poems of others and their songs and slogans were not working.

We spent the night talking about countries, ghettos and citizenship.

I missed Daddy, specially at night. One day, soon, he would be available on the phone. We would make a WhatsApp call and speak to him on video. One day, soon.

'Meanwhile, we must tiptoe around Daddy for a while. Do you understand, Narois?'

I did.

I do.

By then I knew quite a bit about tiptoeing. People were glass. People were shadows.

Daddy would be back by the end of March, I told myself. When the flame of the forest bloomed and the forest of Jahanpanah looked fiery.

Mama-mon's radiation therapy started by the end of February. After the first session, she refused to let me come near her. 'I could be radioactive. Doctors don't give us the whole story,' she said.

They had made a mould, which was the exact shape of her body. She had to lie in it completely still while the giant machine moved around her—all alone in the room that had double walls to protect those who were outside. No one could hear her scream, but they could see her in the camera. If she moved an inch, they had to start all over again. So, she stayed still and pretended she was dead.

'The deader I am, the better the nuclear shower will be.'

I wondered at that simile. Would people under a nuclear attack lie still? Did the people of Hiroshima stay still or run?

One day, the Inspector called Mama-mon and asked as usual, much to her irritation, 'Mrs Imon Dorabjee?'

Mama-mon gritted her teeth and said yes.

'Come to the police station right away. We have something for you.'

He took us to a basement which had many lockers. With a large key he opened one and took out a big black bag.

'Do you recognize this? Is this bag yours?'

'No, we have never seen it before,' Mama-mon said.

The Inspector opened the zipper and asked us to have a look inside.

Mama-mon and I peeked in. There it was—all of it. A large tangle of gold and pearl and ruby, our own treasure trove, recovered from a mystery shipwreck. I put my hand inside and touched the bangles and a three-tiered necklace that belonged to Granny Dorabjee.

The Inspector coughed and cleared his throat. He said he hoped everything was in there. 'I'll give you some time alone,' he said. 'Please take stock and confirm this is all that was missing.'

Mama-mon untangled the necklaces, kept earrings in pairs, kissed the necklace of Burmese rubies. Her hands were shaking from the emotion of meeting ornaments that were like family. I helped her sort, and together we sat in the locker room, watched by a CCTV camera. Not one piece was missing. Everything, even the tiniest broken earring and the tin box that contained my baby teeth, was intact. In the pile, I noticed a small packet and a silk pouch that was not ours. By now I knew a thing or two about duping the police. While the CCTV cameras watched us, I hid my surprise and opened the packet calmly. In it was a nail-art kit. There were twenty artificial nails, the most beautiful rhinestones, stamps, colours—dream tools of a nail artist. One nail had a sparkling galaxy of stars. It was a nail I craved day and night once upon a time, the nail that sometimes tickled me and Kiran. Mama-mon said nothing. We turned our faces away from the camera and opened the silk drawstring pouch. Inside was the bottle of Narois. The scent filled the room when we opened the cork cap.

The Inspector returned, and we told him everything tallied perfectly.

'What about the packet and the silk pouch? Not mentioned in the testimony you gave that morning.'

Cunning as a fox when she wanted to be, Mama-mon said quickly, 'Oh, that is because these aren't ornaments. Just cheap cosmetics. But they are mine. Very much so.'

Inspector turned over the nail art set, gingerly holding up a nail. Then he sniffed the bottle of Narois and said, 'This reminds me of something. I am sure it's a clue.'

He sent someone to fetch Evidence No. 56. The constable came back with the wooden box in which the vial of Narois had been kept, nestled within the keys. We kept our cool and did our pretend-normal face with great success.

Inspector opened the box and sniffed. Scrunching up his nose, he took a deep breath. Next, he took the bottle of Narois from Mama-mon and sniffed it. Then he dived back again into the wooden box with his prying nose.

After a while he gave up and said we could go.

We came home with the ornaments, nail art and the bottle of Narois.

Rani was right—attars are shape-shifters. Narois, safe in the bottle, hadn't given herself up to the Inspector. For me she became the forest smell. For my mother, I hoped she would be Daddy smell.

The bottle of Narois and nail art set seemed to tell us that Rani had snapped off her ties with us forever. 'She has burnt the bridge. This is goodbye.'

Mama-mon: finally understanding, finally accepting.

Now there was nothing to hide.

I felt free.

There was something else we had come home with—a scrap of paper that Aunty Rebecca had left for us. The Inspector handed it over to Mama-mon and said, 'Sometimes it's best to let go.'

On that chit of paper was Kiran's new address. I gazed at the scrawl.

Mama-mon handed me her phone on which I opened Google Maps to measure the distance from our location to hers.

Somehow it no longer mattered. I knew I shouldn't follow the blue route throbbing in front of me. I had to wait.

That evening, Mama-mon and I walked into the forest. A low mist hung over the treetops, and in the falling light it looked blue. When the muezzin's call rang out, the evening lamp was lit at the temple of the forest deity. The smell of phitkari surrounded us.

30. The Paleozoic Age

A plane rumbles past, splitting the sky with its shriek. Unused to big noises, we jump.

'Late-night FedEx from Guangzhou!' Mama-mon's eyes twinkle with that special knowledge.

Now the sky is quiet again and empty. Birds nesting in the saptaparni trees around our flat fall back asleep. We resume our counting—twenty onions, thirty potatoes, thirty-six green beans, half a ginger root. We measure rice and moong daal, spoon aside salt for our daily meals. Daddy would say, if he were here counting with us, that salt can be a vegetable if you so desire. I am old enough to not need milk, but I crave it all the same. Shops are delivering Tetra Paks of it—half a dozen at a time—and Mama-mon says she will consider buying.

At 2 a.m. we finish counting and measuring, and Mama-mon is pleased. 'There will be enough until the end, if the end is near.'

But is the end near? What is an end? When does the end stop being the end and start to begin?

Question away, Dr Ambrita would have said. 'Questions bring answers, and answers are antibiotics for your dreams.'

I am not on Dr Ambrita's yellow couch anymore, and I am not sure I want a cure for my dreams. The medicines have stopped. But I keep up the questions. They help me drown the noise.

So, I jump from one question to another. Playing river and crocodile. Always winning, running ahead of the answers which don't matter.

At dawn, the first strains of Ik Onkar float in from the gurdwara. Through the canopy of trees, Mama-mon and I watch empty roads and starving dogs. Their hungry yowls rent the night.

Far away, Daddy is listening to radio chatter from nearby ships. There are long silences and bursts of static. In my dreams, I join him, bobbing on the Atlantic Ocean, under the cold glow of Gemini and Ursa Major. I spot an iceberg, which Daddy and I scale. Slipping and falling, we reach a flat ledge on which we eat bacon, the bacon lard warming us. In the Northern Atlantic, it is cold as hell. Tomorrow we will catch fish near Ireland. Day after, Daddy and I will stand on the stern and gaze back at the white wake. Maybe we will spot a bloom of glowing planktons. If a hurricane comes, we will head straight into it. But right now, the ocean is as calm and ancient as it was in the Paleozoic Age, long before quakes tore apart one super land. The ocean is a safe place, with a beginning and an end. A place where my Daddy is. A place I visit every night. Sometimes, I see him spotting a humpback whale and announcing proudly to his captain that he has a daughter who is a whale-whisperer, that a beluga smiled at her from its ginormous aquarium in Valencia. Sometimes I see him sinking in slow motion, through various shades of blue, until it's too dark for me to see, and then I wake up and hope he will tell me it was a dream.

March has come. But not Daddy who is still floating in the Atlantic, looking for a boat or a plane that will bring him home. But planes don't fly anymore except late-night FedEx cargo planes from far-off cities, carrying medicines and vaccines.

Friends don't meet anymore, anywhere in the world. Finally, the world is how Mama-mon has always imagined it to be. She helps me list out synonyms for solitary, confined, solitary confinement, isolation and quarantine. We find rhyming words too.

Mama-mon makes a cup of piping hot coffee for herself and lets me have a sip when it has cooled down.

Sometimes, when I miss Kiran and long for her friendship, I enter the address on Google Maps and watch as satellites connect me to her virtually—all the way to where she is, a gentle blue river of empty roads.

Acknowledgements

I lived to tell this story—about that I am grateful.

Jahanpanah Forest, for its shelter and shadows; Mini and Ranjit, for weathering the storm that no parent should have to, with humour, scientific insight and sophistication; Krishna-Ma, for propping me up with her fierce piety; Mandira Moddie, my haven and sister; Nitin Gulati, our in-house Jugnu.

To my friends through thick and thin, the ones who always remembered Mondays—Saugata Mukherjee, first publisher and forever friend; Urmila Dasgupta, for pre-empting my need for warpaint and earrings; Rajat Chaudhuri, keeper and conscience of my writing self; Vandana Shah, for believing and daring me to be ambitious when breath was sparse.

My earnest gratitude to Kavery Nambisan, Saikat Majumdar and Hansda Sowvendra Shekhar, writers I deeply admire. Your words of encouragement are invaluable to me.

HarperCollins India, the home that my books find.

Dharini Bhaskar, my publisher and acquiring editor—our story from submission to offer is the stuff of dreams, reinforcing my belief and hope that all is good with this world. I am grateful that you were perhaps more eager to set Narois out in the world than I was.

Saikat, love of my life and still centre—for dropping anchor while I walked on water. You bring to life what's promised in songs.

About the Author

Lopa Ghosh is an author, columnist and public-health advocate. Her first book, *Revolt of the Fish Eaters*, was published in 2012. Her stories have appeared in *Alchemy: The Tranquebar Book of Erotic Stories*, *The Best Asian Speculative Fiction* and the online magazine *The Antonym*. She is also a columnist with *The Telegraph* and has written for *The Hindu*, Scroll, *Outlook* and academic journals.

An advocacy and communications expert with over twenty years of experience in global health, the UN, the private sector and the media, Lopa is presently senior advisor, policy and communications at the Global Health Advocacy Incubator. She holds postgraduate degrees from the London School of Economics and Jadavpur University. She lives in Delhi with her partner and two children.

HarperCollins *Publishers* India

At HarperCollins India, we believe in telling the best stories and finding the widest readership for our books in every format possible. We started publishing in 1992; a great deal has changed since then, but what has remained constant is the passion with which our authors write their books, the love with which readers receive them, and the sheer joy and excitement that we as publishers feel in being a part of the publishing process.

Over the years, we've had the pleasure of publishing some of the finest writing from the subcontinent and around the world, including several award-winning titles and some of the biggest bestsellers in India's publishing history. But nothing has meant more to us than the fact that millions of people have read the books we published, and that somewhere, a book of ours might have made a difference.

As we look to the future, we go back to that one word—a word which has been a driving force for us all these years.

Read.